STAYING
ON TOP
a Whitman University novel

For: Marissa

☺

LYLA PAYNE
USA Today Bestselling Author

STAYING
ON TOP

a Whitman University novel

xo
Lyla Payne

To Andrea, who has been my best friend for almost thirty years. There has been laughter, hurt, understanding, exasperation, and love, which all add up to a friendship that has shaped my life.

I hope it continues to do so for years to come.

Chapter 1

Sam

"*A*re you Sam Bradford?"

This was getting to be too easy. I didn't know how that made me feel.

I closed my eyes and counted to five. Ten or twenty would have been better, but that seemed like a long time to ignore someone. She sounded pretty, with a lilting, hard-to-place accent—probably Swiss. I guessed tall and blonde, maybe brown eyes, and found exactly that when I swiveled on the bar stool to face her.

"Oh, you are. Hi. I'm Chloe. This is Vera." She jerked her head toward the shorter, less attractive brunette standing a foot behind her. "I'm a huge fan."

They were always huge fans, just not usually of tennis. Girls were fans of things such as the shoes Nike had given me for the season, the way my hair curled in the humidity, or maybe the way my abs looked when I changed out of my sweaty shirt on court. And normally, I didn't mind. Chloe was confident and beautiful, as Swiss girls tended to be, but I'd hoped getting to Basel a few days early would help me avoid the groupies.

Of course, bombing out of Valencia in the second round had helped my early arrival along.

I slid off the stool and dropped some euros on the bar, then grasped her hand. It was warm and soft, everything a girl's hand should be, but I couldn't muster the interest. For all the fun that went along with not having a commitment, lately the shine of the single life had started to wear a little thin. "It's nice to meet you, Chloe."

Disappointment shone in her dark eyes. "You're leaving? I was hoping to buy you a drink."

"If I didn't have to go, I would buy *you* a drink. No way would I let such a beautiful woman pay for booze." I winked and gave her a smile. A pretty blush crept across her pale cheeks, almost changing my mind. "Will you be attending the matches next week?"

She nodded. "Yes. My father's company is one of the sponsors."

"Well, then I'm sure I'll be seeing a lot more of you." I let the double entendre sink in, enjoying the glow of hungry excitement on her face. "Have a lovely night, ladies."

I traded the overly warm interior of the bar for the chill of October in Switzerland, barely glancing at the scenery. The thing about traveling constantly was that every place started to feel the same. Switzerland was beautiful and friendly, and was actually one of the places on my list to consider settling down one day, but tonight a soft hotel bed was all I wanted.

Only a few weeks remained before professional tennis's paltry six-week off-season, and I needed it more than ever this year. The injury my obliques sustained in Melbourne had healed by spring, but a rough five-set semifinal at the US Open had me hurting again in a way that begged for a long rest.

I felt tired—exhausted by the travel; by the practice and play; by women; by my small but invasive circle of friends, managers, and trainers; and by my bloodsucking family. It was impossible to recall the last time I'd been alone. I don't think it had ever happened.

The windows of my hotel, a posh five-star job that cost me thousands of dollars a night after putting up my publicist, manager, coaches, and trainers, glowed in the Swiss evening. The silence of the empty lobby loosened the tension in the back of my neck. As I reached for the elevator buttons I was thinking maybe one drink from the minibar, then bed, when a throat cleared behind me.

Not again. The tournament didn't start for two days—who would have guessed there would be so many women lurking around already?

It wasn't a hopeful girl, though. The desk clerk's face shone with a light sweat, his eyes flitting from the floor, to me, to the front desk, before settling on his toes. His white-blond hair made the redness of his cheeks even more prominent, and his sweat, along with the way he licked his lips, infected me with nerves.

"Mr. Bradford?" He licked his lips again, then darted a glance at my face.

"Yes?"

"There, um . . . seems to be an issue with your credit card. If you would care to step over to the front desk, I'm sure we can make other arrangements."

"What kind of issue?" The travel weariness sank deeper, burrowing into my bones.

"It's been declined by the bank."

"That's not possible." I had no idea what my limit was except that it was extremely high—maybe non-existent, and I spent so much money on a monthly basis on training and travel that there was no way to keep track of my balance. I had an accountant and he hadn't given me any indication of a problem. "Did you try it again?"

"Three times, sir, and we called. There are no funds available." He stepped to the side, motioning to the front desk. The harsh lobby light glinted off his gold name tag, catching his name.

"Listen, Pierre, can we deal with this in the morning? I'll send my manager down first thing."

"I'm afraid not. We'll need a different form of payment on file." Pierre grew bolder with each step toward the desk, as though it held some kind of recharging ability. As though he were Superman and that glossy piece of granite and wood represented his Fortress of Solitude.

If I refused, what would he do? Throw us all out on the street? It seemed unlikely. The presence of press would be enough to deter him; the Swiss were notorious for avoiding the kind of tabloid gossip that places such as England and America ate up like shit from a spoon.

Still, it would be better not to chance it. Despite rumors that I had a reputation for taking advantage of my luck with the ladies, I'd managed to stay off the confirmed gossip radar.

Pierre crossed behind the desk, the ruddiness gone from his cheeks and his expectant eyes on my wallet as

I pulled it from my back pocket. On the tour and in the tennis world, my rep could be summarized as quick-to-smile and laid-back, but this whole day had made me feel anything but easygoing.

There were four cards in my wallet—three, including the one the hotel had on file, were linked to checking accounts. The fourth was a credit card I used to accrue frequent flyer miles. I had a smaller fifth account that I used for personal expenditures, but that card was upstairs in the safe.

I handed him one of the other bank cards, wondering where this mix-up originated but not too worried about it. I'd let Leo, my primary manager, know in the morning and let him figure it out. I rarely talked to my accountant, Neil Saunders. He was an American but spent tons of time abroad with his international clients, including several other tennis players.

"I'm sorry, Mr. Bradford. This one is declined as well."

"This is ridiculous. Something must be wrong with the machine." When he didn't reply, I handed him the last checking account–linked card, unable to stifle my glare.

The flush returned to his cheeks. "I'm very sorry, sir. I'm sure it's some kind of mistake, but it is our policy to have a method of payment on file . . ."

"It's fine, Pierre. Just run it, please. I'm very tired."

Pierre and I both knew that I could cover any bill they could throw at me, in cash even, but apparently policy was policy.

When the third card was declined, the first seed of worry dropped into my gut. There could be a mistake on the part of the hotel, but there didn't seem to be a problem with any of the other guests. The chances that three different banks on two continents had screwed up my authorizations on the same night seemed . . . slim. Slim to none.

My credit card went through on the first try.

"Well, at least I'll get the extra miles," I joked. It sounded strained, even to me, and I hated to show my concern.

Pierre gave me an awkward smile. "I'm sure you'll get it straightened out, sir. Good luck in the tournament and enjoy your stay in Basel."

It weirded me out when people twice my age called me *sir*, employees or not. I might be a millionaire and a third of the way through my career, but I was only twenty-two. Pierre had to be pushing fifty.

"Thank you, Pierre. I'm sorry if I was short with you."

"It's not a problem, sir."

The elevator sped up to the thirtieth floor, the top of this particular establishment. My team of sixteen plus me took up all of the rooms after I paid for two extra to ensure we would be alone. I liked my privacy, and even though the Swiss did a better job regulating paparazzi than most, if I wanted to bring someone such as Chloe and/or her friend home in the next couple of days, I didn't need it splashed on every blog between here and Hawaii.

Her bright blond hair, full breasts, and pink cheeks flashed in my mind. It would probably happen, if I had the good fortune to run into her again. I had a feeling I'd enjoy taking her for a drive, and also that she probably didn't mind sharing the wheel. My favorite kind of girl.

It had been my plan to speak with Leo about the initial financial glitch in the morning, but after having all three bank cards declined, I knocked on his door instead of going straight to my suite. He answered in the space of a couple breaths—he barely slept, even though one of his many jobs was making sure that I did.

"Sam. Everything okay?" Leo's longish blond hair was tousled, as though he'd at least been lounging, his white shirt unbuttoned, his tie askew.

Leo didn't even have ten years on me, but friendship didn't accompany our professional arrangement. He saw himself as the one who had to keep me in line, and he'd told me once that it would be harder to do if we went out drinking and picking up girls together. He worried enough for the both of us plus my parents, who didn't give a shit, and earned big bucks for it.

"I don't know. The hotel clerk stopped me on the way up and said the credit card on file had been declined. They even called the bank."

"Probably a mistake. I'll check with them in the morning and get it cleared up."

"That's what I thought, but none of the bank cards would go through. They took the credit card, so we're fine, but something is definitely going on. I'd prefer to check on it now." It would be harder than usual to sleep, worried that I'd be humiliated trying to grab a *café* in the morning.

Leo opened the door wider in silent invitation. I took it, sinking into the chair next to the windows and rubbing my eyes.

"You look tired. Grab a beer from the bar if you want. You need to use these couple of days to rest up." He grabbed his phone and scrolled through numbers. "I'll give the banks a call."

"It's the middle of the night."

"I have contacts, Sam. That's what you pay people like Neil and me for, remember?"

I shrugged, knocking the cap off a Heineken from the bar and taking a pull. "Thanks. I'm sure you were probably getting ready for bed, too."

"It's fine." He held up a hand, then switched seamlessly to French as he spoke into his phone. "Hello? Yes, may I speak with Herbert, *sil vous plaît? Merci.*"

Someone, I assumed Herbert, came on the line a moment later and I tried halfheartedly to follow the conversation as they continued in French. I spoke some and understood more, same with German, but my Spanish and Russian were flawless. Most of my close friends on the tour were Spaniards, and my last two girlfriends had been Serbian. Aside from that, it was hard to spend as much time in foreign countries as I did and not feel at least a little obligated to learn.

Leo frowned and lowered his voice. I gave up trying to follow the conversation, more tired than ever. When he hung up a moment later, he immediately dialed another number.

"What's going on?"

"I'll tell you in a minute. Let me just make sure we have the facts straight first."

The next conversation took place in German, and then a third in English. That one was the shortest—apparently midnight customer service was harder to come by in the United States than abroad. It didn't surprise me. Leo left a message for the district manager at Chase and then hung up.

His face looked paler than when he'd opened the door. It worried me, especially because Leo took care to maintain a little too much of a tan, in my opinion.

"What's going on, Leo?"

He sat down on the edge of the bed, running hands through his hair before looking me in the eye. "I don't know for sure. We'll have to get in contact with Neil first thing in the morning. I'll leave a message with his office in a minute."

"Okay, well what do you *think* is going on?"

"The accounts at BNP and UBS are empty. The funds were withdrawn by wire transfer at ten p.m. Eastern Standard Time and sent to an account in the Caymans. Untraceable. I assume we're going to find the same at Chase."

About halfway through his speech, the words started to sound far away, as though Leo shouted them through water. My brain and lips felt numb. "How much?" I managed.

"Thirty million, give or take."

Leo sounded as though he were going to throw up. My stomach didn't disagree. Thirty million dollars. Gone.

"There shouldn't have been so much in those accounts. It's supposed to be invested—I thought they maxed out at a million each."

"Your investment accounts must have been moved back into your checking and then withdrawn from there. It would have been easier that way—the investment firms would require fewer authorizations since it was going to another account, not being liquidated." Leo ran a hand through his hair. "Sam, you're fine. You need to focus on tennis; let me worry about this. We'll get ahold of Neil in the morning and I'm sure we'll get all of this straightened out."

I nodded, still feeling like this must be happening to someone else. I was far from broke, but losing thirty million would be a huge blow. As I lay in bed, trying to force my eyes closed, I told myself there were years left in my career. If my goddamn abs would heal up, I could make it back.

Depending on what we found out from Neil, that could end up being my only choice.

Chapter 2

Blair

"*I* am so freaking ready for winter break." Audra tossed her cherry red hair into a bun, then fell backward onto the bed in a dramatic pose that would be more at home on her brother's girlfriend, Ruby, than the levelheaded, even-keeled girl I'd met when we both pledged Kappa Chi.

It made me smile, even though my mind struggled to bounce back from the phone conversation I'd wrapped up with my dad a few minutes ago. "Why? Missing the motherland?"

She rolled her eyes. "I'm not Russian, Blair."

"I know. I just like saying it." I grabbed my Ethical Theory textbook out of my backpack and went back for my notes. "Are you going home?"

"I think so, yeah." She didn't look terribly excited about the prospect.

"Logan staying stateside?" I guessed.

Audra's cheeks turned pink and her hand curled around her phone. "Yes. He's going home to Connecticut."

Something about Audra's boyfriend rubbed me the wrong way. Not having an actual reason to dislike him, however, I kept my negative thoughts to myself. She seemed happy enough. We were only nineteen, and she was my sorority sister, not my actual sister.

"Well, I'm sure you guys will talk as much as always. So, like, a hundred texts a day, average."

Her cheeks reddened further. "Shut up. I can't wait until you meet someone you actually like so I can dish all of this shit back your direction."

"Fat chance. The guys on this campus are a dime a dozen."

"True. If Zachary Flynn couldn't hold your attention, who could?" she mumbled, looking down at her phone when it buzzed.

I didn't bother to answer. She wasn't listening anyway, and I didn't want to talk about Flynn. I had liked him. He hadn't been bad in bed, either, but his notoriety had made me uncomfortable. It had been easy to convince myself it was no big deal, but the first time camera flashes had blinded me coming out of a restaurant, the lies had blown up in my face. Maybe it was because of my dad, or how he'd brought me up, but being noticed—or worse, remembered—gave my hives. Literal ones.

"I'm going to the library," I said, grabbing my textbook and iPad, then shrugging into a jacket. Seventy degrees meant a slight chill in Florida, and even though I'd grown up in Manhattan, it hadn't taken long for my body to adjust to the balmy Southern weather.

"What?" Audra looked up, blinking to dislodge the glassiness hazing her eyes. She'd never had a boyfriend before—probably because she had four slightly scary older brothers—and this Logan thing was out of control. "Why are you going to the library? No one studies at the library."

"I need to, um . . . do some research in the stacks. Some of the reference materials for this take-home test aren't online yet."

For the first time in weeks, Audra's distraction didn't make me want to smack the freckles off her pretty face, because it meant she didn't question my flimsy excuse. Questions weren't welcome. Not when it came to my dad, and certainly not when it came to the part-time "job" I worked at his request.

"Okay. Don't forget about the meeting tonight. We have to review housing applications."

"Got it." Audra and I had been elected—not that we'd run—to oversee the freshmen and sophomores requesting to move into the Kappa Chi house next semester. We were required to fill the house, and since upperclassmen preferred to live off campus we weren't above forcing newbies in to fill up the rooms.

It's how Audra and I had ended up living here as roommates, but that had worked out fine. Much better than my disastrous freshman year trying to keep Kennedy Gilbert from killing herself. She seemed to be doing well, now, and she and her boyfriend, Toby, were living together in a pretty swanky beachfront place. I was happy for her, but not sorry to be living with someone normal. Or someone who had been normal before she started secret dating.

I looked down at my outfit. Yoga pants and a Kappa tee were no good—I needed a skirt and blouse at the least, but my suit would be better. No way would Audra fail to notice me changing clothes, so I gathered the suit and a blouse on their hangers, then paused. "I'm going to stop at the cleaners. Do you want me to take anything for you?"

"Huh? Oh, yeah. Hold on." She put down her phone and slid off the bed, then dragged four dresses and one skirt out of her closet, tossing them on my bed. "Thanks."

That was easy enough, except adding a stop at the cleaner's to my list.

None of my sisters interrupted my escape from the house. I passed through the massive white columns and stepped down into the parking lot, enjoying the cooler brush of air against my cheeks. Autumn was my favorite time in New York. This time of year, late October, was perfect. The trees would be changing, the air would taste crisp and smoky, and the sky would be impossibly huge and blue. I missed it, and not just the weather. The people, more than anything.

Even if I had spent more time ripping them off than getting to know any of them.

The nice thing about the Kappa house being the farthest sorority from main campus was our secluded lot. No one saw as I changed out of my T-shirt and pants and into a skirt and blouse, complete with an annoying pair of old-lady panty hose I'd snuck into my purse. If my dad's lessons had taught me anything at all, it was that the proper appearance did at least 85 percent of the work. And old ladies freaking loved panty hose.

*

Dad had been asking me for more favors than ever since I relocated to Florida, thanks to the abundance of gullible, rich elderly people. The drive to this particular job didn't take long. Twenty minutes or so after leaving campus my GPS said I'd arrived, and a street lined with sprawling faux-brick estates welcomed me to the neighborhood.

Less than three years to go, I thought as I pulled into the driveway and shut off the car, taking a few minutes to clear my head. I'd be done with school, have a degree, and be able to get a real job; I would finally be able to refuse the "work" my dad tossed my direction.

The ever-present worry that I didn't know how to live any other way tried to wriggle past my defenses, but I swiped it away. I could figure it out. Just because a duck had never seen water didn't mean it couldn't swim. Just because I'd grown up stealing didn't mean I couldn't be honest.

It took the space of a few deep breaths to twist my hair into a knot at the nape of my neck and dig my fake FBI credentials from the glove compartment. I slipped them into my jacket pocket and climbed out of my high-end Toyota, which I drove on purpose so as not to intimidate potential marks. Plus, FBI agents didn't drive Beamers like the one Dad had sent me to Whitman in.

The driveway had been recently repoured, and flowering bushes and plants lined the pathway to the massive double front doors. The house was the kind of structure that only rich people in Florida managed to build—more than one story, with an exterior cut to look like brick instead of the stucco that was more appropriate for the environment down here.

All of these huge, sprawling houses and sprawling lawns felt foreign to me. The extra space felt wasteful after living in Manhattan. Some people hated it—the crush of humanity, the never being alone, the constant noise—but after growing up that way, the opposite felt wrong.

An impressively long and loud ding-dong sounded when I pressed the bell. I fixed a friendly but professional smile on my lips and a look of appropriate sympathy in my eyes. My father had stolen over ten million dollars from this woman earlier in the week, but she had another fifty squirreled away in accounts to which she'd retained her access. I was here to change that.

Two years ago the light briefcase would have been slippery in my sweating palm, but today I had no nerves. What had started as an eight-year-old girl playing a game had turned into a job at some point—and into my lifestyle as well as my father's.

The door opened, revealing a tidy African-American woman in an old-fashioned black-and-white maid's uniform. "Afternoon. Can I help you?"

She gave me a tight smile that said she hated her life, one that relaxed the slight knot at the base of my neck. It meant she had no love for her employer, which worked in my favor.

I pulled the badge out of my pocket as though I'd been doing it for years. "I'm Special Agent Cooley with the FBI. I'd like to speak with . . ." I checked a blank notepad on the back of my badge. "Miss Daisy Brown, if she's available."

"Miss Brown is relaxing right now. Can I tell her what this is about?"

"I'm afraid I need to speak with her directly, but you can tell her I'm with the white-collar crime division."

"She ain't gonna know what that means."

"It means we investigate fraud. Like the kind run by questionable accountants who steal money from hardworking ladies such as yourself," I replied dryly.

She eyed me for a few more seconds before opening the door wider and inviting me into the foyer. Step one—get into the house.

"I'll tell Miss Brown you're here. It might be a few minutes. Can I get you something to drink?"

The acid in her tone made me think the beverage would be mostly spit, so I shook my head. "No, thank you. I'll be fine."

The maid left me alone in the foyer. The lack of warmth, or even an invitation to sit, made me wonder why my father had chosen this particular mark and how he'd managed to wrangle the first ten million out of her hands. The house was rattier on the inside than out— the walls had some cracks that needed to be repaired, the wooden floors could use a buff and stain, and the paisley carpet on the stairs was worn thin in the middle. It all added up to the assumption that the mark had money, but she didn't like to spend it.

Maybe Dad was getting bored in his old age. Picking bigger challenges. Fine for him, but I wasn't feeling much like taking on a tough con today. I actually did have an Ethical Theory take-home test to complete before tomorrow.

It was more than twenty minutes before Miss Daisy Brown made an appearance in the foyer. Silk robes draped her soft, curvy figure from head to toe. She had her hair curled up in a style that made me feel as though I'd stepped through the door onto a 1950s film set, and the fact that she had on so many jewels I worried she'd fall down the stairs only added to the image.

"Maise, you can go now. I'll be wanting more fresh cucumbers from the market." Miss Daisy Brown dismissed her help before turning to me, the smile on her face as icy cold as the diamonds around her neck.

The tag on my sensible navy blue suit scratched at my neck and the backs of my knees. The smile on my face felt forced, but she couldn't tell. I held out a hand when the old lady tottered over to me, her ankles wobbly in the three-inch heels that barely brought her even with my five-foot-eight.

"Good morning, Miss Brown. I'm Special Agent Gillian Cooley, with the white-collar crime division at the FBI." She peered at my badge when I held it out. The squint of her eyes told me she needed to be wearing glasses. They probably didn't complement her fashion statement. "I'm here to discuss your recent fallout with accountant Neil Saunders."

Miss Daisy Brown pursed her lips, which were too full, the skin around them too tight. She didn't mind spending the money on fighting a losing battle against time, it seemed. "I don't have anything to say about that."

Great.

Step two—assess the mark's intelligence and level of desperation.

"If you wouldn't mind sitting down with me for just a few minutes, I'd like to ask you a few questions and let you know what our task force is doing to recover the funds lost by you and many others."

Her ears perked up at the mention of others. "I suppose it couldn't hurt to listen to what you've got to say. We can go into the dining room. Maise set out some lemonade."

More like saliva juice.

I followed her through a wide doorway into the ugliest dining room known to man. The walls were covered in black-and-white damask paper and dotted with giant wrought-iron sconces that looked as though they were meant for the outdoors. The table was mahogany and stretched from one end of the room to the other, even though I knew from my research that the woman had no family. She'd never married or had children; she had no one to spend her millions on—not that she'd earned a cent of them. Her grandfather had owned massive amounts of property in Texas that had been flowing with oil. His descendants still lived off the proceeds.

The entire house smelled of kasha and mothballs, along with a potpourri of other scents I had no inclination to pin down. Trying not to breathe through my nose, I slid into an upholstered chair at the dining-room table and pulled a folder from my briefcase. It contained the details of what was stolen from her investment accounts and a forged report as to my father's last-known whereabouts, as well as a nifty little card that claimed to give the FBI permission to include her in the list of victims and continue working on her case. In truth, it added my father as a signatory on her checking accounts and safety deposit box at the local bank.

It was shocking how many financial institutions didn't call to double-check things like signature cards, or even require customers to fill them out in person.

She sat down and stirred three packets of Splenda into a tall glass of yellow lemonade. "Maise is trying to kill me. Today it's forgetting the sugar in the lemonade and not making it pink like I asked. Tomorrow it'll be swapping arsenic for lemons."

I kept my mouth shut about that, but made no move to grab the sweating glass in front of me. "Miss Brown, this will only take a few minutes. I'm here so we can verify the facts of your particular case. If you would like to be included in our investigation, I'll just need a signature."

She took the stapled pieces of paper containing her case specifics and glanced over them. The breath staling in my lungs released when her hawklike eyes slid over the words and numbers instead of studying them. There weren't any mistakes—I knew the scam backward and forward—but I always worried there would be too much information there, or things the FBI wouldn't know, but Neil Saunders, a.k.a. Neil Paddington, would.

She didn't say anything about my having too much information, or start screaming her fool head off for the police. Miss Daisy Brown did pinch her bottom lip, watching me in silence while the rusty wheels turned in her batty old brain.

"What are you gonna do to him? If you find him I mean, which is doubtful since the federal government spends more time with its head up its ass than finding criminals, even petty ones like Neil Saunders."

The mini-tirade ended as quickly as it began, leaving me a little dazed but excited about the prospect of getting her on the topic of revenge and off the path of scrutinizing me. "We're going to set up a sting with the information you and others authorize us to use, lure him out into the open, and arrest him. It's not going to be easy to find him, but these people always make a mistake. And we're there when they do."

She snorted, then downed the rest of her lemonade and wiped her chin. "You're not ever gonna get my ten million bucks back, but let me tell you something—there's more where that came from, and more where that came from, too. The Texas Browns got so much money the likes of my crook accountant and Uncle Sam won't never guess."

Apparently not enough money to buy this broad some class. Or grammar lessons. Instead of engaging with her, I behaved like any good federal employee and ignored her idiotic commentary. It only made her keep blabbering in an attempt to get under my skin, but the tirade ended up in my favor, with signed authorizations for three different banks.

I said my good-byes to Miss Daisy Brown, who waved me away like a gnat trying to kill itself in her lemonade. The little envelopes containing her signature cards, all addressed in my best imitation of her handwriting and bearing her return address, fell out of sight into a mailbox on campus. Dad would have access to three more of her accounts within the week. I wondered if he'd be interested in the likelihood that the woman had millions more buried in her backyard. Possibly in a creepy cat graveyard that may or may not contain the last few men who'd tried to woo her money away.

It seemed unlikely we would get it all, but that was okay. She had some to spare.

Dad had promised me ten million dollars for the last eleven years of free assistance on his cons—I'd been doing more legwork than he had ever since he'd decided living in the States proved too much of a risk. The thought of walking away had entered my mind, for sure, but somewhere along the way this had become what I did. I deserved the money in return for everything I'd surrendered, childhood included, and it was almost over.

Less than three years. Then I would be out of the game, and life could be whatever I wanted.

Chapter 3

Sam

We had not gotten in touch with my accountant, which boded poorly for his being able to help us recover my money, and the distraction had done nothing good for my game. I'd made it into the second week of the tournament in Switzerland by the skin of my teeth, helped along by an injury and a seriously uncharacteristic day of poor play by the top Spaniard. Tomas was a good friend of mine, which was one reason I knew to go after his hamstring.

Tennis was funny that way—practice and party with a guy one day, use every dirty trick in the book to kick his ass on the court the next. Every win meant more prize money, and since it appeared I was thirty million poorer, that had become more important than ever.

The season ended in less than a month—my plane would land in Paris in an hour, and after a week in one of my favorite European cities, all that remained was the Davis Cup and ATP finals. Leo wanted me to focus, to concentrate on the tennis and let him sort out my newfound financial woes. Easier said than done. Even spending the last couple of nights in Basel with Chloe hadn't made me feel better, and that was a damn shame.

My hookups had waned over the past six months. I had spent about seven weeks dating an up-and-coming Aussie girl, and since she'd gotten tired of my "shallowness," there had only been a smattering of one-night stands to take her place. My interest level had been too low to argue with her during the, in my opinion, overly dramatic breakup scene, but I wasn't shallow. It had just been clear to me that the two of us weren't made for any kind of long-term compatibility.

It had surprised me how much I'd like to find something less shallow. Just a little over a year ago I'd met Quinn's girlfriend, Emilie, and I'd kind of thought he was crazy for sticking to one girl, no matter how totally hot.

The idea that I might want to change had started in St. Moritz, when I'd met their friend Blair. She'd made it clear she had no interest in sleeping with me, exclusively or not, but there had been something between us. A spark. I was sure she felt it, too, but I didn't know her well enough to guess at her reasons for not wanting to act on it. Even though it hadn't worked out, the experience had flipped some kind of switch in me.

I'd spent my life embracing cynicism regarding long-term relationships. I thought that feelings couldn't change, that there were families who wanted what was best for one another always, no matter what. It was what felt true to me. It was what I knew.

For a girl like Blair, for a feeling like that . . . for a moment I thought about trying.

The wheels touched down in Paris, bouncing a little and forcing me to brace my hands on my armrests. I went through the motions in customs, which never got easier no matter how many stamps were in my passport. It would be impossible for me to answer a question about the last time I'd been in the States for anything other than business, but that didn't stop customs officials giving me a hard time.

When the front desk clerk pulled me aside at the Parisian hotel's elevator bank, I thought, *No way is this happening again.* Leo and the rest of my team had arrived earlier today and he'd texted to say everything was ready and waiting—including a suite with a massage table all set up.

"*Perdon, Monsieur* Bradford?"

"*Oui?*" I felt so tired. My six-week break couldn't come soon enough. If we weren't poised to win the David Cup, I'd be more than a little tempted to end my season after this tournament.

"I have a message for you." He held out a piece of folded cardstock.

"*Merci,*" I replied, taking the piece of paper and heaving a quiet sigh of relief. No more embarrassing conversations about declined credit cards, at least.

I shoved the message in my back pocket, then shouldered my favorite racket bag when the doors dinged and slid open. Massage tables and sophisticated French girls with strong hands were the only things on my mind as the elevator climbed to the top floor, but apparently Leo had different ideas.

There was a table in my room, along with soothing music and some kind of floral scent hanging in the air, but instead of the pretty face I'd been hoping for, Leo's overly tanned mug waited for me in front of the floor-to-ceiling windows.

I dropped my bag and kicked off my freebie Nikes. "What's up?"

"How was your flight, Sam? Mine was good, thank you for asking."

"Cut the shit, Leo. What have you found out about Neil?"

"He's a ghost. Left the States years ago and hasn't been back, at least according to the passport issued under his name. It hasn't been stamped for ten years, give or take, and that was in the Caymans. But he's a kickass sailor. Owns at least three different boats. He could be anywhere."

"How exactly did he slip through our background check, which I'm going to go ahead and assume we do before hiring people to handle millions of my dollars? Is it just me? Are there others? Is he under investigation, or . . . ?"

"Yes, we do background checks, but according to the FBI, who does have a pretty extensive file, this alias was new around the time we hired him. Their file is all unproven conjecture, which is how he's still operating. I contacted Interpol, and same thing. His clients are all high profile, not the types to share who they're working with financially, and also unlikely to report it when they're been had. They both want a statement but I doubt they'll have any more luck if you give them one."

He paused, taking a swig of something girly—maybe a mimosa. The thought of drinking sweet orange juice turned my stomach. "They suspect he has at least one accomplice, but they have no idea who or how they met, or her role in the scams."

"You came in here and interrupted my massage to tell me we still don't know shit?"

"Pretty much. And to raid your minibar because mine was empty."

"Fantastic. Thanks for everything, Leo, as always."

My phone rang, distracting me from wanting to strangle my manager.

"Hello?" I glared at Leo as he rummaged through my minibar and disappeared through our connecting door with all of my vodka.

"Sammy!"

"Quinn?"

"Do you let someone else call you Sammy now? Say it isn't so!" His voice sounded far away and a little tinny.

I grunted. "Not likely. I believe I've made several attempts to get you to stop."

"If you were better at poker this wouldn't be an issue."

"I'm not bad at poker when a guy who's supposed to be mentoring me my first year on the tour isn't dumping an entire bottle of whiskey down my throat." The mere memory of that night made me gag. I hadn't taken a single sip of whiskey since. "What's up?"

"Do I need a reason to call my favorite baby pro?"

I rolled my eyes even though there was something different in his voice. It popped sweat out on my palms. "Usually."

"There was a segment on some gossip show the other night that insinuated that you're having some financial trouble. Just calling to check."

I sank down on the edge of the bed and pinched the bridge of my nose. "What do you mean by 'insinuated'?"

"By that I mean shaky cell phone video of you at the front desk while multiple credit cards get turned down."

"Fucking fantastic."

"You know this is going to severely hamper your ability to get laid."

"Please. I could get laid if I was homeless," I teased back automatically.

"Probably true. What's going on?"

Quinn was a good friend—a better guy than most people believed, truly—but this was embarrassing. I'd let someone into my life who had ripped me off, and instinct and pride begged me to keep my mouth shut.

Then again, if it was going to be picked up by TMZ before the end of the day, there didn't seem to be much of a point.

"I honestly don't know yet. Looks like my accountant is shady. Leo's still trying to get in touch with him."

"Who are you using?"

"Neil Saunders."

"Huh. Never heard of him." He paused, and in my mind, I saw him staring at the ceiling trying to decide what to say. "Well, if you need a friend, I'll get on the next plane. If you need a loan or anything, I'm good for it."

"Christ, Quinn, I'm not broke."

"I know. I trust the prize money from Switzerland is safe—nice job by the way."

"Thanks." The conversation felt unimportant to me, as did the idea of playing tennis when I should be figuring out what in the fuck was going on with my financial life.

Then again, tennis was all I had. There was no other way to make that money back, and it was good that my abs were holding up.

"I'll be okay, Q."

"What's the plan?"

"Keep playing. Try to figure out what happened."

"You know, the same thing happened to Milos Haughlin a few years ago, and call me crazy, but I swear his accountant's name was Neil." He paused. "Anyway, I thought you'd want to know about the churning of the gossip mill, and that I'm worried about you."

"You know me, man. I'll be fine. How are things with your hot girlfriend? She dump you yet?"

"Amazingly not." His voice carried the smile on his face right through the phone. "Too bad for you."

"How's Toby and . . . everyone else?"

"You mean how's Blair?"

My cheeks felt hot, which was completely fucking ridiculous. I barely knew the girl. It had to be the fact that she'd shut me down not once but several times that kept me so curious. The denial sat on the tip of my tongue for a second before I swallowed it. Lying to Quinn had a tiny rate of success, thanks to the bastard's freakish intuition. "Maybe."

"Sammy, you've got to forget that girl. The more time I spend with her, the less I feel like I have any idea what she's like underneath the man-eating exterior. Not to mention she pretty much thinks you're a stalker."

I let another protest go. I'd texted her three times after we'd met in St. Moritz and one of those times was to invite her to the match in Alabama. When she hadn't shown, I *had* let it go.

"She's fine. She was dating some pretty-boy movie star, but that seems to be over."

"Since when are you up on the happenings of your fellow Whitman Owls? What happened to the standoffish, fuck-the-real-world Quinn Rowland who left me after Wimbledon two years ago?" I paused to heighten my followup, a shit-eating grin on my face that I so wished he could see. "Oh, right. He fell in loooove."

"You're a dick."

"I learned from the best."

"Fair enough. Listen, why don't you come down for a visit in December? It would be good to see you, and your parents are close. Em would love to see you again."

Like being in close proximity to my parents sweetened any deal. "I'd love to see you guys, too. I'll give you a call in a couple of weeks."

We hung up, and despite the depressing and invasive event that prompted the phone call, talking with Quinn had made me feel better. Normal. Sure, I'd lost almost thirty million dollars but, no. There was no "but" to that statement. It was a shit ton of money that I had earned, and I wanted it back. There was no way to know how much longer I'd be able to play. I could blow out a knee tomorrow and be done for good, and then what? I had more money than a lot of people, but not enough to last forever.

My phone beeped with an e-mail notification, something from Nike about my signing a new endorsement contract, which improved my mood a tad further. Then the masseuse arrived. I stripped in the bathroom, donned a towel, and spent the next hour letting her try to rub away my troubles.

Chapter 4

Blair

"Dad, you're not listening. He and I know each other—it's not going to work."

The phone crackled and popped, letting my father's gravelly, urging voice through in spurts. "I hear what you're saying, Pear, but it's a simple problem. Solve it. Your already having a relationship with Sam Bradford means we can't run it the usual way, true, but it puts you in a position to run something of your own. Something unique. Use your charms."

"I don't want to use any kind of charm on that guy. Trust me, it's not a good idea."

"Because he's already gotten you into bed or because he wants to but you don't?"

"How many times have I told you that you and I don't discuss sex?"

My dad sighed. "My prickly Pear. I'm not old-fashioned. I use all of the assets at my disposal to close the deal, and I've never shamed you for doing the same. I want the boy's private accounts. You can get them for me."

"How am I supposed to do that?" His request frustrated me more than usual because it meant reneging on my decision to not have anything to do with the overconfident, devastatingly handsome, ridiculously charming number two tennis player in the world. "I don't even like him."

"You don't have to like him. You have to get him to trust you."

The edge in his voice said this discussion had ended. I'd never been clear on what would happen if I refused to hold up my end of this twisted bargain. Would he stop paying for school? Cut me off altogether? Turn me in to Interpol or the FBI?

I'd already made up my mind to leave the lifestyle behind after graduation—I wouldn't need Dad's money anymore and I had enough aliases and contacts around the world to hide if he tried to throw me under the bus. I didn't think he wouldn't do that, for two reasons. The first being that my dad didn't get emotionally involved enough to get angry. The second being that I had just as much dirt on him, and he had no way of knowing if I'd flip to save my own hide.

He'd used me all these years because I was there and I was free, except for school and general living expenses—and maybe because I'd been cute, and then pretty—but if I disappeared he'd find someone else. Part of the reason I'd recognized Sam's con-man charm was that I'd grown up with it. It was a pretty smoke screen, an artificial heart-patter, and it didn't appeal to me.

Even if the connection I'd felt—the heart-patter—had been more than simple charm, a relationship like that was the last thing I needed. Sam was used to getting what he wanted, but I was not keen to be used and then ignored. That had been my entire life.

It still was my life, I reminded myself. For a few more years. "Fine, Neil. I'll figure it out."

There had never been any hope of convincing him otherwise, which was why I'd sent Sam a note at his hotel in Paris a few weeks ago. The fact that my attempt to break the ice had gone unanswered felt problematic, but I doubted that a guy like him would pass on the opportunity to close a deal he'd been denied. His ego was his sweet spot, for me. Weak spot for him.

"That's my girl. Send me a message when it's done."

"What are we doing for the holidays? Anything?"

Sometimes he liked to play the part of the loving father—usually to work an angle—but my plans would depend on his, and Audra had invited me to Elgin for the winter holiday.

"I don't know. It's going to depend on a few things, probably last minute."

"Where are you?" I asked the question knowing there wouldn't be an answer. Whether he wanted to protect me or himself had never been 100 percent clear, but if and when I saw my father, it would be in the form of a chartered jet with a flight plan filed by one of his many shadow companies, not by me.

"On the water, baby. You know that."

He signed off with that, leaving me with an impossible problem, a marketing exam to study for, and a report for the night's sorority meeting that needed to be prepped.

Audra hadn't been home all day. She was gone more often than not, and when she was here she spent most of the time glued to her phone. The meeting was mandatory, though, and I thought maybe the two of us could hang out afterward.

First things first, though. Sam had ignored the message I'd left—his number had never been added to my phone on purpose, and when I'd gotten a new one it had been lost altogether—so I needed a way to get in touch with him. Which meant biting a rather bitter bullet.

I dragged myself off the bed, out the front door, and into my car. The chill in the afternoon air nipped as badly as it ever would in south Florida, just enough to make me miss Manhattan. My brain turned the Sam Bradford problem over and over in my head until a plausible solution started to take shape.

It went against every instinct, but the answer was the truth. Approaching this con with a lie or a cover wasn't an option, given that he knew the real me, but I still had the element of surprise. My father had been using the name Neil Saunders for the last five years, running long cons with clients like Sam and Daisy, so Sam would have no idea that he was my father.

Unless I told him.

The campus athletic complex parking lot wasn't even half full this time of year. The fall sports were winding down and our football team was on the road. Winter sports were gearing up, but with winter break looming in a few weeks, the gym wasn't swamped. The people inside were those few students using exercise instead of some kind of substance to fuel their studies, and the tennis team, who had conditioning from four to six every evening.

Heat and the smell of sweat smacked me in the face when I entered the indoor practice facilities. I loitered by the door, watching Quinn Rowland where he stood on the far side of a blue and white state-of-the-art tennis court and whacked ball after yellow ball at a line of sweaty students closer to me. He shouted over the sound of squeaking tennis shoes, heavy breathing, and rackets smashing into balls—some of it encouragement, some disappointed-sounding instruction—as the drill continued without a break for another ten minutes.

Some of the players collapsed when he called an end to the practice. Quinn wiped his forehead and swigged some water, his eyebrows going up when he noticed me loitering near the doors.

I gave him my most genuine smile, but judging by the suspicion brightening his impossible blue eyes, it needed some work. His thin white shirt clung to every hard dip and curve across his chest and all of the ripples down his stomach until his upper body disappeared into his shorts. Even with sweaty chunks of black hair sticking to his forehead and a salty smell hovering around him, he was dead fucking sexy. Sexier than Zach Flynn, and sexier than the boy I'd thought I loved in high school.

Or rather, I thought he'd loved me. Both turned out to be false.

"Hey," I smiled, approaching Quinn. "Good workout?"

Quinn flicked a glance at his destroyed athletes. "They'll be in shape by spring. Whether or not that means they'll be able to play decent tennis remains to be seen."

"I'm sure you can do something with them."

"Thanks." He grabbed a towel and wiped the back of his neck, those keen blue eyes studying me the whole time. The guy missed nothing. "What are you doing here? Thinking of playing?"

"Me? Hell no. I enjoy a good tennis match, but no way I'm willingly putting my life in your hands." The pause that followed felt awkward, but I forced my voice to emerge at my leisure. "I lost Sam's number and wanted to text him. Can you give it to me?"

"Why?"

I forced myself to meet his gaze. "What do you mean, why?"

"I mean, I heard he didn't make much of a secret of his interest in Switzerland last spring, and I know for a fact he invited you to sit in his box at his first tournament back, and you blew him off both times, so . . . why now?"

It occurred to me now that perhaps the drive would have been better spent figuring out how to con Quinn Rowland rather than Sam Bradford. Of the two of them, Quinn struck me as the more suspicious. Then again, since my dad had recently lifted thirty million off of Sam, I had to assume he would no longer be the trusting, happy-go-lucky guy I remembered, either.

Luckily, I was at least as smart as Quinn, and I had the advantage of knowing what game we were playing, at least at the moment. "Well, when Sam and I met, I had a thing for Flynn, and then we dated. That ship has sailed, and I can't help but wonder if I missed out on something with your friend."

Quinn's eyebrows went back up. "So, it doesn't bother you anymore that he's a pro tennis player with girls swooning at his feet all over the world?"

"I'm not saying we're going to get married, Rowland. Christ. Are you his mother now? I just hate the idea of always wondering what would have happened, since even though I told him I wasn't interested, I felt something between us."

This time I waited out the awkward pause. The best thing to bring to any negotiation was the ability to walk away, and I had other ways of getting to Sam Bradford. Perhaps not ways as convenient or simple, but ways nonetheless.

"Give me your phone."

Victory. I handed it over and watched as he added Sam to my contacts, then took it back and returned it to my purse. "Thanks."

"I don't trust you."

"Sam's a big boy, Rowland. He can make his own decisions."

"Fair enough." He broke into a dazzling smile, dissolving the oddly combative moment hanging between us. "So what are you doing tonight? Are you finished for break?"

"I have a marketing exam tomorrow, then yes. What are you and Emilie doing for Thanksgiving?" I barely knew Emilie Swanson, or Quinn for that matter, but I preferred the attention and questions not be directed at me.

The flicker of distrust in his eyes said he didn't miss my redirection. "We're spending it with her family, since she figures I can't mouth off too much over a one-day meal. Christmas we're traveling Eastern Europe."

"Do you mouth off often?"

"I can't handle anyone who wants to make her feel like she's not amazing."

The sweet honesty in his voice shook something at my core. It was so much rarer than people believed to hear truth spill from someone's lips without any kind of agenda or caveat behind it. The two of them were a legend on Whitman's campus since they'd gotten together almost two years ago, and even for me—a huge cynic—it was hard not to be touched.

It was almost painful to see it. To know it existed. Because it made me hope.

"Okay, well, thanks."

"No problem." He winked. "Have fun. I've never heard any complaints."

"I'm glad you said that. You being sweet throws my worldview off kilter, but you being gross makes total sense."

"I'm part of your worldview?"

"Coming to Whitman? Sure. You're a legend. Or you were." He still kind of was, just for different reasons, but the last thing Quinn needed was a bigger ego.

"I'm good with that. Gotta have stories to tell the grandkids one day. And now, I have someone to imagine grandkids with. Double win."

"Double win."

I said good-bye and wandered back out to the parking lot, trying to steady my shaken foundation. Since I'd been old enough to understand how babies were made, I knew that I didn't want one. The idea that I could ever be normal enough to fix myself, never mind not fuck up someone else, didn't seem possible.

The idea that I could find someone I'd want to be yoked to for the rest of my life seemed even less likely. Or that anyone would want to be tied that way to me.

I wasn't seeing my dad for Thanksgiving. Until our conversation today, I'd figured on staying at Whitman, maybe trying to get a jump on studying for finals or figuring out my schedule for next semester. Financial reports were due to Kappa Chi nationals before the end of the year, as well.

Now, it appeared I'd be traveling.

When I got back to the Kappa house, I pulled up my computer to find out where Sam was at the moment— it didn't qualify as stalking if his whereabouts were easily found on the Internet. It appeared the season had just ended for the year, so it was hard to say. The American team had finished third in the Davis Cup, due in no small part to Sam's efforts, and he'd ended his year with his number two ranking firmly in place. If everything stayed the same next season, he had a legitimate shot at grabbing number one from Javier Trevino, the Spaniard who had held the spot for the past three years—who, also according to the Internet, was also Sam's practice partner.

There was disturbingly little information and even less gossip about Sam Bradford, aside from the typical ladies'-man assumptions. I found nothing that told me where he lived in the off-season, where he liked to vacation, or who he'd supposedly been dating—the gossip sites did have archives under his name, mostly because he'd dated more than his fair share of hot models and/or actresses, but nothing current popped on a Google search.

His parents lived in Boca, at least officially, but they struck me as the kind of people who weren't ashamed to ride their son's financial coattails. Living this kind of life all of these years had given me several gifts, but none came in handier than my ability to read people with a pretty high reliability. I was almost never wrong. Sam's parents were greedy assholes. I'd bet my hair on it, and I had a shameless, narcissistic love for my hair.

Stalking wasn't getting my anywhere, and the sorority meeting started in fewer than ten minutes. I took a deep breath, grabbed my phone, and scrolled through my contacts. There was nothing under Sam or Bradford, and I rolled my eyes, thinking I should have known better. Now I had to guess where Quinn had stored his friend's number.

An entry for Monster Dick jumped out at me. I was sure I'd never added that one, though I did tend to give nicknames to the boys I met at the bars, or even ones I dated. Flynn had been Pretty Boy in my phone the entire two or three months we'd been together.

I shook my head and typed out a message—short and sweet, and following nothing but instinct.

47

Hey, this is Blair Paddington, Quinn's friend from Whitman. I'm not sure if you remember me from St. Moritz, but I was thinking about you and thought I'd say hi. Hit me back if you have time to chat for a few.

I typed and deleted an exclamation point a few times, then typed and deleted a smiley face, then did the same with an XO before dropping the phone with a groan. It was better to leave it, since I'd been so insistent on not being interested. Especially since he'd just been taken for millions of dollars, Sam would be wary. Changing my behavior too drastically could work against me—even texting him could be too much, but I didn't have much of a choice.

In the end, I texted the private investigator we had on retainer instead. He was sleazy as fuck, but he could tell me where Sam would be on Sunday. It would be better that way—showing up out of the blue. With the story I'd decided to use, I'd still look like a stalker but it would work.

Audra pushed the door open a minute later and slung her backpack onto the thin carpet. Her cheeks were pink and her eyes sparkled like emeralds. "Hey. What are you up to?"

"Nothing. Just getting ready for the meeting."

"I know, I'll hurry." She kicked off her flip-flops and jeans, then stripped her tight shirt over her abdomen. "What's going on tonight? Is it going to be a long one?"

I shook my head, applying some lip gloss and tugging a rust-colored cardigan over my black-and-white dress. Most of the girls hated formal meetings, but they weren't so bad. Dressing up had always been fun to me—in fact, it had been one of the things Dad used to hook me into the con life as a little girl. "No. Reminding everyone that their dues and incidentals need to be paid before they go home for Christmas, and I think solidifying a location for spring formal. You have plans with Logan later?"

"No. They have a meeting, too, and he has a big exam tomorrow. I was hoping we could hang out, actually."

I smiled, still surprised that her friendship inspired that reaction in me. Friends had never been encouraged. They asked too many questions. "That would be awesome. I'm ready for my marketing exam tomorrow, and I'm leaving town Saturday, so it'll be nice."

"Where are you going?" She asked, her voice muffled by a navy blue ruffled sheath.

It brought out the green in her eyes, reminding me how pretty the Scottish girl was, and making me think again how too good she was for Logan Shapiro.

"I'm meeting my dad overseas for a few days."

"You aren't going to miss the rest of the semester again, are you?" Concern lit her expression as she swept her lashes with mascara.

"I don't think so. Last year was a family emergency." *Lie.* It had been to set up a few of Dad's clients in the Caymans. "This is vacation."

49

Not technically a lie. It seemed as though I might be having a forced fling with Sam Bradford, if talking him into trusting me turned out to be as difficult as expected. Thinking about it twisted my lips into a grimace. Plenty of girls would willingly take my place, but there were way too many reasons this was a terrible idea. Dad hadn't wanted to hear any of them, though, even though it could very possibly mean curtains on my time at Whitman.

I was used to moving, though, and I could graduate from anywhere with a marketing degree. The plan to get Sam to trust me would work, but I hadn't thought of a way to come out the other end still smelling like roses. He would tell Quinn what I really am, and my life here would become a living hell, at best.

Audra watched me, her expression curious. "What are you thinking about? You looked so sad for a second."

"Did I?" I forced a smile, unused to having other people watching *me*. "I was thinking about how I hardly see you since you've started dating Logan."

"I know." Audra reached out and squeezed my hand. "I'm going to do better at managing my time. Plus, the sex has to slow down eventually, right? Like, the honeymoon period only lasts so long?"

Knowing the answer to that question would require having been with someone long enough to find out. "That's what I hear."

"Cole has been bugging me about why I never spend time at their house anymore, too. The excuses of not wanting to hang out with old grad students and sorority duties only goes so far."

"I can't believe he doesn't know who you're dating, Audra. Whitman isn't that big of a campus. He's going to find out sooner or later, and don't you think it's going to hurt his feelings that you didn't tell him about a guy you're so obviously crazy about?"

"I'm more worried about what piece of Logan he'll hurt if he finds out at all."

I rolled my eyes and grabbed the folder of financial reports off my desk. "The Stuart brothers can't possibly have expected you to never date a single soul until you married. Right?"

She shrugged and slipped into a pair of heels, declining to answer the question. "Ready?"

We left the room together, her knee-length skirt and mine making swishing noises in the empty hallway. It bothered me that Audra was so keen on keeping her relationship a secret from her brothers. If Logan was a good, upstanding guy then she would trust him to win her family over . . . wouldn't she?

Spending years watching other people—brothers and sisters, parents and children—meant that I knew them well enough to scent their weak spots. It taught me nothing about how to live inside a family unit. There were surely more complications than I could guess, so maybe Audra deserved some slack.

But if she and Logan were still dating when I got back from Christmas break then my sleazy private investigator would have another project. I lived by my instincts. I'd learned to trust them, and even though

Audra would probably hate me as much as everyone else once she found out about my dad and what we'd done to Sam, she was the closest thing I'd ever had to a friend. My greasy worry over this obsessive relationship wouldn't go away until I figured out the source.

We lined up in alphabetical order to enter the Chapter Room. The other girls bitched about the formality and traditions. It was kind of a pain to follow them to the letter every time, but it made this experience feel special to me. Like we were part of a giant family, one that had been formed a hundred years ago by a group of women not too unlike us, and we all still belonged to one another, bound together by the little things that we'd done together over and over.

When I reached down to make sure my phone was on silent, I saw a text message from Captain Sleazeball, the private investigator.

Westin hotel in Melbourne, and according to my sources, has plans to spend the majority of the next two months in the area. I've sent the address and room number to your private e-mail account. Let me know if you require any additional specifics.

Great. Fucking Australia. Despite what I'd told Audra, it looked as if I might not be able to finish the semester on campus. It would be tricky, since I'd used the family emergency excuse last spring, but my professors would probably let me take the finals remotely. I was a good student, and they trusted my devotion to academia. Taking into consideration the fact that plenty of Whitman students had less-than-average lifestyles, with the right explanation, they'd be falling over themselves to let me finish from the road.

The music started in the Chapter Room and the line of chattering sorority girls fell silent. We stepped through the white-painted doors, and I took my place at the table toward the front. I watched the rest of them file into rows of cloth-adorned folding chairs, wearing their Kappa Chi letters on their chests and varying expressions of interest.

They were the only sisters I'd ever have, the only family who had ever chosen me. Like true families, even the girls I didn't particularly like, I loved. A hole opened up in my chest at the thought of losing a single one of them.

I couldn't afford to think like that. They weren't family, which meant I didn't get to keep them. It had been a hard, early, lesson in the days and weeks after my mother's death.

Chapter 5

Sam

$\mathcal{I}$'d opted out of Thanksgiving with my family. They didn't know about the stolen money yet, but they had seen the same gossip on the news that Quinn had. They'd been relentlessly asking me to explain, unwilling to accept my "it was a mistake" explanation.

Not unwilling. Afraid. If I lost everything, so did they, and my parents had no intention of getting a job other than following me around the world. The only member of my family that I felt close to was my cousin Melody. She was three years older than me and a successful book editor in New York City, and we'd been close ever since she'd spent a year traveling with me during college.

She'd never once asked me for money. It shouldn't matter, but it did.

Summer held Melbourne tight in its grasp. Choosing to come here for my six weeks off had multiple benefits, the warm weather being a big one. The massive time difference and jet lag followed close behind, because it also meant that I wouldn't be expected home for Christmas, since the Australian hardcourt season began at the beginning of the new year.

Basically, I could wallow here for the next month and a half without anyone bothering me. I was not typically a wallower, but this one had been earned. Fucking Neil.

This morning had disappeared into a haze of burning muscles and sticky buckets of sweat. The five-mile run on the beach, followed by an hour in the weight room, then a two-hour practice had done wonders for my state of mind, but I needed a shower worse than a homeless person.

I let myself into my suite at the Westin, then stopped cold at the sight of Blair Paddington, who didn't disappear after a hard blink. She sat on the love seat, looking as beautiful as the last time I'd seen her, which I realized in that moment had been far too long ago. Her hands were steady as she poured tea from a silver pot into delicate, rose-painted china, then dumped in a lump of sugar and stirred. The bored gaze that met mine was dark brown, almost black, like an inviting cup of coffee. Matching hair tumbled past her shoulders, begging me to run my fingers through it, to fist my hands in it.

"Are you going to stand there with your mouth hanging open or say hello?"

The indolent tone freed me of the thought that she might be a dream. It dumped me into reality, a place where this girl who lived halfway around the world did not belong. It also reminded me that she'd been pretty rough in her many refusals to my advances, and my dignity replied.

"I don't typically say hello to people who let themselves into my private space without asking. Or being invited."

She shrugged, an odd and out-of-place gesture in response to my statement. "Tea?"

"No, thank you."

"Would you rather have coffee? I ordered both."

And no doubt charged it to my room. "No. I don't drink caffeine."

"Ah, gotcha. I'll remember next time."

The shock of seeing her here started to wear off, and suspicion replaced it. It was so unlike me to not take things in stride or assume the best of people, and the subtle change made me hate Neil Saunders even more. In another life—five weeks ago—my assumption would have been that she had finally given in to her unvoiced desires and sought me out.

Sure, I would have wondered how she found me and how she weaseled her way into my room, but remaining friends with Quinn had taught me that the kids at Whitman had the kind of money that fueled the wet dreams of even my fellow tennis pros. Not to mention that Blair's beauty and charm could probably talk some unsuspecting CIA agent out of a key to the White House.

"What are you doing in Melbourne?"

"I would have assumed your first question would have been about how I managed to get into your room."

"Or find my hotel, but yes. The answers to all three of those questions are going to be necessary if you don't want me to call security and have you hauled out of here."

"I thought you liked me." She pouted.

The curve of her bottom lip almost distracted me. Almost. "I barely know you. Which I've recently come to realize can actually be an issue."

She sighed and then sipped the steaming cup of what smelled like vanilla chai. I'd spent enough time in Europe to discern my teas. After a few moments of silence she stood and stretched. Blair was all lithe movements and smooth skin, reminding me of a cat as she slipped past me and opened the doors that led out to the balcony.

A whiff of citrusy perfume tickled my nose as I followed her into the balmy late morning. The sound of the waves crashing on the shore dove into my center and soothed the worry tightening my stomach, another reason I'd chosen this particular spot for the remainder of my rehab and downtime. When Blair turned, resting her elbows on the ledge of the wrought-iron balcony, my heart stammered in an attempt to find an even rhythm. Even though the hesitance in her gaze said her appearance had nothing to do with a romantic change of heart, it couldn't stop the thought of how perfect she looked with the salty breeze toying with her hair.

"I'm not here because I changed my mind about dating you. I'm here because of what recently transpired between you and your accountant, Neil . . . Saunders, is it?" She smirked, but the mirth didn't reach her dark eyes.

My heart stopped altogether. "How do you know about that? Who have you told?"

"Take it easy. I haven't told anyone and I'm not going to. I know what happened because Neil Saunders is a pseudonym for big-time con man Neil Paddington." She paused, watching me closely, then continued when she received silence. "And Neil Paddington just happens to be my father."

She waited while the news sank in, looking strangely as though she was prepared to wince away from a swift punch but ready to stick her jaw out to meet it at the same time. Neil, who had conned me and ripped me off for over thirty million, was Blair's father. It didn't seem any weirder than anything else since he'd betrayed my trust, though, and I tried my best to stifle my confusion and surprise.

The past several years, since my career really took off, I'd let other people handle the details of my life. Before that, I'd been much more involved and despite what people—probably including Blair—thought, I wasn't a dumb jock. That I'd come off looking like an ignorant, trusting dumbass hurt almost more than losing the money. Almost.

"That still doesn't explain what you're doing here." It did sort of explain how she found me, since her father seemed to know whatever he wanted whenever he wanted. Her smile was explanation enough as far as getting into my room, but I planned to talk to the hotel manager about it at my earliest opportunity. Hot girl or not, letting people into my space was not cool.

"I want to help you get it back."

"Get it back . . ." I repeated slowly, not understanding where this was going. "The money? Why? And, more importantly, how?"

"You might guess that I didn't have the most fantastic childhood. My father is a ghost, even to me, and I haven't seen him in over two years." Blair tucked a piece of hair that was caught in the breeze behind her ear. Her fingers trembled and she took a deep breath before continuing. "I want to find him. You want to find him. I thought we could help each other out."

"If you haven't talked to him, how do you know I was one of his . . . cons?" I couldn't bring myself to say "victim."

"I said I hadn't seen him. The FBI is all over my ass—has been since before I could drive—to help them find and arrest my dad. I'm tired of this shit. Of being watched, of being treated like a criminal by association. I don't want to deal with it anymore. But I *have* talked to him. He doesn't keep his life or his cons a secret from me."

"So you knew he was going to steal from me before it happened?" Just talking about the money made my mouth go dry. "How could you do that to me?"

"First of all, I barely know you, remember? Second of all, I don't know the names of all of his marks. I know he's been running long cons, mostly international, mostly high-profile clients, as Neil Saunders for the past four to five years. I saw the blip on TMZ's radar about your credit card being declined and asked the next time we talked. End of story."

Her voice softened and she reached out a hand, resting it on my forearm. Despite the surreal nature of this entire conversation, my muscles twitched in response to her silky skin against mine.

"So, you find out some guy you barely know—and didn't want to know, by the way—just lost the bulk of the money he's earned with fucking sweat and time and a lot of other things I can't bitch about, and your immediate reaction is to fly halfway around the world to ask me to join you on a manhunt for your father. Do you even have a clue where he is?"

A knock at the door interrupted her reply, whatever it was going to be, and she slipped past me back into the room. It took me aback, the way she moved purposefully through my space in her bare feet, but it also felt strangely as though it had been happening my entire life. As though the wrong scenario was one in which she *hadn't* ordered multiple courses of room service without asking.

Blair signed the receipt and thanked the porter, then flopped back on the couch and put her feet up on the coffee table. "Could you be a dear and pour the champagne? I'm old-fashioned about things like that."

"About pouring your own beverage?" I asked, more curious about her than ever.

I picked up the bottle of champagne and worked on the cork, my mind racing. Blair had grown up the daughter of a con man. What that entailed I had no idea, but she appeared a bundle of contradictions. The girl who butted her way into my room and spent my money, the one who didn't pour her own champagne, the one who claimed to be bothered by the effects of her father's enterprise, the one who wanted to help me.

She had said that, hadn't she? That his criminal activities bothered her?

I shook my head, trying to clear it. The situation with Neil suggested that more caution was needed in my personal life, and as pretty as Blair was, as sincere as she seemed, and as much as I would really, really like to take her clothes off of her . . . who's to say she wasn't a chip off the ol' block?

She shrugged in response to my question about pouring her own drinks. The thin strap of her sundress slid down her tanned shoulder and I forgot what was happening.

It was a nice four seconds.

"I think that, while feminism has its merits, we've lost a few niceties along the way." She took the flute of champagne from my fingers, smiling. "Like having someone bring us a drink and being okay with it."

"I'm okay with it."

I poured my own glass and settled in the overstuffed chair next to the love seat to keep some distance between us, unwilling to let the sparks I felt around her cloud my judgment.

"So, what do you think? Do you want to help each other out?"

"There are many, many ways I can envision the two of us helping each other out," I replied without thinking. "But as far as finding your dad . . . I mean, what good would that do?"

She ignored my suggestive statement. "We find him, we turn him in, the FBI helps you get your money back. It's not that hard to figure out."

Maybe not, but something bothered me. I couldn't put my finger on what, and maybe it wasn't anything at all. Maybe I was paranoid, and I should go ahead and count her appearance as a blessing fallen from the sky, but . . . "You would do that? Turn in your own dad?"

To her credit, she paused. Something flickered in her eyes, there and then gone before I could pin it down or even begin to figure out what caused it. In its place, a mask of indifference that I so did *not* believe, descended.

"Honestly? I don't know what I'll do when the moment comes. But I want to see him, and if you know where he is you'll have enough leverage to at least get your money back. Win-win, right?"

It sounded right. But also wrong.

I mean, I wanted my money back. Badly. My still-questionable obliques scared the piss out of me—the idea that it could all be over in a moment and I'd be left with nothing. No way to make money, nothing to fall back on, since 80 percent of my life had been dedicated to this sport. Her offer tempted me, to say the least.

"What's your plan? Use the same private investigator you used to find me?" Another knock at the door closed her mouth, which was distracting as fuck. "Jesus, are we having a ten-course breakfast?"

"No. I was hungry after this stupid long flight but I didn't want to waste any time. I'll give you the cash, if you want, but I mean . . . you kind of owe me."

"*Owe* you? Your father ripped me off—I'm guessing you'll get your fair share of that sooner or later."

"I don't know about fair. That's not really a concept near and dear to my father's heart."

She let in another porter, this one bringing waffles, fresh fruit, and biscuits with jam. Thank God no Vegemite, because as much as I loved this country, that shit was an atrocity.

"You think I owe you because you're offering to find your dad. Except you have no idea where he is, either."

"When did I say that? No one knows my dad and his habits better than I do—shit, no one else knows my dad and his habits at all. I can find him. I know it. But . . ." She cut her waffle, flicking a dubious glance my direction.

"But what?"

"I'll need your financial details in order to lure him out of hiding when I find him."

"I'm sorry, when *you* find him?" She went still, but there was no way that was happening. "I have six weeks off. If you're going to find your dad, I'm going with you. And I'm sorry, but I wouldn't give my financial details to Jesus right now."

"You don't have to do that, Sam. You can trust me. I'll be faster on my own, and my dad's defenses won't be up if it's just me, and . . ."

"You can stop talking. I'm coming with you."

Annoyance tangled with frustration tightened the muscles in her face. Now she looked more like the Blair

Paddington I'd met in Switzerland, the girl who had unwillingly lit such a fire of interest inside me.

"No, you're not. I'm going alone, and I can try to get your money back or not. Without your details, he has no reason to meet me, and I have no way to get your money back. I came to offer you my help, not to babysit you on a trek across the world."

"Excuse me, but there would be no babysitting. I have contacts and friends in a dozen countries, speak five languages, and have the desire for justice on my side. In what way would I be a hindrance to you?"

"First of all, I didn't invite you. Second, my father has pretty specific security mechanisms in place, and you're pretty high profile, which means he could find you anywhere in the world in under ten minutes. How do you think I did it?"

"So, if that's true, what makes you think he can't find you even faster? You're his daughter. If you take me with you, I promise to pull my weight and give you a percentage of anything I recover." It was a last-ditch move, a shot in the dark, but my curiosity overrode everything else.

I wanted to see how Blair would react to me offering her money in order to right a wrong.

"I don't want your money, Sam. What kind of person do you think I am?"

The breath I'd been holding gushed out of my lungs and I smiled at her. It seemed to take her aback, but the loosening of the tension in my gut felt great. If she was like her father, with little to no moral compass, she wouldn't have turned down a fee.

That's what I'd have to believe to go forward. To at least trust her enough not to lead me down a dark alley and kick me in the nuts.

"So we'll go together? Fly under the radar?"

She squinted up at me. "You know what that means, right? No fancy hotels, no room service, no staying with your friends or taking chartered jets. It's going to be . . . different."

"For you, too." After a moment she nodded reluctantly. I grinned because I wanted to see if she would return it, and warmth spread over my skin when she did. "So, do you think we'll need to wear disguises?"

*

"Are you *sure* you want to come?" Blair asked me for at least the fiftieth time in the past twenty-four hours, pursing her lips as she slammed charging cords into her backpack. "I'm sure it's not going to be good for your training schedule. And the time change is going to be a bitch to deal with when you come back for the start of the season."

"Yes, I'm sure, but thanks for coming up with new reasons for me to stay. The others were getting stale." No reaction. "Besides, we'll be on the move and you can be my new hitting partner. You up for it?"

This time she rolled her eyes, shouldering her pack in a way that drew my eyes to her breasts under her tight black tank top. "I'm going to assume you mean tennis, not some *other* kind of hitting. And I don't play."

"I'm still coming. And by that I mean coming along, not some *other* kind of coming, although we are going to be spending a lot of time together so I hope you're prepared to control yourself in that department."

"I think I'll manage," she said with a snort. "Are you ready?"

"Yep. We're all checked out, and I have enough cash and euros on me to pay an international ransom. Are you going to tell me where we're headed first now?"

"You mean you're not going to follow me blindly, no questions asked? I knew that it would never have worked between us."

I stepped closer, inhaling her perfume and purposefully invading her personal space, not missing the hitch in her breath when we drew close enough to touch. Blair had been flirtier since she came to my room this morning, still trying to change my mind but also ready to accept my company on her trek. Her cocoa eyes gazed up into mine, a confusion of thoughts parading through them. I couldn't catch a single one, but most of them I didn't like.

I bent down until our faces were inches apart, loving that she leaned in to me instead of backing away. Blair likely didn't shy away from much. "Trust me, Blair, if we were involved, I would lead or follow, whichever you wanted at the time. I do it all."

She tipped her chin up, but not before a delicate shudder told me she wasn't immune to the crackling tension between us. "Maybe so, but given your confidence and reputation, I'd need to see multiple blood test results to go anywhere near your bare skin."

Protests or not, she leaned closer when I took another step forward, swaying as though fighting the desire to touch me. "Is that what bothers you? That you wouldn't be the only one?" I slapped her ass a little harder than necessary, and when she bit her lip I got a hard-on I would have to hide.

Her recovery didn't take long, and the dirty look she shot me could wither a rose in the middle of summer. "Rule number one—don't ever touch my ass again. Rule number two, I've never been a one-and-only kind of girl, but this entire partnership is fragile enough without adding sex to the mix. I think we'd be best off keeping it simple."

"Agreed. Nothing fancy, then. And I agree to your rules, with one exception—I won't touch you again until you *ask* me to."

"Fair enough. Let's go."

I could tell by the look on her face that she thought resisting me would be possible, but the lust neither one of us could quite hide made me wonder if we wouldn't end up in bed together sooner or later. Even though it was hard to feel badly about that, the whole thing tickled my newfound suspicious bone. Blair had been so dead set against even a harmless fling with me, she'd turned down at least five requests for a date and refused to come to my tennis tournament. What had changed?

It could be that nothing had changed, because no matter her protests, the attraction between us couldn't be one-sided. She felt it, and I felt it. Maybe she had gotten tired of fighting it.

Maybe. But she showed up out of nowhere, claimed to be the daughter of my accountant and that she wanted to help me. My unwillingness to let her go without me had been met with . . . flirtation. As much as I wanted to, I couldn't trust it.

Instead of overthinking it, I followed her swaying hips down the hotel stairs—all twenty flights of them—and into a cab. A *cab*. I couldn't remember the last time a car hadn't been waiting for me, but according to Blair's assessment of her father's reach, the flying-under-the-radar plan was necessary. If we used our connections, he would know.

And this was only the beginning. We were flying *coach* all the way to fucking Austria.

It had been a long time since no one had waited on me hand and foot, but that wasn't even my biggest concern—it was the germs. It wasn't my manliest quality, and I didn't share my issue with many people because it was a bigger problem than I liked to admit, but they freaked me out. And I was pretty sure I was the only guy on the tennis tour with a full-fledged plan for the zombie apocalypse.

Because it *was* going to happen. It was only a matter of time before germs adapted further and turned on us, the microscopic little hellbeasts, and we were all brain-rotted zombies. I didn't want to think about how many of them lived on commercial airlines or were currently trying to find a way through my pants in the cab.

"Why are you making that face?" Blair asked, watching me with a mixture of amusement and concern from her side of the taxi.

I stared at her legs, half turned on and half horrified that her bare skin was touching the cracked black leather that had been touched by countless other bare legs. It wasn't an incapacitating obsessive-compulsive fear of germs, but I went out of my way to avoid certain things. And, fine, the incapacitating level of my problem might not be far off.

Blair didn't need to know my secrets, or weaknesses. It made me uncomfortable enough that she'd read my face with such ease. "Nothing. Just thinking."

"You know, if taking a taxi bothers you this much, this is going to be one long trek."

"Maybe we'll find him in Austria."

"You have no idea how badly I'm hoping that's the case." She wrinkled her nose. "You're sitting in the middle on the flight, by the way."

We lapsed back into silence when I didn't argue with her. Arguing could turn into a full-time job with the two of us, and I had no interest in a nine-to-five. I had a bag full of sleeping aids in the shape of pills. She'll be sorry she didn't give me the window when I pass out on her lap and leave a drool puddle between her legs.

No. Do not think about anything between her legs.

"The taxi doesn't bother me."

She gave me a look that said she didn't buy my protest but was already tired of arguing with me, too. I had no idea how she read me like that—we hadn't spent hardly any time together and I had no idea what she was thinking. Ever.

My phone buzzed with a text message from my cousin Melody, asking if she could come spend Christmas with me. I replied with an excited yes; it would be nice to not be alone on the holiday for the first time in years. Then a message came in from Leo, wanting to know where in the hell I'd gotten off to, and I had to break the news that I was leaving the country for an undetermined amount of time.

There was no way Blair could miss the angry buzzing of my phone created by his flurry of pissed-off protests, and I caught her eyebrow raised in between my hurried responses. "You're not the only one who's less than thrilled about my decision to blow off a few days of training."

"You know—"

"Save your breath."

Once we checked our bags and went through security, we settled at a table in the airport Starbucks without discussing it. Blair ordered a black coffee and stirred in cinnamon, vanilla, and Splenda. I ordered a decaffeinated tea.

"Okay, so now that I've proven my willingness to follow blindly and we can't possibly be overheard by anyone who cares, Miss Paranoid, how about you share a little bit about where we might be going on this little impromptu adventure."

I still wasn't convinced this would end up doing me any good. Even if we did find Neil, why would he give me my money back? What if he was more of a badass con man than a weaselly one and tried to, like, get rid of me or something?

Part of me wanted to forget the thirty mil and nurse my wounds in Australia, make sure my body was ready for the season in six weeks, and focus on replacing what had been stolen.

The beautiful, irritating, mysterious girl across from me shouldn't have anything to do with my decision, yet she did. She'd been on my mind, in my fantasies, for months, and this gave me the opportunity to spend time with her, get to know her. It made me entertain the ridiculous notion that maybe this entire thing happened so that the universe could force her to get to know me.

It couldn't stop the insistent burble underneath all of that, the quiet, certain whisper that I couldn't trust her.

"Sure, we can talk about it." Blair bent down, her silky chocolate hair spilling over her arm as she reached into her bag. Her fingers smoothed the wrinkles out of a piece of notebook paper. I tried not to imagine how they would feel on my skin, how her hair would tickle my cheeks.

"So, there are five places that have always been my dad's favorites. Every time he's asked to see me in the past five or six years, it's been in one of these places . . . but he's always had me flown in to a private airport and driven to his house, so it's hard for me to guess exact locations."

"And one is in Austria. It's a big country."

"I know, but I know what airport I flew in to and how long the ride was to his house."

71

"General direction?"

"You know, you really don't fit the dumb jock image."

"You say that like you're disappointed." I smiled, trying to soften my response. "Do I have a dumb jock image?"

She shrugged, and the pink tinge to her cheeks surprised me. "I don't really keep up, honestly. I'm not . . . comfortable with the whole idea of notoriety."

"Is that why things didn't work out with you and Flynn?"

Blair's head snapped up, her fingers curling around the edge of the paper. "How do you know about me and Flynn?"

"Is it a secret?" The twisted expression on her face didn't lessen. "Quinn."

"Oh. Right." Her shoulders relaxed. "Anyway, yes, that was one of the reasons things didn't work out with Flynn. Although I'm not sure what 'work out means,' since we're, like, nineteen years old. We had fun for a while. I didn't like the idea of the cellulite on my ass being circled in national magazines."

"I've spent a good amount of time staring at your ass, and it looks damn good."

"Yeah, well, you haven't seen it naked."

"I think we could remedy that. I mean, if you're concerned. I could even photograph it if you want."

"*Anyway,* the car in Austria headed south from the airport in Villach, crossed the Slovenian border, and took me to a town in the mountains. It wasn't too small." She turned her phone around so I could see the map of the area she'd pulled up. "I'm guessing Jesenice."

"Wait, so we're going to Slovenia? Why not fly there, then?"

"Because we can't take the chance of flying into a smaller airport. It's easier to get lost in Vienna, and we can drive from there." As though on cue, a tinny voice announced our flight. Blair pulled her hair up into a bun and grabbed her backpack. "You know, you can still stay here."

"Nice try, gorgeous." She flinched at the very honest compliment, which made me smile. I had no idea why it made me smile to cause her discomfort, but it seemed I had more than a few miles to figure it out.

Chapter 6

Blair

Sam's hot breath blew across my neck, rustling strands of hair that tickled my skin. It felt a little wet, but I couldn't see well enough to figure out if he was drooling on me and, really, there wasn't much point in knowing the answer.

I could not believe that he was slumped against me on the last leg of an impossibly long coach flight from Melbourne instead of in Australia where he belonged. This was not part of the plan, even though in the back of my mind it had been a possibility. I figured my surface honesty would have him groveling at my feet, ready to give me any and all required information so that I could fake finding my dad and bringing him to justice.

It made me respect him more that he wouldn't bite, but the distrust he'd earned by being taken by my father had made him suspicious. It made me unexpectedly sad. Even though dating Sam hadn't appealed to me for many reasons, his carefree, embracing attitude toward the world had warmed me in St. Moritz. It was rare to find someone who had made it all the way into his twenties—and been successful along the way—who hadn't acquired a certain amount of cynicism and bitchiness. Myself included.

Sam hadn't been putting it on, though. He simply lived each moment as though it was its own tiny story, then closed the book and moved on.

It was how my father lived, but with an entirely different agenda. It was how *I* lived, because of the life I'd been born into, but it didn't come naturally to me. I wanted to keep something. Watching Sam had made me sad then—for myself. For what I'd never had.

Watching him now made me sad for him. Or humanity in general, I didn't know.

I suspected it had a little to do with why I hadn't shoved his head off my collarbone two hours ago. And I would be lying if I denied the heat between us, or the fact that touching him was like a drug I had no desire to quit cold turkey. It had taken every last ounce of self-restraint not to lean up and kiss him in the hotel room.

It had been over thirty hours since we left Australia, and I had never missed my father's arsenal of private jets more in my life. We'd stopped in China and Holland, which didn't seem like it could possibly be the fastest route to Austria. If I didn't get my feet on solid ground for more than a couple of hours I was going to flip out—it would have been easier to take the sleeping pills Sam had offered, but one of us had to be sober to make sure we made our connecting flights. He'd popped them every few hours and slept more than he'd been awake.

Lucky bastard.

Hopefully whatever had freaked him out about being awake on the plane wouldn't be an issue in a car, because the drive from Vienna to Jesenice would be at least three hours and I had exhausted my supply of caffeine pills. Sleep was becoming an inevitability.

The pilot announced that we would be touching down in about twenty minutes. I elbowed Sam, not gently, disproportionately pleased at his pained grunt.

He sat up slowly, squinting out the window and self-consciously wiping the corners of his mouth. "Where are we?"

My fingers itched to check my chest and shoulder for drool, but I ignored them. "We're landing in Vienna. Are you going to be okay to drive?"

"To Slovenia?"

"Yes."

"Won't your dad's vast network of spies be able to see us if we rent a car?" He yawned, unaware of how badly he made me want to slap him and kiss him with equal fervor, then peeked at me out of the corner of his eye.

Maybe not so unaware.

He seemed to think me paranoid, to assume my estimation of my dad's omniscient nature higher than the reality. In truth, I wasn't positive how closely Neil monitored his marks—or me, for that matter. It didn't really matter. We weren't going anywhere near my dad. All of the stops I had planned hadn't been utilized since before my mother died, as far as I knew. The crazier the trek, the more uncomfortable the travel, the faster Sam would wear down and cough up the signatures I needed.

He would go back to his life a few million lighter and I would go . . . wherever I went.

I hesitated to answer his question about the rental car, unwilling to argue with him or to let him farther into my secret life. He was along for the ride now, though, and there would be consequences to pay at the end of this sham partnership. Those couldn't be helped.

It wasn't as if he wouldn't notice committing a felony.

"We're not going to rent a car," I whispered. "We're going to . . . borrow one."

"Borrow one?" His golden brown eyebrows shot up. "You have a friend in Vienna?"

"Not exactly. Why, do you?" Borrowing a car from a friend would be preferable to boosting one, even if I did plan to give it back.

"No." Sam gave me a strange look, his typically soft brown eyes sharp and probing. "What does *not exactly* mean?"

The woman sitting on the aisle, who hadn't slept a wink but had recognized Sam the moment we sat down, shifted. Her head tilted toward us, and her constant and obvious eavesdropping made me wonder if I should have said yes to his cheeky suggestion of a disguise.

"Can we talk about this once we have more privacy?"

He shrugged, unbuckling his seat belt and grabbing his bag from under the seat as the wheels touched down in Austria. I followed suit and the two of us disembarked with a couple hundred other passengers who looked as tired as I felt. Sam, for his part, appeared way too perky and refreshed for someone who had slept half bent over on a plane. The woman who had been sitting next to us grabbed him at the top of the Jetway.

"Could I have an autograph? It's for my daughter. She's a big fan."

The spiderweb of lines around her eyes and lips put her in her fifties, probably, and I supposed her dark brown, brittle hair came courtesy of a box and a drugstore. She had been pretty once, though, and the smile she turned on Sam dropped years from her face.

"I don't believe you could possibly have a daughter old enough to watch tennis." He rummaged around in his pack and came up with a tennis ball, then signed it with a wink. "There you go."

She hurried away toward baggage claim, her cheeks red and cracked wide with a grin. Sam's smile widened when he saw the look on my face, which I imagined was somewhere between incredulous and disgusted.

"What? Jealous?"

"Hardly. I'd just forgotten what a shameless flirt you are." I would never admit it, but I did feel the slightest twinge of . . . not jealousy. But something. Irritation?

"It goes with the territory."

I snorted. "Right. Because you can't be good at tennis *and* be an asshole to fans. No one has ever done that."

The smile slipped from his face, not disappearing, just shrinking. Even asleep on the plane, his lips had curled up at the corners. Not that I'd been staring.

"I know you want to think the worst of me, and I suppose you must have your reasons for that, but I'm not an asshole. A bit of a whore, if you want to be judgy about it, but never an asshole."

A funny feeling, shame or maybe guilt, took root in my stomach. It was foreign—a virus that my father had long ago vaccinated me against, and my body attacked it now. How Sam Bradford lived his life was none of my business. There had been good people in my path before and it had never stopped me. It wouldn't now. I was almost out.

"I don't care who you flirt with or where you stick your penis, but I *do* care about how long this whole endeavor keeps me away from school. So, if you could *try* to focus."

"Okay. Fine. No funny business." He reached out and tugged on the hairs that had fallen out of my bun, loosening the whole thing until it flopped low on my neck. "With anyone but you."

I groaned and trailed after him as he wound his way toward the ground transportation. My neck tingled where his fingers had landed and my own lips tried to twitch into an unused smile. Once outside he turned to me, eyebrows raised, but I hailed a cab and asked the driver to take us to a restaurant in a quiet, cheap neighborhood in the city.

Twenty minutes later we stood on an uneven street. The sun's rays reached fingers over the horizon, scrabbling for purchase against the night. Austria in late November meant freezing cold. Sam looked refreshed, his cheeks a healthy pink and the chilly wind ruffling his wavy brown hair. I felt disgusting after thirty-five hours of travel, but he may as well have stepped out of a shampoo commercial. That fact boosted my level of grumpiness, which helped me ignore the twinge of desire in my stomach, at least for the moment.

I could not be attracted to him *and* rip him off. One of them had to go, and thanks to my dad, it had to be the former.

My eyes adjusted to the lightening dawn. We were alone on the street, at least at the moment, and I could feel Sam's silent questions pummeling me. Instead of having a conversation about it—which would mean protests—I moved, expecting him to follow. My tennis shoes made little noise on the old streets. The first car on the street had a blinking red alarm light, the second was too nice to not be missed. The third and fourth had locked doors, but the fifth was the jackpot.

The doors on the beat-up, dark blue Volkswagen Jetta were unlocked and the keys fell into my lap when I tugged on the sun visor. The standard transmission didn't trip me up, though it had been a while since I'd driven one in Europe. Shifting with the left hand never felt natural.

The passenger door opened and Sam's face appeared. "Um, what exactly do you think you're fucking doing?"

"Borrowing a car, like I said." The more clandestine and illegal the trip became, the faster Sam would lose interest. I crossed mental fingers that stealing a car would be the place he balked.

"We're not stealing a car, Blair. People know who I am. Between the two of us, we have access to millions of dollars."

"Look, you don't know my dad like I do. He has security and IT people on twenty-four-hour payroll, monitoring me and all of his clients. If either of us uses our ID to rent a car, we're screwed. If you're not down with doing this my way, then give me the information I need to do it myself and go back to Melbourne. Otherwise, get your ass in the car before we get caught."

The truth was, my dad's con business was a two-man enterprise—me being man number two. He used a few shady individuals, like the PI and the occasional property manager, on a contract basis but, with one exception, they didn't know shit about his real business.

I could find my dad if I really wanted to, at least I thought I could, and he probably wasn't monitoring Sam's movements. He'd worked contacts to verify whether or not Sam had reported the theft to Interpol and the FBI, but that was as far as it went.

He had reported it—or his manager, Leo, had. Law enforcement dutifully added Sam's name to the list of victims swindled by Neil Saunders, a.k.a. Neil Paddington, a.k.a. a few other names that had been compromised over the years, but they didn't have a clue where to start. Or finish.

Indecision skittered across Sam's classic cheekbones and down his strong jaw. The desire to see this thing through warred with his knee-jerk response to stealing, the entire thought process laid bare in his too-honest eyes. An arrest could damage his career, his only way to make back what my father had taken, and that thought had to weigh heavy on him, too.

I was counting on it. I wanted him out of my hair, and this new and uncomfortable conflict out of my gut.

Instead, he folded his six-foot-three frame into the tiny car and buckled his seat belt. "Let's go."

"You sure?"

"Yes. Can you drive this thing?"

"I can do lots of things."

He didn't respond to my teasing statement, telling me that I'd been closer to making him fold his cards than I'd suspected. Dammit. Where would he draw the line? Every man had a breaking point, an invisible line in the sand his code of morals wouldn't let him cross. I needed to find Sam's so I could get on with my life.

The car rumbled to life and slid into gear under my guidance, and we rolled down the street and around the corner. I thought about what my dad had said about using all of the tools available to me, feeling sick to my stomach again, and not because I didn't *want* to sleep with Sam. Reconnecting with him had made our spark impossible to ignore, and the constant heat under my skin was only going to get harder to dismiss as harmless.

But that was *my* line in the sand. My body had always been mine—the one thing safe from my dad and his life, because no matter how many times he suggested such a thing, he'd never forced me and I'd always figured out another way to make it work. As much as I lusted after the lanky, too-confident, handsome guy in the passenger seat, I would have to do it again.

"Can you check and see if there's a map in the glove box? My phone battery is shot."

He complied without argument, finding a map of Austria and the surrounding region, then directed me toward the best route to Slovenia in a quiet voice. A few hundred yards farther he reached over and put his hand over mine.

Tingles soaked into my skin, raising hairs and goose bumps up my arm and neck that only had a little to do with his cold fingers. I jerked free. "What?"

"You're exhausted, Blair. Pull over and I'll drive."

"No. If we get caught this way you can say I kidnapped you." Despite my protest, the heaviness of my eyelids moved my foot from the gas to the brakes.

Sam chuckled, the sound warm behind the chill of his touch. "Come on, gorgeous. No one's going to believe you wrestled me into a stolen car, and you don't have a weapon . . . do you?"

"Not on me," I said with a quick smile.

"Good to know."

I pulled up the parking brake, leaving the car in neutral and reaching for the door handle. Sam headed for the front of the car, so I crossed at the rear. My fatigue and guilt were making my body respond despite all of my self-righteous internal lectures about steering clear. Avoiding close proximity wasn't an option, so my self-control needed to buck up.

We settled back into the car and it felt good to let Sam take charge. The whir of the wheels against the pavement, the wind outside, and the sun climbing over the horizon tugged me toward sleep faster than I would have thought possible.

It crossed my mind that Sam might drive us to the closest police station, but even that worry couldn't keep me awake. He might not agree with my methods, but he wanted his money, and he was smart enough to know that I was the only way he'd ever see it again.

He would keep driving. I could sleep the sleep of a girl who knew exactly what waited at our destination—an empty house on the side of a mountain.

*

"Hey, gorgeous. Time to wake up."

I left my eyes closed for a few seconds after my brain registered Sam's request, until the situation in which I'd fallen asleep came back. It felt nice to wake up to a voice that sounded sorry to disturb me. Much better than the alarm clock on my phone that roused me for 8 a.m. classes. Not to mention what the huskiness and close proximity did to my heart.

Sam Bradford possessed many, many assets that made girls around the world swoon in their tennis skirts—and climb out of them—but the rich quality of his voice, the way it gave me the ability to picture the look on his face, the expression in his eyes, ranked highest on my list.

Of course, I hadn't seen all of his assets.

In that moment, in between the blessed nothingness of sleep and waking to the reality of this debacle, avoiding the inevitable seemed silly. The reaction between my legs at the mere thought of going to bed with him suggested that it wouldn't be a disappointment.

Shaking off sleep and, with it, pointless fantasizing, I opened my eyes and stretched the kinks out of my neck. My breath tasted like week-old anchovies. A package of mints in my purse helped, but I waited until the fuzziness of lust faded before trusting my voice. "Where are we?"

"About three miles outside of Jesenice. Do you want to drive or give me directions?"

A second later, I remembered this part of the con. *Sheesh.* Sleeping had erased half of my brain, it seemed, had made me think Sam and I were college kids on a tour of Europe with nothing to concern me but when we'd give in to the tension between us.

The plan was to appear to be that couple on holiday, even though we weren't that. One of us had to remember that fact, and since Sam had no idea what he'd actually signed up for, that person had to be me.

"I don't know exactly where we're going." A road sign that promised food at an upcoming turn caught my attention. "Let's get some breakfast and I'll work some contacts, see what I can find out."

"I'm not even going to ask what that means."

"That's probably best." I smiled, unsure why. Maybe because Sam did it first.

He steered the car into the half-full parking lot of a restaurant. Jesenice was a small community nestled among mountains—beautiful and friendly enough, and more undiscovered than many places, at least as far as tourists were concerned. It made finding restaurants that didn't give me the willies a little difficult. I'd spent perhaps a collective month here, a couple of two-week stays back when my mother had been alive. More than ten years had passed since she'd left me alone, since her attempts to keep me from my father's life had been thwarted by cancer.

It felt good to have my feet on solid ground, even if it was dusty gravel and the sunlight had done even less to dispel the chill in the air at the higher altitude. A Whitman hoodie helped warm me up. I noticed Sam pull a Nike jacket out of his pack and shook my head. "Nope. You're recognizable enough as it is, and putting you in Nike will make things click in people's heads."

He looked around at the mostly-empty parking lot, empty streets, and the ranges of hills surrounding us. "What people?"

"Hey, you're the one who got all excited about disguises." I shrugged. "It's up to you."

I hid a smile as he tossed the jacket into the Jetta's backseat, then turned and trudged inside the restaurant. The interior was rustic and a little rundown, the booths sporting worn patches and rips in the vinyl, paint graying and seeming to sag off the walls. The other patrons glanced at us without much curiosity, returning to their conversations and coffee after quick glances.

Sam and I both ordered tea and breakfast, then stared at each other over steaming cups. My brain continued to feel sluggish, proof that the three hours of sleep in the past forty didn't amount to nearly enough.

My phone distracted me from staring at Sam, and I pretended to send e-mails and texts, to research maps, for the next twenty minutes. He stared off into space, then at me, then at the two other patrons in a lazy pattern until our breakfast of eggs and potatoes landed on the table in front of us. I dug in, realizing that I hadn't eaten anything but airport food since the room service in Melbourne. We ate in silence, which would have been weird except it wasn't. It hadn't occurred to me before now, but Sam and I spent a lot of time not talking. The comfort level between us increased without words to get in the way.

Of course, that might just be the discomfort of a girl who lied when she spoke.

The alarm I'd set on my phone went off, giving a single beep that mimicked the sound of my e-mail. I looked down to check the nonexistent message, then met Sam's gaze. "I think we have the address."

"That was fast."

"Finding the addresses isn't hard. I've taken care of communicating with our tax attorney ever since my mom died, so I just sent him an e-mail and asked for last year's tax returns. The property tax deductions were listed with addresses. Only one in Slovenia."

"When did your mother die?"

A little voice in the back of my head berated me for bringing her up. Too late now. "When I was eight. Cancer."

"I'm sorry. That's hard—the knowing. The watching."

He spoke like someone who knew from experience, but commiserating had never helped. Sympathy grated on my patience and pity made me want to throw up. "It was less than six weeks, beginning to end. Not much waiting. Not as much pain as some. It was a long time ago."

Sam opened his mouth like he wanted to say more. In his eyes I glimpsed more than one of those hated, common responses, and in mine he must have seen my determination to be fine about the whole thing. He put tea in his mouth instead of letting words come out, and the gesture flooded me with equal parts relief and concern.

It shouldn't be so simple for him to read me. That ability could bring down this entire operation. "You ready?"

He finished his tea and nodded, dropping euros on the table to pay the check before I could ask if he wanted to split it, then stood. We nodded at the waitress, who smiled and went to count her money. For all the languages Sam claimed to speak, Slovene didn't rank, and neither did Croatian or Serbian, the second and third most common languages in the country. I didn't speak any of them, either, and we'd ordered our breakfast by pointing.

Sam seemed more comfortable than me with not being able to communicate. It made me feel unprepared; I rarely traveled places without knowing the language.

I would have to get used to it, or at least pretend to, since I didn't speak Serbian or Arabic, the primary languages in our next two red-herring stops. When we returned to the car I slid behind the wheel and steered onto the vaguely familiar path to one of my father's mountain homes.

"I'm surprised you don't speak Serbian. Aren't, like, half the ranked players on the pro tour from there right now? Including your most recent ex?"

His knuckles were white where they gripped the seat belt. "Not half, no. And I thought you didn't keep up with tennis."

"Are you nervous or something?" I responded, happy to change the subject. I loved tennis, and had watched the major tournaments and rankings since my mother had signed me up for lessons in second grade. But I had told Sam the opposite.

Dammit, that was sloppy.

"No, I'm totally comfortable riding in a stolen Jetta along mountain passes with a girl behind the wheel who spends more time in her own head than paying attention. No worries."

He had done it again—seen right through my exterior. The mountain scenery—all rocks and trees and bright blue sky—had barely registered while my mind worked ahead on the problems to come, such as whether or not my dad would have any security at the house.

"I'm paying attention, doofus. It's like with tennis—you never look where you're going to put the ball, right?"

"Says the girl with no interest in tennis."

"Okay, fine. I like tennis."

"And you play."

"And I play."

"Well enough to be my hitting partner while we're away?"

"Don't push your luck, Bradford. I'll drive us off this cliff right now."

"That is so not funny."

Chapter 7

*L*uck had been on my side for what seemed like the first time since my dad had sent me to complete the swindle on Sam. No one had been watching the house in Jesenice. There must be a regular maid service, because the place smelled like lemons and the sheets on the bed were soft and clean.

They tempted me; we could spend the day and night, get some good sleep, and move on tomorrow. But making Sam's life more comfortable wasn't going to get me what I wanted. Needed.

Which was to get the fuck out of there before I lost control. It was the only thing I had.

"This place is amazing. Seriously. I never want to leave."

Sam wandered the front room of the house, which ran a little cold to my tastes, but was inarguable impressive. Ceramic tiles stretched out under our feet, meeting a wall of windows that overlooked a mountain pass. The sharp drop had freaked me out a bit as a girl, due to my fear of heights—I couldn't even read the chapters in *A Game of Thrones* that took place in the open-air jail cells at the Eyrie without my palms sweating. Large ceiling fans stirred the comfortable air above our heads and the off-white, overstuffed furniture lent an atmosphere of comfort that couldn't be farther from the truth.

But Sam looked at home in this room, surrounded by these things that had been bought with other people's money. Standing with his back to me, hands in his pockets, staring into the abyss, I was hard-pressed to recall anything that had looked so . . . handsome. Desirable. Male.

The boys I had dated at Whitman and before, even Flynn, were just that—boys. Cute, or hot, or sexy, but not handsome. Not comfortable in their own skin. I had a feeling that Sam looked exactly as he did now in every single room he ever walked into, and it made me jealous. I had spent my life pretending and it appeared this guy never did.

It made me hate him as much as I wanted him.

"Well, we're going to have to leave. Dad's not here and I need to get back to school, so on to the next option." I picked up my bag, avoiding his gaze. The scent of my body inside two-day worn clothes made me squirm, but hot showers were a comfort, so they were off the list, at least as long as he would let me get away with it.

"Where are we going next? Croatia? Serbia? Maybe some scary Arab country?"

The suggestions stopped me. "What made you guess those places?"

"Nothing. Let's go." He shouldered his pack. "Can I take that bottle of Germ-X from the kitchen?"

"Sure, I don't care. But answer my question."

He paused, glancing back out the window as though he thought jumping might be preferable, then sighed. "I keep a list of nonextradition countries taped inside my passport."

"What in the hell for? You don't strike me as the kind of guy who's going to need to seek international asylum."

"It's part of my zombie-apocalypse plan."

"If you don't want to tell me, just say so."

"That's the reason. I'm prepared, that's all."

"Prepared like you have a blanket and flashlight in the trunk of your car, or prepared like you hired someone to build you a fully stocked underground bunker in your backyard?"

"I don't drive my own car, nor do I have a backyard."

"Those are examples. I'm trying to gauge your level of doomsdayishness."

"That's not a word."

"Okay, but seriously, zombies? Out of all the things to be afraid of in this world—terrorists, North Korea, global warming, thieving accountants . . . you're prepared for zombies?"

Sam didn't reply. He grabbed the bottle of hand sanitizer from the kitchen on our way out through the garage, then climbed into the Jetta's passenger seat. I wasn't looking forward to more driving, but it appeared I didn't have a choice.

The engine turned over and I told myself it didn't matter why Sam had a list of nonextradition countries stored in his brain.

Except it might.

Discomfort tightened in a knot between my shoulders. Everything my dad had ever taught me, all the tricks I'd learned when forced to react in the middle of a con . . . they all boiled down to one thing: get to know your mark. Know their hopes, their fears, the desires that drove them, and eventually, one of those things would lead you to the answer of how to fool them.

But every last molecule in my body warned me that getting too close to Sam was dangerous. We already shared some kind of weird sexual charge, a fact that had made it way harder than it should have been to turn him down in St. Moritz and again last spring. The bottom line was that I didn't trust myself with him, and that made me feel as though bugs crawled over my skin.

My self-control, my ability to not get emotionally involved, helped me survive.

"So, did I guess right? Where are we going?"

"We're going to Serbia, so yes."

"You want me to get us a car there that we don't have to steal?"

"Borrow. We borrowed this one, and yes, if you can find one we can borrow there, that would be preferable. As long as we don't have to go too far out of our way to pick it up and it can't be traced back to you." I risked a glance his direction, noticing that his hands weren't clutching the seat belt quite as tightly as they did on the way up to the house. Progress. "We're taking the train to Ljubljana."

"My middle-European geography isn't the best, but I'm pretty sure that's not in Serbia."

"It's not. The train goes there from Jesenice. From there we take the bus to Belgrade."

This time my peek caught a poorly hidden expression of horror, along with an actual shudder that worked its way down his spine. "The *bus*? Do you know how long that's going to take? Have you ever *been* on a bus?"

I shrugged, trying my damnedest to hide a smile. We could fly or even drive in half the time, but that would be too easy, and it didn't fit with the image I'd painted of my dad. I'd never been on a bus, but Sam didn't know that and he didn't need to. It couldn't be that bad. "About ten hours total, according to my phone's calculations. We take the bus through Croatia, then across the Serbian border to Belgrade. The towns where our passports are stamped are small and probably aren't digital. It's a good plan."

In the lengthy pause that followed, I could almost hear his stubborn will crumbling. That this—a ten-hour train and bus ride in countries that were more than a little behind the rest of the world when it came to comfort and hygiene—would be the thing that made Sam flee for a first class ticket on the soonest international flight.

It only served to pique the curiosity I didn't want to admit to. What kind of person rationalized stealing a car but balked at taking a bus for half a day?

It appeared I would never find out, because a few breaths later, Sam agreed.

"Okay, fine. The bus it is, and never let it be said that Sam Bradford isn't up for adventure." He reached out a hand toward the back of my neck, but stopped short the second before his fingertips brushed my skin.

I felt the heat of them, the rub of his hard-earned callouses, and fought the instinct to lean into his touch. He pulled his hand back and settled it in his lap. I told myself I wasn't sorry.

"Sorry. I almost forgot about our deal."

"What deal?" I asked, feeling out of sorts. What did it mean, that he could make my brain fuzzy by *almost* touching me?

"That I wouldn't touch you again until you asked." He paused. "Are you asking?"

I shook my head, unwilling to trust my voice not to sound as shaky as my insides felt.

"Noted." The way he said it made me think he'd noted a few other things, too. "Belgrade is perfect, actually. My friend Marija still spends most of her off-season there."

An image of the tall, shapely girl with shiny black hair and a smile that had landed her more modeling contracts than tennis titles appeared in my head. I gritted my teeth. "She really goes back to Serbia? Don't most of you guys live in, like, Monaco or Majorca during your six weeks off?"

"Again, a strange amount of tennis-world knowledge for a girl who 'doesn't keep up.' But you're right. Marija is involved in funding orphanages in Serbia, and since she spends so much time away during the season with her commitments, she goes home for the holiday."

"How nice." That sounded snotty even to me. Jesus. Was I really bashing a girl who went home to a country still struggling in many ways to shake off a war to work with orphans?

"It *is* nice. *She's* nice, and I'm sure we'll be able to borrow a car."

"Hopefully it's not too flashy and doesn't come with a driver."

"She has a big family, I'm sure we can scare up something appropriate. I'll call her. What's the matter with you?"

"Nothing. Don't use your phone. We'll use one at the train station."

"Can I send her a Facebook message so she'll answer the call? Girls like Marija don't answer calls from unfamiliar numbers."

"Dude, no girls answer calls from unfamiliar numbers." I took a deep breath, telling myself to chill the fuck out. So, we were going to borrow a car from Marija Peronovic. No big deal. Maybe she would give me her autograph. I'm sure my dad could put her signature to good use. "Go ahead and message her."

"Good thing I have a permanent international data plan." He got out his phone and started typing. "Speaking of cars, what are we going to do with this one?"

"Leave it at the train station. Once we're somewhere we can rest, I'll use a public Internet café to e-mail the police back in Vienna with the location." I flashed him a smile. "See? Borrowed. We'll even fill it up with gas first. No harm."

97

"You really are a strange girl, Blair Paddington. I think it's one reason I liked you right off the bat in Switzerland."

I swallowed, ignoring the little leap-and-flip my heart did in my chest. "Or you were trying to sleep with every girl you came across and I was ruining your goal."

"You know, I can't help my reputation. Or that people like me, girls included." He lapsed into silence for the briefest of seconds. "In fact, I think we should get to know each other better so you can realize you like me, too. I mean, we're trapped in a car, then a train, then a bus. What else will kill the time?"

"Sleeping?" I suggested. "Eating? Reading? Anything?"

"The fact that you're trying so hard not to get closer to me during this whole trip only proves that you have feelings you're trying to avoid, you know. If you really didn't feel that . . . thing between us, you wouldn't be such a bitch."

"Oh, so I'm a bitch now?"

"You know you are. It's your thing. It might work for you as far as putting the people off that you want to avoid, but I find it charming. For the record."

"Fantastic." More like he enjoyed a challenge. After watching him play tennis for the past five years, I should have guessed that none of this would go down as I'd hoped.

Sam Bradford the tennis player loved being the challenger. His level of play had dipped since becoming number two in the world, and he'd been knocked out of more than one tournament early by nothing other than his own lazy game.

But put him up against the number one in the world, and he sparkled. Kicked ass, ran down every ball, aced every other serve. He was bored playing those first weeks of a tournament—which wasn't good for his career, or his winnings—because it was too easy. The conclusion foregone.

It was clear to me now that I had gone about this the wrong way. The more obstacles I put in his way on this road to getting his money back, the more determined he would become to get there, with or without me, but it was too late to change my story about us needing to stay inconspicuous now.

Dammit.

It was the same with me. Thwarting his advances only made Sam more intent on wooing me. Maybe if I made myself look like an easier conquest he would lose interest. It was worth a try. Or it would be, if I could trust myself not to believe my own gig.

The problems that could arise from my pretending to like him would begin and end with the reality that I *did* like him, and with the way my blood heated every time we accidentally brushed against each other, it would be stupid to assume we wouldn't end up in bed.

"I don't want to play a game."

"Fine. But you're still going to like me."

Sam hadn't drawn his line in the sand. I had, but the more time we spent together, the harder it was to see, or to remember why I'd etched it there in the first place.

Chapter 8

Sam

*T*he Croatian, then Bosnian landscape held my attention for quite a while. Fields of wheat and maybe barley stretched across the foreground, dotted with bales of hay and the occasional grouping of livestock. I glimpsed grapevines and wineries, and we crossed bridges over more than one sparkling, impossibly clear lake complete with crashing waterfalls. The Dinaric Alps reached toward the sky, silent sentinels in the distance. I'd seen those up close, since they sat nearer the coast, but I'd never spent time in the interior of the country.

It all made what would be a six-plus hour ride a little more bearable.

The inside of the bus left more to be desired. Aside from the smell, which I'd identified as a potpourri of impressive body odor, stale breath, and unwashed hair, the bench seats were an army green plastic that reminded me of the behemoth that had dropped me off at elementary school. Pieces of stained yellow foam and the occasional spring poked through faded cracks. Trash—cigarette butts, balled-up scraps of paper, discarded straws and toothpicks—and droppings of what I hoped wasn't feces smudged the rubber aisle runner, and the few characters who joined us on this journey were suspect at best.

No families, just a gaunt, pale couple with sunken eyes and a twitchiness that infected my nerves, a bunch of men traveling alone, and one fat woman, all of whom, in my rampant imagination, might already be infected with the zombie virus. At best, they were connected to some sort of European ring of organ thieves determined to sell at least one of my kidneys on the black market.

I was quite keen on keeping them both.

Once I put a stop to a pointless internal monologue about all of the potential ways riding on this bus was probably going to kill me, it dawned on me that something had changed between the train from Jesenice and boarding this bus in Croatia—Blair had stopped fighting me at every turn. She'd stopped avoiding my gaze, quit making a face every time I opened my mouth, and had even let her hand brush against my leg the couple of times she'd leaned down to get something out of her bag.

"You two nice couple," the fat woman said as she tottered past, apparently intent on finding a seat closer to the back. Probably in case the meth heads went into withdrawal. Or maybe there had been a falling out among the organ thieves.

"Oh, no, we're just—" I stuttered, my voice dusty from the last twenty minutes of silence.

"Yes!" Blair interrupted, turning a hundred-watt smile on the woman and leaning in to my side in the process. "We're on holiday and wanted to do something different, so we're touring the countryside. It's so lovely."

"Yes, yes. Lovely couple. Thank you."

Obviously the woman's English left a little something to be desired, but given that I didn't understand diddly-squat of any local dialect except the tiny percentage of German that was spoken here, pointing that out seemed more than a little insensitive.

She moved on, her giant muumuu and dirt-streaked coat slapping the bench seats on her way past. It seemed Blair had more ideas on this whole cover thing than she had shared with me. We were a couple on an adventurous holiday, now. I turned to her and raised my eyebrow in a silent question we both knew wouldn't get answered. Instead of asking it, I choose something more innocuous in an attempt to get her talking again. "I was thinking maybe I should dye my hair, what do you think? Since we're all keen on the backstories and undercover now."

"I was thinking you should shave it."

"You must be kidding."

"Are you attached to those sunny brown locks, Bradford? How manly of you."

"Thank you for noticing the magnificence of the exact color. The highlights are all natural, too."

She snorted, but her voice wasn't quite right. It kept fading when it should have punched me, too soft for the banter that had so far defined our time together. Blair had been quiet for the last half hour or so. I thought she'd fallen asleep before she answered that lady.

I breathed deep as she leaned across me to peer outside, her breasts, barely contained by a tank top and hoodie, brushing my arm. She rested her head against the window, which was propped open at the top, eyes closed. I shut my own, breathing her in and trying not to pop a boner against her belly while trying to remember how long it had been since I'd gotten laid.

Longer than usual, for sure, and my intense reaction to the smell and heat of her was about ten seconds from embarrassing me. I shifted in an attempt to put space between her torso and my crotch. It earned me a curious look, but it didn't last long. She looked a little sick. "Are you okay?"

"Do I look okay to you?"

"I mean, you still look good. Green's a nice color on you." As hard as I tried, I could not keep the smirk off my face or out of my voice. Blair had been none-too-subtle about the assumption that I would be the one most uncomfortable on the bus.

"I get motion sick, sometimes, especially on the hillier parts. The smell isn't helping."

One of our fellow passengers had some kind of mutant BO that had been making my eyes water since boarding this bucket of bolts two hundred miles ago in Ljubljana—which, for all my world travels, I still couldn't pronounce.

"You were fine in the car. And on the train." I wanted to reach up and rub her back to offer comfort, but I had promised not to touch her until she asked. Stupid.

"I know. I guess the terrain wasn't so bad? It's better when I'm driving, too." She pushed off the window, brushing harder against me as she settled back in her seat. "Distract me."

A million filthy thoughts sputtered through my mind, urging my hard-on toward painful, but if she was softening toward me now wasn't the time to be dirty. "What are you majoring in?"

"Boring." She sighed. "Marketing."

"Okay, fine. What do you want to do with your marketing degree, Blair Paddington?"

"I think I'd like to work in higher education. Recruitment, maybe."

"You could talk me into about anything."

"Is every conversation just an excuse to make a suggestive comment?"

I shrugged, then gave her a smile. "I can't help it. My mind is one-track with you this close."

"Try harder." She crossed her arms, features twisting into a grumpy expression that was starting to turn me on. I heard a hitch in her breath, and her tongue snaked out to lick her cherry red lips.

It took every ounce of focus to bite back a groan. I didn't know how much longer I could keep my promise not to touch her. The heat vibrating in the space between us suggested that's about all it would take to set off a chain reaction.

"What was it like growing up with your dad?" I tried, suspecting Blair wouldn't come within ten yards of giving me an honest answer to that one.

"What was it like growing up with *your* dad?" she fired back, splotches of red appearing on her cheeks.

"Not too memorable, but not horrible," I replied, trying to model a normal response for her. Nothing about my parents was a secret. My financial divorce from them at age sixteen had been the talk of the tennis world, as had my subsequent decision to still let them join me on tour when they asked. "They got me into tennis, so I'm thankful for that. I spent the majority of my childhood traveling, and they spent the majority of my teenage years spending the money I made."

"They sound sweet." Her voice dripped with sarcasm.

"They're not evil or anything, they just never had money. I could have been worse off."

"You could have been better off, too." Blair's hand, resting on her thigh, twitched and then inched its way toward mine.

I held my breath waiting for the contact. My body went perfectly still, like a thirteen-year-old boy on his first date in a movie theater, anticipating that very first moment when his hand touched the girl he'd been fantasizing about for months.

When her skin hit mine—just the outside of her pinky finger against the outside of mine—the little spark that shot up my arm shocked me, but still, instinct urged me to stay still. She reminded me of an animal in the woods, one trying to decide whether or not to take the carrot out of my hand. Scaring her away was the last thing I wanted.

That realization surprised me, too. Why, with my ability to go through life happy and satisfied and unfettered, alongside girls who wanted to be in my company, had this one sparked such an interest for me?

It could be as simple as the fact that she didn't seem like other girls, but I thought it was more than that. I'd thought that we could go through this trip together, and if we didn't end up acting on the feelings between us, it would be easy to shake it off. Somewhere in the past three days, that had changed. Not ever knowing what it was like to be with her—really be with her—would take some time to get over. Maybe a long time.

Nothing sounded worse than finding out.

"I'm guessing neither of us hit the lottery in the parent department." I nudged her finger with mine. "Tell me more about your dad."

She hesitated. Her finger rested against mine now, relaxed. "It was . . . fun. His life. At least for a while. He wasn't like other dads. Especially after my mom died, it was like he and I against the world. And it took me a while to realize that the little games we played were cons."

"You helped him steal from people?" My stomach clenched. Poor kid. Who got their ten-year-old mixed up in international crime?

She tensed, drawing her hand back into her lap. I missed it as though she'd taken mine with her, as though her hand was a ghost appendage that I felt even though a surgeon had removed it.

"I'm not judging," I rushed to explain. "You were just a kid. I'm . . . I don't know. Sad."

"You don't need to be sad for me, Sam. I had a more privileged youth than about ninety-five percent of the population, and no matter what he made me do, my dad never mistreated me. He loves me, in his way."

"But you're tired of it. The stigma."

"I didn't know I was helping him. I refused to keep doing it as soon as I realized what was going on." She flicked a glance at me for the briefest of moments, then looked away.

Without another thought to my previous promise, I reached up and slid my hand along her jaw, turning her head toward me. The expression in her deep brown eyes eluded me. The truth of her thoughts, of her feelings, hid behind things such as resentment and pride, and her daring me to say that she should regret her unorthodox childhood.

"I don't blame you for what happened to me, Blair, and no one else your dad conned can blame you, either. He's the criminal. He's the one who should have known better." I smiled, my heart doing a stutter-step when she lifted the corner of her lips in response.

I couldn't decide if her pissy face or her smile made me want her more.

"You're a good guy, Sam. I know because otherwise he wouldn't have seen you as an easy mark. You're *too* nice. You trust people too easily." The smile fell away. "I'm jealous of that, a little. The way I grew up, especially after my dad's lifestyle came out . . . I'm not sure I'm capable of trust."

I felt like a dumbass. After all she had seen and done, she must think I was a real idiot for falling for her dad's bogus scheme. It didn't stop my hand from tracing a line down her neck, over her shoulder, and down her arm until it settled on top of hers. Her skin was so silky, so smooth, and contradicted her prickly personality. "Maybe your way is better. At least people can't take advantage of you."

"Somewhere in the middle is the sweet spot, Sam. You can't trust everyone. People are assholes, on the large." She bit her lip and stared out the window. "But not trusting anyone isn't the greatest life plan, either."

The speaker on the bus crackled to life, screeching loud enough to set my teeth on edge before the driver's voice burst through the static. Most of it was unintelligible—all of it was in Croatian. "Did you catch any of that? I'm pretty sure I caught nothing."

"Not really, but we should be about ten minutes or so from the last stop in Bosnia. Next up, Belgrade!"

"I never thought I'd be so happy to hear someone say that."

Belgrade was not my favorite place in the world even though plenty of people thrived in its cosmopolitan atmosphere. It didn't even rank in my top fifty, but the people I knew from Serbia were some of my favorites. Aside from Marija, who was hot as fuck and sweet besides, the Serbians on the tour—and there were plenty of them—had a great sense of humor. Jokesters, the lot.

"I'm going to get out at the station and stretch my legs. Try to settle my stomach. It should help me get through the last couple of hours." She leaned closer and lowered her voice. "Maybe the stinky guy will get off here, too."

The smell of her body wasn't quite as nice as it had been when we both had access to showers every day, and I could only imagine that my own wasn't too pleasant. Still, Blair smelled nothing like the reek of the man stinking up the bus. Blair's scent of salt and sweat and skin mingled into something earthy and somehow sexy.

Then again, maybe as a professional athlete, I was prone to find things like sweat and dirt a little sexier than most guys.

"Why are you whispering? Even if he could hear us over the rattle and cough of this junker bus, what are the chances he understands English?"

"Here's a pro tip for you, world traveler. Always assume everyone knows how to speak English."

"Fair point."

More people spoke English than anything else, especially in the Western world. I knew that, but we seemed so far away from everything out here. Like maybe we *were* two college lovers backpacking their way through Thanksgiving break, intent on seeing new things and experiencing them together.

I wouldn't mind being that guy. Especially if Blair would consent to being the girl.

Whether or not she would under normal circumstances, she kind of had agreed to it for now. The cover had been her idea, so she couldn't get mad at me for playing it up. Especially now that she'd been the one to touch me first—and she hadn't complained when I'd done the same. We were making progress. My initial reaction was pleasure, because nothing would improve this little vacation more than getting to know Blair well enough to have a little fun, but then our conversation a few minutes ago replayed in the back of my mind.

You can't trust everyone, Sam. People are assholes.

Her included? It was hard to admit, but that she had spent time working cons with her dad bothered me. The way she'd tensed up when she'd admitted it triggered a negative response, too—almost like she hadn't meant to tell me the truth. If it was the truth.

No. I was being stupid, overly paranoid because of the situation. She had found me, not the other way around. She wanted to help. And Quinn knew her. He would warn me if he thought she was dirty—not in a fun way.

The bus shuddered to a stop a few minutes later, every bolt and joint creaking and groaning in protest. It bellowed a huge cloud of exhaust, the odor overtaking anything else that might have found its way onto the curb as I followed Blair into the Bosnian evening.

"Are we close to the border? Like, will they check our passports here?"

"I don't know. Don't think so." She wandered down the platform, away from the thin crowd of our fellow passengers.

Some seemed to be getting air and stretching their legs, grabbing snacks from the smattering of vending machines or braving the toilets, but others hurried away, intent on getting home, maybe, or catching another bus to somewhere else.

"So, what are the chances your dad is hiding out in Serbia? I mean, I know they don't have a nonextradition treaty, and those places are pretty hard to come by these days, but still. It's not that parts of it aren't nice, but it's not an easy place to spend thirty million dollars of my money."

Blair didn't reply, leaning on the crooked wooden railing and staring off toward the mountains. The November air had a sharp chill to it, one that made me shiver, but even out here with no jacket, she didn't seem to feel it. Or it didn't bother her, maybe.

"Where are you from? Originally?" It seemed as though she piqued my curiosity more with each passing day, instead of the opposite, which was more typical for me. I wanted to understand what made her tick, guess the reasons she tried to ignore our chemistry so I could convince her to ignore them.

"New York City." Even though she faced away from me, the smile was clear in her voice.

"You loved it there."

"I still do. But Florida is okay."

"Florida's a shithole, Blair, and as two people who have seen a good portion of the world, we're uniquely qualified to make that assessment."

"The weather is nice."

"You don't seem to mind the cold."

She turned then, the wind whipping long strands of brown hair in front of her face. When she brushed them away, her cheeks were red, her dark eyes bright. "I like the chill. I miss the seasons while I'm in Florida. You're from there, though, aren't you?"

There she went again, spouting offhand knowledge that she really shouldn't have. It was possible that Quinn or Toby had mentioned it, or even that I had said something to her while we were in St. Moritz—heaven knew I wasn't sober enough while we were there to recall the details of every conversation—but it had happened enough times now that I knew she had to be lying. About being a tennis fan or not being attracted to me, I couldn't be sure. And it made my stomach twist into an impressive knot.

I liked her. I had since we first met, and there didn't seem to be much point in denying the fact to her or myself, but I had to remind myself to be careful. "Yes. My parents are from central Florida—the middle of the shithole, as it were—but we moved to Bradenton when I started training seriously."

"Where do you live in the off-season? Melbourne?"

I hated that question. People asked it all the time—reporters, friends, nosy fans—because most players had that place they loved. Sometimes the home they were born into, sometimes one they had fallen in love with and adopted along the way, but not me. My six weeks off were spent wherever sounded good at the time. More of them *had* been spent in Melbourne than other places, because that's where the new season began and it was nice to not have to rush, but that was the only reason. I had no more affection for Australia than anywhere else.

It didn't take a shrink to know that it was because home had never been a place of solace for me. The road had given me a life. Refuge. Love. As much as I adored women, enjoyed being in relationships, they'd never had any chance of surviving. My family had cured me of a burning desire to create one of my own—what the tennis world gave me was enough.

*

I had dozed off with less than an hour to go before we arrived in Belgrade. A loud pop and Blair's fingers squeezing my thigh startled me awake.

"What?"

Her hand flew from my leg to cover my mouth, but her sharp gaze stayed focused on the front of the bus. Mine followed, and a second later, cold fear froze my limbs.

The meth-head guy had a gun.

I pulled her hand off my face and squeezed it between my palms, then slumped down in the seat, tugging her with me so our heads were out of sight.

"What's happening?" I whispered.

She shook her head, the faint, leftover smell of her shampoo tickling my nose. "He started yelling, then a lady screamed, then he fired the gun."

"What's he yelling about?"

"I don't even know what language he's speaking," she said so softly it barely carried over the sound of the engine.

Great. I knew the two of us were going to be in trouble trying to traverse less-traveled European countries like normal people—ones who knew how to handle crises that might pop up—but being on a bus with a loaded gun was outside even my wild imaginings.

For her part, Blair looked unimpressed. The fact that she'd grabbed on to me so hard when it started proved that it frightened her, but now she appeared more annoyed than anything as she peered around the edge of the seat to get a better look.

Her fingers twitched between my palms but she didn't pull away.

"What's happening?"

"Shut up, I'm trying to listen," she hissed back.

The man and woman continued to shriek at each other in what sounded like babble, and a moment later Blair slid back my direction. Her teeth worried her bottom lip, but other than that, she still didn't seem too bothered by the fact that a maniac with a gun paced the aisle. "He thinks the woman he's with is cheating on him. Maybe with his brother."

"How do you figure?"

"A few Latin roots here and there, plus his hand gestures and the fact that she's yelling back now." She shook her head. "It's the *Maury Show*. You've got to be fucking kidding me."

The bus swerved toward the shoulder of the uneven road, slamming our hips together. I let go of her hand and caught her around the shoulders, steadying us both against the window. My hands were shaking, and even though it was stupid, I hoped she didn't notice.

More shouting erupted from up front, along with another gunshot that made us both duck on instinct, and the bus swerved back into the proper lane. I guessed the driver's plan to pull over and deal with this crisis while not moving had failed.

"Fuck this shit," Blair muttered, and stood up before I could stop her.

To her credit, she didn't straighten all the way, leaving her chest and torso covered by the seat, but if you asked me she should have been more concerned about her head.

Then again, these seats weren't stopping a bullet. If the asshole decided to spray the back of the bus, both of us were going to be Swiss cheese.

"Excuse me!"

Her voice rang over the shrieked argument, too loud, too confrontational. Awe over her balls warred with embarrassment over my cowering, with neither winning out over my worry.

"Is there any way you could put the gun away and sit your ass down? The rest of us would like to arrive in Belgrade alive, and we're only, like, ten minutes from the station. You can just pick up where you left off there." She paused, waiting for a response maybe, but the rest of the bus had a similar reaction to mine—stunned silence. *"Hinsetzen? Schnauze? Ja?"*

The glance she threw me seemed to ask an opinion on her German. It was translatable, though whether it would be understood was another story. I gave her a baffled nod. I inched upward until my eyes cleared the top of the seat, just in time to see all hell break loose.

Blair's mouth had shocked the gunman into silence, and two of the bigger organ thieves took advantage of the distraction and rushed him. His gun arm flailed. They wrestled and shouted while the bus swerved again. A shot exploded. Someone screamed and I grabbed Blair around the waist, yanking her down on my lap and curling around her body.

The commotion ceased as quickly as it began. My heart pounded so hard against Blair's back there was no way she didn't feel it, and my arms trembled from holding on to her so tight. My eyes were closed and I had to work at opening them for several seconds—the feeling of her breathing said she was alive, but fear that there would be blood everywhere kept ice in my veins.

"Sam."

I gulped some more air. "Yeah?"

"I can't breathe."

"Oh my god, are you hurt? Did he shoot you?"

"No, dumbass. You're squeezing the shit out of me."

"Oh." I loosened my grip and opened my eyes, already feeling a little stupid and expecting to see exasperation and contempt in her gaze. She maneuvered on my lap until she straddled me, and then smiled. For some reason, her reaction swapped my cold fear for hot anger. "What in the hell were you thinking? He could have shot you!"

"Somebody had to do something before the driver freaked out and drove us over a cliff."

"You didn't even know what was going on, or what kind of crazy he is! It didn't have to be you."

"I was willing. Everyone else was sitting on their hands. Ergo, it had to be me."

"Blair."

She cut me off by placing her palms on my cheeks, hesitating for the tiniest of seconds, then leaning forward to press her lips against mine.

The kiss was soft, so unlike Blair that it took me by surprise. I slid my hands to her hips, squeezing hard enough to keep her in place. She scooted forward on my lap, her palms drifting to my chest while her fingers brushed the exposed skin at the base of my throat.

Her touch drove out my fear and replaced it with shuddering desire, and I tangled a hand in her hair. The slip of her tongue against my bottom lip shot boiling need into my gut and I opened my mouth, greedy for the taste of her.

What began as a kiss, maybe to thank me for trying to protect her, maybe born of the relief of surviving a harrowing incident, turned into something animalistic inside ten seconds. Her chest pressed against mine as her fingers dug into my scalp and our tongues tangled with far more urgency than was appropriate for a very public place.

I didn't care.

It was as though my hands had minds of their own. They explored until they found the hem of her sweatshirt, then the tank top underneath, reveling in the softness of the skin on her back.

Blair gasped against my lips, the tiny, incredible admission of pleasure bringing me back to the present. As much as I didn't want to let her slip away, we had to stop or end up being the second horrifying thing our poor fellow passengers would witness today.

I didn't remove my hands, though. Now that she'd touched me, now that she'd proven that her body felt the same pull as mine, going back was off the table. She laid her forehead against mine, eyes closed, until both of us could breathe normally.

"I knew you were hot for me, Blair Paddington," I whispered with a smile.

She sat up and crossed her arms, avoiding my gaze. "Whatever. I just thought it was sweet that you tried to protect me. Even if it came a little late."

"Don't do that." Her eyes snapped to mine, and I held on to her gaze, refusing to let her look away again. "There was nothing sweet about that kiss, and I never come late. I'm a right-on-time kind of guy."

That made her smile, even if she didn't seem to want to. "Fine. I might be attracted to you, but that's it. I don't *like* you or anything, so go ahead and unswell your head accordingly."

"I don't like you, either. You're a pain in my ass, you do crazy shit like stand up in front of men holding guns, and I'm considering the idea that you could be the Antichrist." I ran my hands over the bare skin of her back, then trailed my fingers around front, skimming the softness under her bra. The way her eyes fluttered made me ache to pull her against me, but dammit, we were still on the bus. "But you're a fucking sexy devil."

"You really are an idiot."

"But I'm hot?"

She rolled her eyes and climbed off my lap, turning to check out the scene that had started all of this. I almost wanted to thank the psycho with the weapon for helping me break down the emotional barriers Blair had spent who knows how long erecting. Even though she'd kissed me as though she wanted to fuck me right here, even though she'd acknowledged the crackling attraction that felt as natural as breathing, I had an inkling that getting her to admit to any feelings would be harder than pulling teeth out of a rabid raccoon.

Instead of pressing—and also to give me time to deep-breathe away my boner—I followed her gaze. The bus driver had pulled over at some point during our make-out session, which must have gone on a little longer than it had seemed to, and the two burly men who had corralled the gun-wielder had escorted him off the bus.

One of them was talking to him, a hand on his shoulder, and the previously frightening crazy person now looked to be sobbing on the side of the road. The woman who had sparked such passion sat in silence, knitting something lumpy and purple. She didn't look up when the two men boarded the bus without her boyfriend or whatever he was, and said nothing when the driver pulled away, leaving him behind in the frigid night.

We were close enough to Belgrade that he wouldn't have to walk far to get a ride, find shelter, or call someone, so it was hard to feel badly for him. Especially since he could have killed us.

Blair said nothing as the bus puffed and puttered the remaining ten minutes to the bus station. She sat carefully next to me, near enough that we shared heat but far enough to keep us from touching, with a faint smile on her lips. I realized my own mouth sported a matching one and shook it away. Goofiness would never help me into the bed of a girl such as Blair Paddington.

It still surprised me that even after the kiss—which I could not stop thinking about—I was still more curious about what was going on in her head than between her legs.

And that helped me stop smiling for good.

Chapter 9

Blair

I could not stop thinking about that kiss. It had been
an impulse, a result of high adrenaline and base wonder
that he had tried to protect me. Or, that's what I'd
thought before my lips touched his.

I could barely recall what happened after that. It was
a haze of lust and heat and tongues, of his hands on my
skin, of the frustrating desire to be closer to him. The
reaction had been instinctual, coded into my DNA, and
the force of it left my head in a fog. Scooting away
from Sam had done nothing to dim the electric current
of desire humming underneath my skin.

We needed more space from each other than a bus
could provide, and by the time we pulled into the
Belgrade station, I was happier to see Serbia than
anyone had a right to be.

That is, until the sight of the all-too-perfect Marija
Peronovic greeted me inside the dingy terminal.

After five days of nonstop travel, wrinkled clothes,
and no shower, Sam and I fit in with the rest of our
bedraggled travel companions a little too seamlessly.
Marija freaking glowed, from the shiny ebony hair that
hung to the middle of her back to the long inky lashes
framing her bright blue eyes and the tanned legs that
were completely out of place in the Serbian winter. She

must have had a dress or skirt on, but it wasn't visible under the soft blue of her wool coat.

She smiled at Sam, happiness and welcome lighting her beautiful face, and opened her arms for a hug. The girl had been one of my favorites to watch for years, and her spunky attitude with the press always planted me in her camp, but when her manicured fingers locked around Sam's back, I wanted to claw her eyes out.

Which was stupid. Sam wasn't mine, and I didn't want him to be. No matter what I'd told the woman on the train, we were not lovers exploring Europe on Thanksgiving break. I was here to get access to his bank accounts by whatever means necessary, and kissing him couldn't change that. *Wouldn't* change that, even if I wanted it to.

Which I didn't.

Sam and Marija had spent months and months on the road together for years. If they'd wanted to have sex or date, they'd had plenty of opportunity already—and who's to say they hadn't? The familiarity and ease between them as they caught up in soft voices suggested a level of comfort that could be more than friendship.

I touched my lips, then snatched my hand away when I realized what I was doing. So, Sam was a good kisser. So, it felt as though his lips were made of magnets perfectly tuned to a frequency in mine. All it meant was that, if this job did come to getting naked with him, I might actually enjoy it.

The tingle between my thighs at the thought said I would *definitely* enjoy it—or even want it—but as hard as it was to admit that to myself, I couldn't do it like this. Lying to him.

I needed to stop dripping with lust and focus on the task at hand. Earn Sam's trust. Make him believe I was on his side by pretending to ferret out my father's current location. When we "failed," talk him out of his bank account information so that I could continue the "search" on my own. End of story.

Still, would it be so bad to enjoy myself while doing my due diligence?

"Hello, earth to Blair . . ."

Sam's voice knocked me out of a frustrating loop of not-logic. "Sorry, what?"

"What were you thinking about just then? Your face looked exactly like the one on a possum treed by a dog."

"That's flattering."

Silence hung in the air between the three of us until he accepted there wouldn't be any more information forthcoming about my state of mind.

"I was introducing you to Marija." He nodded toward her as though he were speaking to some kind of daft child, or a recluse who didn't own a television. "Marija, this is Blair Paddington, a friend of Quinn's."

"Any friend of Sam and Quinn's is a friend of mine," she replied in perfect, perky English. Even though she played for Serbia, she'd trained in the United States since she was ten years old. Common enough knowledge. "Would you like to go?"

"Wait, where are we going?" I turned to Sam. "I thought we were just borrowing a car."

"Calm down, devil girl. We are borrowing a car; it's at Marija's house. And since it's almost midnight, I was thinking we could grab a shower and catch a few hours of horizontal sleep."

Agreeing meant going against everything I had been telling him since we set out on this misguided field trip, but the mere mention of a hot shower brought tears to my eyes. I stunk like four-day-old body odor, and even though it wouldn't have stopped me from making out with him for another twenty minutes, Sam didn't smell so hot, either.

In fact, I was pretty sure Marija had taken a few steps back after hugging him. Using her house didn't make much of a difference to me, but with the omniscient picture I had painted of my father, it could send up imaginary warning flags for Sam.

Still, it was midnight. We would leave first thing in the morning. It would be okay.

I nodded. "Okay. But we need to be out of there early."

Sam groaned, then reached over to slide my backpack off my shoulders.

I grabbed for it. "What are you doing?"

"Trying to be nice. It's heavy."

"And it will be lighter if you carry it? I'm fine." My shoulders ached, my back wrenched every time I moved, and the balls of my feet were as sore as if I'd hiked Michigan Avenue in stilettos, but letting him carry my bag felt like an admission of something. Weakness, maybe.

I didn't want to go there. I'd already gone enough places today that frightened me—in front of a gun and onto Sam Bradford's lap—and it was hard to say which was more terrifying.

"Fine. Whatever."

He turned and strode toward the bus terminal door, skirting a couple of men in dingy business suits and a family with five kids, all of whom were running in different directions. Marija looked at me as though she wanted to say something but couldn't figure out what. She gave up after a minute and shrugged, then followed Sam. I trailed after them both, taking a six-year-old elbow to the ass on the way. The girl babbled something that appeared to be an apology, an endearing, half-toothless grin easing my irritation.

I smiled back and patted her arm, then stepped out into the blustery night.

*

Marija's house lived up to the image in my mind and then some, even if it was ugly as sin. The tan and chocolate stucco and wooden beams stretched four stories high and resembled an especially grand vision of how I imagined the cabin in the woods that belonged to the seven dwarves.

I kept my opinion to myself, largely because I was too tired to even think about opening my mouth and also because now that the idea of a shower and bed were within reach, doing anything to screw that up seemed like a particularly bad idea.

"Are you two hungry?"

Sam's eyes wandered toward me, waiting on my answer. I wished he would stop playing the gentleman; we all knew he was nothing more than an overgrown man-child who had never wanted for a damn thing.

"A little, but I don't want food as much as I want a shower. Or sleep," I admitted.

Marija nodded. "I'll have the servants bring a little something up to your rooms. You can get ready for bed and have a snack before you crash."

"Thank you, Mari." Sam kissed her cheek, then headed toward the giant winding staircase.

It climbed out of the center of the great room, which had too much brown and ivory furniture, an abundance of rugs, end tables, and antiques, and *way* too much velvet. The floor was slate, or made to look like slate, and my lack of sleep made me slip a few times.

"Yes, thank you," I echoed.

"You know," she said, her voice taking on the same tone she used when someone in the press had talked to her as if she were a dumb blonde. "I haven't asked exactly what's going on here, or why the two of you showed up in Belgrade needing to borrow a car in the middle of the night, and quite frankly, I'm not sure it's in my best interest to know."

When neither of us offered a negative or affirmative response, she crossed her arms, stuck out her hip, and fixed Sam with a look that I swear made him shift to cover his balls.

"My family has a lot of respect in this city, and we've been consistently aboveboard with all of our business dealings. I run a successful charity involving orphans. If helping you and your surly little friend here fucks that up, I am not going to be happy."

Sam sighed. "Trust me, Mari. No one wants you to be unhappy, least of all anyone who has ever seen it happen—which includes me. I've had a small issue in my personal life that Blair is helping me rectify, but we're not doing anything illegal or anything that could affect your family in any way. Right, Blair?"

It was true that no harm would come to Marija or her family's reputation by us being here, but the image of my father as an international force needed to be maintained. "I'm sure everything will work out fine. Really."

I left enough of an ambiguous trail in the words to make Marija squint her eyes and Sam roll his, but she didn't stop us this time when we started up the stairs.

A maid waited at the top, a silent woman who probably didn't speak much English, and she showed us to a pair of guest rooms connected by an all-white bathroom. Even the fluffy towels were white. And monogrammed. It was like Texas in there.

"You want the girly room, or does that offend your feminist sensibilities as badly as my trying to carry your bag did?" Sam's voice had a gravelly twist that was new to me, and the expression of annoyance in his eyes surprised me, too.

"Are you mad at me because I wouldn't let you carry my bag?"

"No." He ran a hand through his longish hair, which mussed it more than usual given the amount of grease that had built up during our travels. "I don't know. It's not just that, it's . . . you scared me today, Blair. I got distracted when you kissed me, because holy hell, but now that you're standing a good four feet away, all I feel is angry. You can't go around risking your life like that. Like it doesn't matter."

Silence rolled in between us, thick and tangible like a dense fog. It swirled around our ankles, then rose to our calves, then higher until it seemed to strangle the life out of any words that might have any meaning. Despite what I'd said after our kiss, I wasn't sure how I felt about Sam. I didn't know if I liked him, if I was interested in more than his body or his money, and sharing parts of my real self with people didn't come easily for me.

Or come at all.

"Sam, I'm really tired. Too tired for an existential discussion on the importance of one person's life in the grand scheme of the world, so can I please take a shower and we can talk about this in the morning?"

"Sure. But you and I both know we won't talk about this in the morning."

He gave me a small smile, one that might mean he'd forgiven my rash behavior on the bus and my inability to even attempt an emotional connection with him, or it could mean nothing at all.

"Thank you."

The room he'd given me had a huge white canopied bed with piles and piles of gold and purple blankets and pillows. It looked like heaven, like something the Egyptian gods had imagined during their more decadent musings, and I forgot all about fighting with Sam.

Even though the bathroom reminded me of a space fit for a mental hospital, the shower felt amazing. The scalding water turned my skin pink. Days of dirt washed off me and swirled down the drain, and the bottles of shampoo and conditioner were foreign and smelled delicious. There was even a razor, which I used to shave my legs, as well as other parts of me that wouldn't need the attention had the thought of sleeping with Sam not lodged in my brain.

I dug toothpaste and my toothbrush out of my backpack, tugging the giant white towel tighter around my chest and rubbing a circle of steam off the mirror. My reflection appeared leaps and bounds better than it had before I'd stepped under the spray, and no doubt the stench coming off me had been eliminated, but the circles under my eyes left plenty to be desired.

The door swung open as I rinsed and spit, framing Sam's impressive stature. He had on a pair of Florida Gators basketball shorts and nothing else. The tanned muscles rippling across his chest and down his stacked abs pooled heat in my stomach that dripped lower until it weakened my knees. My hormones were out of control.

He was just a mark. A sexy mark that was currently looking at me as though he was picturing me without the towel, who was making my breasts tingle and my head feel light with a mere look, but still. Just a mark.

Just a mark.

"I'm almost finished," I managed, turning back to the sink under the guise of rinsing one more time. In reality, my face felt as though it were melting off, and the self-satisfied smirk on Sam's face said he knew exactly why.

"Trust me, I can tell when you're almost finished."

I choked on the water, then covered it up with a cough. Despite the air I liked to give off at Whitman, and in general, my experience with super-aggressive men was less than some girls. Another side effect of keeping to myself, and of my father being a large, intimidating man. Handling a confident guy such as Sam Bradford would take a skill set I had to admit I might not have. Which was maybe another reason I'd blown him off from the beginning.

Once I felt more under control I laid down my toothbrush, turned off the water, and spun to face him. He was still gorgeous, but this time I was ready for it. Instead of swooning like a damn Delta, I gave him the sauciest smile I could muster. "All yours."

"What is?"

"Whatever you want, of course. Isn't that how your life works?"

I left the bathroom before he could come up with an answer, feeling pretty proud of my comeback in the face of his incessant dirty talk—which I secretly loved.

My self-satisfaction crashed when I felt his hand on my elbow. He spun me around, then gathered me flush against him. With the knot at the top of my towel barely holding, the majority of my breasts were smashed against his bare chest, strands of hair tickling my skin in a delicious way. His eyes—light brown, like maple syrup—stared into mine with an intensity that spread goose bumps all over my body.

Sam lifted a finger, tracing my bottom lip. "First of all, I don't take what I want unless it's being expressly offered. Second, don't offer unless you mean it."

"Mean what?" My voice sounded breathless and far away.

Now that I'd kissed him and touched him, had imagined having more of him, it was like a drug. I knew I shouldn't do it, that sleeping with him needlessly complicated everything, but that moment on the train had bashed a hole in the dam, and desire seeped through everywhere.

"I haven't made a secret of the fact that I want you, not since the first day we met. Then, it was because you're hot as shit and I spent hours imagining your ass in my hands." He paused, studying my reaction.

Which was probably somewhere between surprise and take-me-now.

"Now it's still those things, but it's also because you drive me insane. Because you're a mystery I want to figure out, and because nothing but you is going to make this ache go away. But what do *you* want, Blair? Because you've gone from despising me to kissing me like your life depended on it in half a day and I'm trying to keep up." He used a hand to guide me onto my tiptoes, bringing our lips within inches of each other, his eyes still searching mine.

I wanted to close the distance. I wanted to feel his lips on mine, to drop the towel, tug him to the bed, to feel his *everything* on mine, but the words stuck in my throat. My body felt frozen and alight at the same time, which didn't seem possible.

Yet, I recognized the feeling. It wasn't new for me to want something, but not be able to have it because of my father. Because of my life. Because of my fucked-up head.

This *was* the first time that I'd wanted something for me that aligned with what my father had asked, and it made me feel slimy and dirty, and nothing like a girl who Sam deserved, even for only a little while. I wanted him, but it bothered me that this was all a sham. Pretend.

Even if my feelings weren't, he wouldn't see the distinction once he learned the truth.

"I don't know," I finally replied.

Disappointment fell over the eagerness on his face. He dropped his arms and I shivered, feeling not only cold but cast away. But this was my life. I didn't get to have what I wanted without consequences—in this case, feeling at best like a liar, at worst, some kind of prostitute.

Before I could decide whether or not to explain or what I could possibly say, Sam went into the bathroom and closed the door.

Chapter 10

Despite being more tired than I could ever remember being in my life, I'd spent the last three hours tossing and turning in the bed, which turned out to be a little too soft.

Except it wasn't the bed. It was this stupid trip. It was me and Sam, and the fact that an ache had lodged between my legs and throbbed every time I thought of him in his shorts, him with his arms around me, him asking what I wanted.

Saying that he wanted me.

I thought about taking care of it myself in order to get some sleep—not to mention it might be days before I had a room to myself again—but I didn't want to get off. I wanted Sam.

It would be simple to get up, walk through the bathroom connecting our rooms, and wake him up. Take what I wanted and banish all of the lame, exhausting, self-centered thoughts to the back of my head.

So what if my dad basically told me to sleep with him? So what if I was lying to him about whose side I was on or what we were doing?

And if I would never see him again once I got what I wanted?

His problem, not mine.

Except it felt wrong. It had never really felt wrong to take part in Dad's shit. It was how things were, and I did it because he was my father and he asked. And I liked it, sometimes. The being close to him. Sharing something with someone, especially because I didn't have anyone else.

The root of my discomfort wasn't sleeping with Sam. It was that helping my dad take the rest of his money felt wrong, too. Before I'd gone to St. Moritz, he'd been the guy I'd watched on television for the past four or five years. Cocky, handsome, talented. He had money to burn, like all of Dad's cons, which always eased any potential guilt.

The difference between Sam and people like Miss Daisy—other than the fact that I knew him now—was that even if he played a game for a living, he had worked his ass off for that money. He wouldn't be able to earn more, not indefinitely, and once his career ended, what would he do?

It's not your problem, Blair. And you know what else isn't your problem? Whether or not it hurts his feelings that you slept with him and then stole from him.

Holy Jesus, now my brain had joined forces with the rest of me.

Maybe I was overthinking this whole thing. I wanted him. He wanted me. He'd never been a guy who wanted a serious relationship, and I was incapable of having one.

Who cared about the rest of it?

I tossed the covers off my legs, shivering when my feet hit the cold floor, and paused in front of the bathroom mirror to smooth my hair and swish mouthwash over my teeth. I took a deep breath, then pushed open the door that connected to Sam's room.

"Fancy meeting you here."

His deep baritone slid from the shadows and I jumped, covering my mouth to stifle a shriek. "What are you doing?"

"The same thing you're doing, I imagine. Coming to see if I could make you change your mind about offering yourself to me." He took a step forward.

I took a step back. We repeated that dance a few more times, until we were both in the bathroom and my ass was pressed up against the vanity. His features were soft but visible in the orange night-light glow, eyes bright with a restrained desire that shot straight down my spine.

"Well?"

I licked my lips, unable to look away from the intensity of his gaze, unable to verbally give him the go-ahead because talking about feelings and emotions and sex didn't come easily to me. Instead, I reached up, looped my arms around his neck, and crushed his lips to mine.

Sam didn't waste a moment going slow. Maybe he was afraid I'd change my mind, or maybe he'd been lying awake imagining all the ways we could fit together the same way I had been.

His tongue parted my lips, searching my mouth until it found mine, then tangled with it. Strong hands grabbed my ass and he groaned into me.

"Yes. Better than I thought," he murmured, then lifted me up onto the counter.

The proof of his excitement pressed into my crotch, tightening the fabric of my pajama shorts and rubbing in a way that ripped an involuntary whimper from my throat. He felt so good against me I couldn't imagine what he would feel like inside me—and I wanted to know.

I reached out, running my fingers over every muscle, down every ab, delighting as they tightened under the scrape of my fingernails. His hands left my rear and lifted my tank top over my head, leaving me naked from the waist up, shivering in the cool nighttime air.

My hips bucked and my hands fisted in his hair when his hot lips closed over my nipple. Again, no warm-up, no pretense, just breath and tongue and a firm nip of the teeth until my senses fled, leaving me grinding helplessly against him. When he moved to torture my other breast I struggled with his shorts, finally shoving them down over his hips and taking his hardness in my palm.

My strokes distracted him from his mission to drive me completely insane and his fingers hooked in the waistband of my shorts, dispensing with them, too.

He growled. "No underwear? God, I wish I had stayed in bed and let you come to me."

Fingers teased the backs of my thighs then swirled inward, hitting places that made me shudder and bite my lip, then moving down to dip inside me. I'd been wet with anticipation before I'd come in here but now he slipped one finger, then another, in and out of me with ease.

"Christ. I don't want to wait." He paused, seeming to want some kind of go-ahead from me, even though it was painfully and embarrassingly obvious that I was more than ready.

"Do you have anything?" I asked, sounding too breathless. Please say he had something.

He crooked a smile. "Who do you think you're talking to? Don't move."

It felt strange, sitting naked on the bathroom counter, but I fought the urge to slide off. Sex made me uncomfortable. Not that I didn't enjoy it, or want it, or intellectually know that what went on in my bedroom was similar to what went on in beds across the world, but . . . I felt silly anyway.

I felt sillier when Sam returned wearing a different pair of shorts and no condom.

"So . . . I don't have anything."

My brain screamed that I didn't care, but my body was having none of that. I wanted Sam, but it didn't mean I could afford to be unrealistic about his past.

I crossed my arms over my breasts in a lame attempt to hide my nakedness. My arms didn't go nearly far enough, and before I could reach for my clothes, Sam tugged on my wrists.

"Don't do that. Don't cover up."

"I want to."

"Why? What's changed?"

What had changed was that I could handle being naked and vulnerable during sex, but not without it. I

137

figured on using a good portion of the money I'd earned working for my dad on a good therapist, but for today, prancing around naked in front of a guy I hadn't just slept with made me feel as though hives were breaking out across my skin.

I scratched at one on my shoulder, still covered, and eyed him. "Nothing."

"You are a funny little devil," he murmured, then leaned forward and scooped me into his arms.

"What are you doing?" I demanded as he strode easily back into his bedroom.

"Bringing you to bed with me."

"But you just said . . ."

"I said we couldn't have sex. I'd be happy to pleasure you another way, if you'd like, or give you a T-shirt and tuck you in, if you prefer that. But I haven't been able to sleep thinking of you in the other room, and how much better it would be if you were in here."

"You want to cuddle?" The idea did not amuse me in the slightest.

"I mean, we're going to be driving tomorrow, right? Don't you want me to get some sleep?"

"You're a grown-up, Sam. I'm sure you manage to get to sleep alone all the time." I grabbed a discarded T-shirt off the dresser, trying my best to ignore how it smelled like him, and slipped it over my head. "I'm not really into cuddling."

"The first option, then?" He winked and reached for me, frowning when I stepped out of range. "Blair, seriously. Why are you acting like this? I thought when we met sneaking into each other's rooms in the middle of the night that it meant you were into it. Did I imagine that whole scene in the bathroom? Is this a dream? Am I in *Inception*?"

He looked around like a suspicious animal, sniffing the air, and in spite of everything, I felt a smile tug at my lips. It made me feel more exposed than being naked but no matter how hard I tried, it wouldn't go away.

Sam leaned over and kissed my nose. "You're really pretty when you smile. For a devil."

"I don't want anything from you."

That earned me an eyebrow raise. "Oh?"

My face heated at the memory of myself undressed and writhing under his touch, his mouth. "Well, nothing you can give me tonight, anyway."

"Blair, I have many talents and despite what you seem to think, I'm not selfish."

"No. I mean . . . I'll lie down, if it's that big of a deal to you, but that's it."

"You're pretty fucked up, aren't you."

It wasn't a question, and he didn't say it in a way that made me feel stupid or unwanted. I hated that he could see the broken pieces of me so easily but had no idea that my entire purpose here was to defraud him further.

Then again, maybe he did. Sam had great instincts—he would have made a great con man in another life, one where he didn't wear his thoughts on his face and let them tumble out of his mouth unchecked.

He sat down on the bed, stretching in a way that displayed every single one of his abs. I looked away before I decided to borrow another girl's personality and asked him to finish what he started, at least on me. It was safer on the other side of the bed.

"Can I have a pair of shorts or something?"

"This is the only pair I have. And since you wouldn't let me bring anything other than a backpack, I've only got two pairs of underwear and they're both dirty. Speaking of which, we should have asked Mari if we could do laundry."

That would have been smart, actually. I had one clean pair left but that was it.

"Besides, I prefer you without it," he whispered, lying back and tugging me toward him. His hands ran up my thighs and over my ass, giving it a light smack.

"Okay, that's enough touching," I said, hoping my words distracted him from noticing my involuntary shiver.

He didn't protest at the distance I put between us, the smile on his face palpable in the dark room.

"I don't want anything from you other than sex," I clarified after several moments of silence. Guilt burned in my blood, insisting that he hear those words, that he understood. That when this was over he couldn't accuse me of promising things I couldn't deliver?

Even if it wasn't true. It was the only way to prove to myself that the two things—the money and the pleasure—were not connected.

"I don't even like you, devil girl. Remember?" His voice was quiet, blurred around the edges as though he was nearly asleep, or maybe he didn't quite know what to make of this situation. This conversation. "Maybe I have a hankering for some good hate sex."

It killed me that I couldn't sniff out the reason behind his tone. Reading people came naturally, but Sam turned the tables. He sensed things about me, but I was in the dark about how to win more than his attraction.

"You promise?" I rolled over to face him, wondering if his expression would help. "Not even a little?"

"Hell, no. You're a pain in the ass."

I didn't learn anything from his face, because the words trailed off as he fell asleep, his pinky finger twitching against mine. But that didn't stop me from watching him for a long, long time.

*

I woke up when the first light of dawn peered between the wooden-slat blinds. Sam's deep, steady breathing almost lulled me back to sleep, but the idea of living a half-naked, awkward morning-after-not-sex scene didn't appeal to me.

The memory of last night in the bathroom embarrassed me more than it probably should, more than it would embarrass girls such as Audra or Ruby, girls who had a healthy worldview about sex. Then again, they hadn't spent their lives developing the inability to trust other people, and that couldn't be fixed today. Avoidance it was.

I inched my way out of bed, lifting Sam's heavy arm, which had somehow found its way across my belly in the middle of the night. He sighed and shifted, then rolled over and settled back into a light snore.

The empty space of my room both welcomed and mocked me. It couldn't be normal, to feel better able to breathe here than in bed with a super-sexy, smart, flirty millionaire.

Sam might be the most normal person I'd ever met, but nothing in my nineteen years had been average. That fact used to give me perverse pleasure, but not anymore. Normal had started to intrigue me. Maybe because it would always elude me.

I stripped off Sam's shirt and tossed it on the floor, then threw my own dirty clothes on top of the pile. In spite of not wanting to wake him, it didn't seem nice to go find a washing machine without taking his things along.

He didn't move a muscle while I grabbed the handful of clothes from his backpack and the pair of discarded underwear in front of the closet. Marija would have to deal with me in a sheet, because there wasn't anything to put on in the meantime except my last pair of clean underwear.

The floor in the hallway and on the stairs chilled the soles of my feet. The first thing I saw at the bottom was Marija, sitting on her beige love seat with a newspaper and a cup of coffee.

I cleared my throat and she looked up, prettier than anyone had a right to be at sunrise. A stab of jealousy went through me, hot and unexpected, and totally stupid since all she'd done was be beautiful—not her fault.

"Good morning, Blair." Her sharp gaze dropped to the clothes in my arms. "Laundry?"

"If you don't mind."

She set her steaming coffee on the end table and unfolded her long legs, getting gracefully to her feet. "I can take them."

I hugged the stinky garments to my chest without thinking. "No, I'll do it. Just show me where. Or tell me. You don't have to get up."

"I'm already up," she said with a bemused smile. "And I really don't mind."

"Okay. Fine."

Marija led the way through the kitchen and into a mudroom, where a sleek, modern set of appliances waited with open lids.

"Thanks."

I expected her to leave when I set about the business of adding soap and setting the machine, but she leaned against the door frame and watched me. And blocked my only exit.

"You don't like to let people help you, do you?"

"It's not that." Marija didn't respond to my obvious lie, but her continued stare drove an uncomfortable knot between my shoulders. "I'm used to taking care of myself, that's all."

"You're different than Sam's usual girl. He's easygoing and he attracts the same. Easy in, easy out. No muss, no fuss." She cocked her head. "You're definitely fuss, Blair. But if you muss him, you'll have to deal with me. I don't know what's going on here, but it smells bad. He's a good guy—a little too much so, probably."

"I'm not Sam's girl, so I guess you don't have to worry."

"Hmm. We'll see."

She wandered off, leaving me a ball of tension. I finished dumping in soap and set the dial to the shortest wash possible. When I made my way back to the living room, I found her at the foot of the stairs, two piles of clothes in her hands.

"Here. One for you, one for him. There will be breakfast in the kitchen in a few minutes."

"Thanks." It was hard enough for me to get out that one word, so I didn't try for any more.

Marija wasn't unique—others along the way had sensed something off about me or my story, or my dad, and we'd had to bail on that con and find another. Some people were gifted with greater intuition than others, for sure, the same way some people sensed ghosts or whatever. Like an extra sense, or at least a super-honed bullshit meter.

We would be gone soon, but it wouldn't stop her from warning Sam.

I tossed the clothes on the bed in my room, wishing I could hide under that too-soft pile of bedding until this entire situation melted away. The sound of running water snuck under the bathroom door, signaling Sam indulging in a second shower, which hadn't been part of the plan. I walked over and tapped on the door, then tried the knob when he didn't respond, cracking the door just far enough to make sure I wasn't going to see anything I didn't . . . well, not that I didn't *want* to, but that I shouldn't assume I could.

"Sam?" Despite my best efforts, my eye wandered to the half-steamed mirror, my breath catching at the sight of his naked body though the all-glass shower.

"Yeah?" he shouted back, not pausing in his soaping pattern.

"I'm leaving clean clothes on the counter for you, and Marija says there's breakfast."

"Okay, I'll be down in a few minutes." He paused, then glanced over his shoulder at the mirror and caught me staring. "Unless you want to join me."

I backed up and shut the door without answering. My mouth had dried and my gut twisted at the mere thought of touching him; I had to get farther away. Marija's clothes fit me pretty well, if they were hers and not just extras—rich people always seemed to have some laying around—but the yoga pants were a little bit long.

The socks warmed my toes, though, and the hooded sweater eased the chill bumps on my arms. By the time I slid into a chair in the empty kitchen and grabbed a croissant and a slice of bacon, my nerves had settled. When Sam appeared a few minutes later, hair damp and smelling freshly washed, my heart gave a couple of quick thuds before easing back into a steady beat.

There. I could be in the same room with him and not jump his bones. Mind over matter. *In fact,* I thought as he poured a cup of coffee and sat across from me, *we should get to the business at hand.*

145

"We might as well run over to my dad's Belgrade house while the clothes are washing. Then we can get out of here as soon as we're done."

He eyed me over a piece of toast. "If your dad's not there, you mean."

"Of course," I covered smoothly, sipping my own coffee. "Maybe today will be the end of the journey. You never know."

"I think I'd be sad if it was."

I looked up to find a strange expression in his eyes—a little bit of sorrow, some of the thrumming lust that had become familiar, and something else harder to pin down.

"Why? You don't want your money back?"

He sighed and sat back, the chair popping under his weight. "No, I want my money back. You ready?"

Going out in public in yoga pants wasn't something I did off campus, but what the hell. I didn't know anyone in Belgrade, and it was early. Hopefully the Serbian people weren't judgy as far as fashion went. "Sure."

"Let me get my shoes on and see which car Marija wants us to take."

Of course she had more than one spare. Why wouldn't she?

I waited in the living room, pretending not to care that Sam and Marija talked too softly in the next room for me to overhear. When they emerged, he had a frown on his face that reinfected me with worry, and she had a fire in her eyes that made me tired.

"Well?"

"You two can take the black Mercedes. My parents are in Monaco for the month, and I typically take the Jag when I need to drive myself."

"Thank you," I managed again. It seemed to be the best I could do when it came to acknowledging her hospitality, especially since she so obviously wished that I didn't come as part of Sam's unexpected visit to Serbia.

Marija gave him one last pointed look, then jerked her head toward the kitchen. "Garage is through the laundry room. Keys are in it."

Sam leaned over and pressed a kiss to her head. "Thanks, Mari. We'll bring it back safe and sound."

She nodded, leaning into his lips for a second too long. "I might be out at a meeting this afternoon. Help yourself to anything in the kitchen, or the staff can prepare lunch."

It was on the tip of my tongue to snap that we could make our own lunch, and that we would be gone before mooching another meal, but I couldn't figure out why. She knew that Sam wasn't used to preparing meals. I assumed Sam dined out, ate room service, or took advantage of spreads at his events. Dad and I had a cook before I went to college, and even though the dining hall left something to be desired, it sufficed.

We left through the laundry room, where someone had moved our clothes from the washing machine to the dryer, stepping into the garage. It had an air of disuse, of cleanliness, that didn't match up with my mental image of such a place, and the black Mercedes gleamed in the sunlight streaming through the windows on the doors.

It smelled new, and the leather of the passenger seat was shiny and stiff under my legs. Sam and I clicked our seat belts into place at the same time, and he ran his fingers over the sun visor until he found the opener and the garage door rumbled up behind us. Dust motes trembled in the blast of sunshine as we backed out into the day, still not speaking.

Instead of thinking about how Marija's helpfulness irritated me, I pulled up a map to the old Belgrade mansion on my phone, then hit "start" on the navigation app.

"It's down on the shore of the Danube," I said as it pulled up directions. "Doesn't look like far."

He paused at the end of the driveway, squinting into the sun. His hands gripped the steering wheel so tightly that his knuckles turned white, and breath went in his nose, then blew out his mouth.

The picture of nerves, or anger, made me cold. The idea that Marija had voiced her suspicions or, worse, done some digging and found out more about my dad and my life, throbbed in the base of my skull.

"Why are you being so cold to Mari when she's helping us?"

"I'm not."

"Blair, you are. If I didn't know better, I'd say you were jealous. But you've made it very clear that you have only limited interest in me, and she's my friend. She's doing us a favor. Stop treating her like she's some kind of insect buzzing around your face."

The quiet force of his request hit me square in the chest. It swelled the shame and guilt I'd acquired over the past week so big that it was hard to swallow. He was right. There was no reason to be bitter with Marija just because she'd come unwittingly into the landscape of my con. It happened all the time. I had to roll with it or risk making Sam more suspicious than he already was.

"I'm sorry. You're right. I'll be nicer to her." I swallowed, finally, and managed to choke down enough of my pride to say what needed to be said. "I guess I've been getting used to having you to myself, that's all. It felt strange having someone else around."

"But you're not jealous." He glanced over at me, eyes holding mine.

"Why would I be jealous? Are you guys a thing?"

He shook his head. "Not for a long time, and never seriously. She's a good girl. Lots of fun, super loyal. Great instincts. Doesn't trust you, though."

There it was—the bomb I'd been waiting for since he'd stopped driving. Marija had voiced her suspicions to him while they were on their own. The part of me that knew how special it was to have caring, protective friends respected her. The rest of me, which was trying to accomplish something specific, wanted to tear her hair out for making my job even harder.

"She said as much. Very protective of you, for a never-serious fling."

He shrugged again. "The tour's an interesting place, Blair. Its own kind of life."

When more seconds ticked past without him stepping on the gas, my palms started to sweat. It felt like some kind of crossroads, here, as though he was waiting on me to say something, to share something, to defend myself against Marija's accusations. If he started to trust her instead of me, I might as well go home and wait for whatever retribution my father had planned.

I took a deep breath and found a truth stuck to the side of my heart. Peeling it away cost me, but it would be worth it if it made Sam feel better. "I know about living inside a bubble, Sam. Inside a life that people think they understand. I grew up that way. My neighbors, my teachers, the kids at school . . . they saw Blair Paddington in her Upper East Side penthouse, with her big-time accountant father and full-time staff and thought that, despite the lack of a mother, my life must be better than the average. They had no idea that my nights and weekends were spent swindling people out of their fortunes with my toothless fourth-grade smile. That my dad looked at my innocent little-girl face and only saw what he could gain by using it."

His hand snuck over and covered mine, fingers squeezing. I fought the urge to pull away and, after a moment, comfort and warmth started seeping through my skin. The breath I took shuddered and my throat burned—the confession had turned out to be something I needed to say as badly as Sam needed to hear it. "Be thankful that other people live inside your strange world, Sam. It may not be normal, but at least you're not alone."

"I'm sorry, Blair."

I laughed, trying to dispel the emotion built up in my chest. "For what? It's not your fault."

"That you've been alone for so long. For saying you're fucked up." He tipped my chin up so I had to look at him. "I mean, you are. But you've earned it."

"So we're good?" I asked, the hopeful tone in my voice catching me off guard.

It freaked me the fuck out that I couldn't tell fantasy from reality anymore. I'd been with Sam a little over a week, only eight days, and everything I felt sure of had started to slip away. The harder I dug my fingers into it, the faster it poured through them.

"We're good, Blair. I trust Mari's instincts, but you're a special case. I've spent every hour with you for a week solid, plus those few days last spring, and you're probably the hardest person to read that I've ever met."

Little did he know that he read me better than anyone. He just didn't want to believe I'd rip him off. Yet.

My phone finally uploaded a map and the electronic voice startled us both with directions out of Mari's neighborhood. It was a short ten-minute drive across the older part of Belgrade to the rivers. I'd never been to the house here, but the addresses were stored in my phone and my dad had a particular taste and style when it came to real estate—opulent and modern, lots of glass, set high on a hill if possible, where the commoners could look on and genuflect before his superiority.

There were a few e-mails from my professors, which I returned, and a text from Audra making sure everything was okay—I replied to that, too. Sam had taken a couple of calls from his management team on the train yesterday, but we'd started to ignore our phones. It felt as though we were living inside a film, or a book, or some kind of alternate reality that would dissolve if too many people peeked behind the curtain. By some unspoken agreement, we'd delayed the inevitable crash and burn by separating ourselves from the world. Our respective worlds, because we didn't share one. Could never share one.

Sam had to move his hand from mine to pilot the standard transmission. My fingers twitched more than once, suggesting that I reach over and lay a hand on his leg, begging to touch him, but I didn't listen. Being with Sam confused me. I needed some time, some silence, to try to figure out exactly how to proceed.

It didn't help that, more than once in my mostly sleepless night, I entertained the idea of helping him find my dad for real. Stop pretending. Get his money back.

I couldn't do that. Sacrifice my future, end up with nothing in exchange for the childhood my father had stolen from me . . . not for a guy I barely knew.

Except it didn't seem as though I barely knew Sam. Not anymore. Maybe not ever again.

The electronic voice said we'd turned on the right street, which made sense because there was nothing but a *No Trespassing* sign to greet us. No other houses dotted either side of the lengthy drive, which opened up to a gorgeous view of the Danube a few thousand yards in.

The house at the top of a steep cliff had Neil Paddington written all over it, from the manicured grounds to its ostentatious appearance. The entire glass-covered front, which overlooked the water and houses down below, glittered. The rest of the house appeared to be modeled after a Manhattan high-rise as opposed to the turn-of-the-century Gothic influence prevalent in the historic areas of Belgrade. It stood out, didn't fit. It made people look, if only to comment on how ugly it was.

I hated it.

If the day ever came when I was setting up a home, either for myself or—though I didn't believe it would come to be—a family, it would be the complete opposite. Cozy. Smaller. Maybe old and drafty—different from the houses in the area, but the same, too.

"Maybe park here," I suggested. We were still a couple hundred yards from the house's driveway, and there were trees on the left side of the road that could hide our approach.

There shouldn't be anyone here. As far as I knew, my father hadn't used this house in years. He'd never brought me here on an impromptu visit, and even though Belgrade had surprised me with its beauty and sophistication, it wasn't my father's kind of place. He'd probably bought the house here because of the country's nonextradition status with plans to spend no time here unless it became necessary.

As far as I knew, with the exception of my mother's unexpected passing, nothing bad ever happened to my father. Not even close calls. All the millions of dollars he'd conned, all of the Interpol and FBI files opened and maintained, hadn't led to a single arrest. He'd never spent a minute behind bars or in an interrogation room. I had my doubts that he ever would.

Sam parked the car on the soft earth, then took the keys out of the ignition and peered up ahead. "Doesn't look like anyone is here."

The place did have a deserted air about it. There were no other cars in the driveway, but there wouldn't be even if Dad were here. "Well, he's good at making it look like that. We're here. Let's go check it out."

We got out of the car and trekked up the road. Halfway there he took my hand and, again, I didn't stop him. For a hundred yards I pretended the two of us were lovers on fall break, enjoying Belgrade, visiting Sam's friend from the tennis world, maybe going to visit my dad—who in this pretend version of life was normal and loving. The kind of dad who wanted to meet the guy his daughter was interested in, who might even puff out his chest in an attempt to intimidate the young man into good behavior.

The vision collapsed as we snuck around the back of the house to the garage door. They always had keypads and they always had the same code—my parents' wedding anniversary.

I punched it in and waited for the door to rise. We entered the house, which bore an eerie similarity to the one we'd explored in Jesenice. The windows let in too much sun, making us squint in the high-ceilinged living room. Everything was white—the walls, the hard-looking furniture, the tiled floors. Like Marija's bathroom only bigger, more cavernous, and it left me with a strangely exposed feeling that planted a seed of worry.

"I don't think he's here, but let's take a look around. Quickly."

Sam shot me a look. "What's wrong?"

"I don't know. I have a bad feeling. You don't?"

"Not really," he answered after a quick self-assessment. "I mean, it's not like I feel great about anything that's happened since I got ripped off, though, so my meter is a bit off."

"Let's just hurry, okay? I'll take the front of the house, you take the back."

He nodded and we split up. I hustled through the kitchen, dining room, den, office, laundry room, and parlor before heading back to the living room. Sam strode back in a few minutes later, a piece of paper clutched between his fingers.

"What's that?" I asked at the same moment the strange peal of European police sirens split open the peaceful morning air.

We both froze, our eyes locked on each other, and listened. They were definitely moving closer.

My eyes swept the room automatically, doing the thing my father had taught me to do first in every single home I entered. Conning was best done in public, or on the person's porch or on a walk around their property—inside there were too many potential land mines. Hidden cameras; microphones; people that could be tucked away in other rooms, too far to see but close enough to hear. It had seemed like paranoia ten years ago, but with the kind of technology the average person owned these days it had become more and more likely.

Blinking red lights inside the vents caught my eye. I put a finger to my lips and turned, moving through the rooms I'd already checked. There were blinking red lights in those vents, too.

I didn't know if my father had seen us, heard us, or if we had done nothing but trip an alarm system, but now wasn't the time to sit around and figure it out.

Chapter 11

Sam

I'd followed Blair's eyes to the vents. The blinking red lights were innocuous to me, but they seemed to mean something to her—nothing good. They had to be cameras, or some kind of alarm. The sirens grew louder, inched closer, and the muscles in my legs tightened, aching to move.

When she came back into the living room, the snapping tension in her eyes made everything real. The control with which she moved, the calm flowing from her, helped me breathe.

She was a constant contradiction. A bundle of nerves in situations I considered normal, chill when we were about to get arrested for trespassing.

"What do we do?"

"We need to get out of here, obviously," she whispered.

"There's not another road, so there's no way back to the car."

Blair gave me a look that said *duh*, so I decided to stop thinking out loud. Instead I worried silently about Mari's car and how she was going to explain why it was abandoned out there.

"What did you see in the bedrooms? Is there a balcony? What's behind the house?"

The low volume of her voice and the pounding of my heart in my ears made it hard to decipher her questions. It finally made sense and I closed my eyes, trying to remember.

"We're a little short on time, here."

"Your impatience isn't helping," I murmured. "Okay. There's a balcony that overlooks the river off the master bedroom. The rest of it is woods. Undeveloped."

She walked off without answering me. I followed in silence as she poked her head into a couple of rooms before finding the master. We both went in and she closed the door, then yanked open the French doors leading to the balcony.

We peered together over the railing, cold morning air freezing the nervous sweat on my skin. Blair shivered and it crossed my mind to offer her my jacket. My mind, my autopilot, had been derailed by the sound of those police sirens, though. And the idea that they were coming here for us.

She turned to me, dark eyes stoic. "We have to jump."

"Jump? Are you crazy?"

"It's not too far to the river—sixty feet at the most. It's the only way we're not going to get caught."

"So what if we get caught?" I hadn't thought too much about this whole trip until I stood facing a sixty-foot jump into a freezing cold river, but Leo would kill me for running around trying to find Neil on my own. My trainer would kill me if I got injured. If the fall didn't. "You're his daughter, right? Don't you have some kind of right to be here?"

"That's not really the point, is it? We get caught, they contact my dad to check out my story and verify that we're not trespassing, and your jig is up. If we don't surprise my dad, it's over. He knows we're looking, he disappears." She crossed her arms, her expression almost lazy. "It's up to you, Bradford. What do you want to do?"

"How do you know the river is deep enough to handle us from this height? What if someone drove a car into the water and we smash into it? I mean, I want my money back, Blair, but I don't want to die."

"I don't want to die either, Sam, Christ. The Danube is at one of its deepest points in Belgrade, where it joins with the Sava." She paused, closing her eyes for the briefest of seconds. "And I know it's safe. There are pictures of my mom cliff jumping from this spot, before they built the house here. She was a daredevil."

I wished we had more time so I could ask her a follow-up, get her to talk more about her mom and how her life might have been different, but the sirens had given way to ominous silence. A thud sounded from inside the house.

The idea of losing all that money still made me sick to my stomach. The thought that I could play all of these years, put all that stress on my body, and come out of it with hardly anything to show destroyed the last of my resolve and I nodded. And I wasn't ready to leave. "Okay. I trust you, Blair. Let's go."

"Together."

Her hand slipped into mine and it felt good. Like this five-foot-eight, wiry, damaged girl would keep me safe. Or maybe that I would be okay as long as she was with me.

Either way, her touch calmed the adrenaline slamming my heart into my rib cage. The two of us climbed over the railing, balancing on the lip on the outside. Her fingers tightened around mine.

"One. Two." Pause. "Three."

We jumped together without discussing it, leaping as far away from the shore as we could. The balcony hung over the water by a good eight to ten feet, and we managed to push out another five on our own. In the instant before my stomach flew up into my throat, I thought, *We're going to be okay.*

The water smacked my feet hard, as though someone had whacked the bottom of them with one of Quinn's fraternity paddles. It was cold. Painful even through the soles of my shoes. The water closed over my head and I lost Blair's hand in the swirl of freezing liquid. Bubbles—little ones, big ones, popped from my lips and tickled my skin as my arms swirled, trying to tell up from down and propel me the right way.

Sunlight signaled the surface and I kicked upward, a little surprised that stinging feet seemed to be the worst of my injuries. I broke the surface and gulped bitter air. I whipped around, water droplets spraying from my hair as I searched for Blair. The relief at the sight of her dark hair bobbing a few feet away almost made me throw up and I took three big strokes to her side to pull her against me.

She threw her body against mine and wrapped her strong legs around my waist. My body responded even before her lips found mine. Her tongue slid along my upper lip then toyed with mine until my blood heated. We were frozen from head to toe but our mouths were hot, pressed together and searching for a way to be closer. We kissed for longer than we should have, but I didn't want to stop.

Good sense returned with the knowledge that as badly as I wanted this girl, now was not the time.

At the moment, I *was* regretting my lie about not having a condom last night, though.

"We need to move," I murmured into her lips. "This can be continued once my balls aren't shrunk up against my body for warmth."

She tightened her legs around me, disproving my remark.

"Fine. Once the police can't look over the balcony and wonder about people swimming in a freezing cold river, then."

"Okay."

Blair gave me a smile and started making her way over to the far bank. There was something different in her smile, in the easy way she moved, and like her burst of passion last night, it befuddled me.

My body knew what it wanted—had known since last spring. It wasn't hard to figure out. But Blair was a different story. She had been pretty damn adamant about what she *didn't* want since last spring, and even when she'd shown up and offered to help me in

Melbourne, her attitude about getting involved with me hadn't changed.

I was having trouble putting my finger on when exactly it had, and the fact that it felt . . . sudden somehow, or as though she was giving in against her better judgment, bothered me. At least, it had last night. That kiss just now, the languid pleasure on her face, had felt genuine. Filled with desire, not guilt.

If she had been that way last night, I would have grabbed the condom and gone for it.

The mud and loose debris on the bank slipped underneath my soaking wet tennis shoes, which were ruined. I didn't want to think about what it said about me that I cared. There were boxes and boxes of similar or identical product manufactured especially for me, but I couldn't get new ones until I was back in Australia and off the road.

I looked at Blair, her chestnut hair soaked and stuck to her cheeks and forehead, panting with the effort of the swim and the remnants of adrenaline.

She caught me looking and grinned. "I can't believe we just did that."

"What? It was your idea! Remember the whole 'we're going to be fine' speech you gave me up there?" I jerked my chin upward, unable to stop myself from smiling back at her.

Happy Blair was a powerful thing to resist.

"I know, and I was telling the truth, it's just . . ." Her smiled slipped. "It feels awesome to do something my mom did, even if we jumped off a house and not a cliff."

I put an arm around her, a shiver transferring from her to me. The space between us warmed up after a few minutes, spreading outward from where we were pressed together.

She looked up at me, her cheeks pink, eyes bright. "We need to do a better job with our cover story, especially now that the cops are involved. I don't think they're going to bust their brains trying to figure out where we went, but they will if my dad asks. If he cooperates and hands over the video feed from the house they'll know what we look like, and even though you're scruffy and not dressed very nice, your face is still pretty damn recognizable."

"What do you want me to do about my face?"

"Personally? Not a damn thing." She winked, starting a painful, thawing ache between my legs. "But glasses, maybe? A hat?"

"You want to dress me like a hipster."

"Sure. And we should do a better job playing a couple. If anyone asked the other passengers on that bus, they wouldn't say we were together."

"They would if they saw us dry humping on the seat after we almost died."

Her cheeks bloomed red. "We didn't almost die, and we were just kissing. You're such a drama queen."

"That's why they pay me the big bucks." I stood up before her red cheeks, soft looks, and bright eyes undid me further, then held down a hand and hauled her to her feet beside me. "Fine. I'll get some glasses."

"Also, we've got a couple of problems. First, I'm guessing both of our phones are ruined."

My heart sank, then stuttered as I remembered something awesome. "No! At least, I don't think mine is—I got a free sample of that new spray shit that's supposed to make anything waterproof. Check it out."

I dug my phone out of my pocket and pressed the home button. It flickered on as though it hadn't been submerged in river water, which was crazy. I'd seen one of the first demos on the *Today Show*. They threw a bunch of ketchup and mustard on Matt Lauer.

"That is fucking crazy," she breathed, taking it from me. "Do you mind?"

She started scrolling through my contacts before I could respond, finding Mari's cell phone number and hitting dial. "What are you—?"

"Marija? Hi, it's Blair. Listen, I know I promised you that there wouldn't be any trouble for you or your family if you helped us, but Sammy and I have run into a little snag." She paused. "What? Oh. I don't know why I just called him Sammy. My lips are numb." Her cheeks reddened again, probably from the realization that Mari would think her lips were numb from an entirely different activity. "Anyway, you need to call the police and report your parents' Mercedes stolen. Say you just noticed and you don't know how long it's been gone, since your parents are out of town and you've been using a driver—they'll believe you. We're going to catch a taxi back to your place, grab our things, and get out."

I motioned for the phone, which Blair handed over. "Hey, Mari. I'm really sorry about this, and I'm sorry to ask you for something else, but I saw an old

Volkswagen in the garage, does it run? Can we take it? I promise to get it back to you."

"Sam, I don't care about that shitty car. My dad only keeps it because it's the car he taught me to drive with and he's a sentimental sap. Are you okay?"

The concern in her voice touched me. I looked down at my body, soaked and a little worse for the wear, then glanced at Blair, who resembled a drowned cat. The expression on her face reflected longing and resignation, and it cut me straight through the chest.

We were both a mess, but someone cared enough about me to ask if I was okay. Had anyone ever asked Blair the same thing and truly wanted to hear the answer? Her friends at Whitman seemed nice enough, they seemed as though they liked her—especially her roommate, Audra—but what did I know? I'd spent a brief few days with them, and we hadn't been sober the majority of the time.

"I'm fine," I told Mari after a pause. "We'll be by in the next thirty minutes. Thank you, and I promise to explain every last detail of what's going on when I see you in Australia next month."

"You'd better. Take care of yourself, please. And for God's sake, don't trust every single person who looks up at you with big doe eyes and says you can."

Mari hung up before I could reply, which was fine since figuring out a response that wouldn't raise Blair's hackles would have been difficult. I put the phone in my pocket and reached out, tugging her into my chest before she could protest.

Her body went rigid against mine, her arms tucked in, forearms against my chest. But the longer I held her, my chin resting on the top of her head, the more Blair relaxed. Finally, her arms went around my back and her chest sank into mine.

"Are you okay?" I asked, my breath steaming in the cold morning.

She nodded. When we pulled apart, I saw the tears in her eyes but chose to ignore them. This girl wouldn't hate anything more than me seeing her cry, except maybe me making a big deal out of it. Maybe she wouldn't let me give her much, but that I could do.

*

We made it back to Mari's, changed clothes, grabbed our packs, and took the Volkswagen without any trouble. Two police cars passed us on the way out of her neighborhood, but the fact that we avoided that situation made me feel better about involving my friend.

It also made me feel better that Blair cared enough about not getting Mari into trouble to make that call at the first opportunity. The way she'd treated her had bothered me more than a little—having an attitude with me for no apparent reason was one thing, but doing it to a friend was something else altogether.

I would never compare growing up in the tennis world to anything more stressful, such as growing up an orphan or a foster kid, but our community was bonded in a similar way. We didn't always get along, and there were some who were better friends than others, but we were family.

"Okay, so where next?" I asked, ready to type a destination into my phone since Blair's was toast from the dip in the Danube.

"Well, I'm thinking we'll try Santorini next."

"Greece. Excellent. Huge improvement, in my opinion."

"You're a beach guy as opposed to a mountains guy, I take it?"

"I'm a warm weather guy, honestly, and Greece has beaches *and* mountains. What's not to like?"

"An unstable economy? Impossible travel? Mistreated donkeys?"

"Wait, you're telling me you don't like Greece?" I asked as she navigated toward an interstate based on the road signs, though I had no idea how since they were in Serbian. "How are you reading those signs? Are you an alien? A pod person?"

She shrugged. "I've traveled a lot, Sam, probably about as much as you. But I'm guessing I've done quite a bit more driving abroad—or at least more paying attention. Interstate signs all look the same, and obviously I can read the numbers."

"Okay, but how do you know which way to go once you find it?"

"I have a good sense of direction. Born that way."

The highway loomed up ahead, and Blair navigated us south. The map on my phone said Greece was about

552 miles from here, almost directly to the south. "Let's get back to you not liking Greece."

"It's not that I don't like it. It's just not my favorite place that I've visited, that's all."

"What *is* your favorite place you've visited?" It was the first time in a long time that I'd asked a girl such a throwaway question and been dying to hear the answer. It occurred to me that the girls I'd been spending time with since forever hadn't been that hard to figure out.

I was enjoying the challenge.

"Probably Romania. Brasov. I really love Ephesus, too, though."

"Those are super-random places. I've never been to either one."

"That's one reason I like them—despite Brasov being close to Dracula's castle, it's not a huge tourist destination. And Turkey's instability keeps people away, even though the coastal areas are fairly safe."

"When do you have time to travel to such remote locations? What about school?"

I watched a veil slip over her animated features at the question. Questions about likes and dislikes, fine. Ones that might reveal anything about her life, not okay. Noted.

"I'm doing fine in school, and the teachers at Whitman are progressive. High school was the same way."

Another question, one about her father and whether he had dragged her all of those places to steal money from weak-minded people such as me, dried up when she steered us off the highway. A small cluster of restaurants, hotels, gas stations, and other side-of-the-highway staples clustered at the bottom. "Where are we going?"

"The car needs gas, and you need a disguise. Plus, I'm hungry." She pointed. "There."

A McDonald's nestled next to a cheap drugstore across the street. She parked at the store, then unbuckled and dragged me inside and over to the racks of glasses.

"You pick some out, I'm going to find you a hat. And some razors for me."

She wandered off before I could contemplate the reason for her sudden concern about grooming. Instead I spun the racks, looking for the most unlike-me pair of glasses they had available, finally settling on an oversized, horn-rimmed pair that made me look like a hipster liberal-arts professor at some hippie school.

They worked better at disguising me than I would have thought, especially with the week-old scruff crawling over my jaw and lip. It itched something fierce, but when I'd said something about shaving Blair had nixed that idea right away. Itchy was better than her holding me down and bleaching my hair or something equally ridiculous.

"I have to say, you pull off the sexy nerd look better than I would have guessed." Her gaze found mine in the mirror, happy again and maybe even a little excited.

"You think I'm sexy?" I teased.

"I would think you would be used to girls calling you sexy by now," she tried to backpedal, holding out a knit cap that would be at home in any number of

169

Abercrombie ads. She also cradled a pay-as-you-go phone and two pairs of rubber flip-flops.

I turned around and pinched the hat between two fingers, trying my best not to wrinkle my nose. "I'm not used to *you* saying I'm sexy. Or using your words when it comes to me at all."

"Whatever. Yes, I think you're hot, okay?"

I moved closer so no one who happened to speak English could overhear. "And you want me?"

"I think I made that clear last night."

It annoyed me that she sounded embarrassed. "Being attracted to someone or asking for what you want isn't anything to feel shameful about, Blair. I think it was pretty obvious that I wanted you, too, and you're beautiful and sexy and maddening and perfect. Please don't feel like you have to hide from me, or be anything other than what you are. Who you are."

"What if you don't like who I am?"

The weight of the moment fell around my shoulders like an iron cloak, heavy and uncomfortable and unfamiliar. My life off the court contained happy, carefree people and situations, because I dealt with enough pressure in the day-to-day life of my career. As much as I liked Blair, as much as I wanted her, this scared me.

Mostly because I didn't know how to handle it.

"It doesn't matter if I like it, you can't be anyone else." I tweaked her nose, trying to ignore the bare anguish in her dark eyes. "Besides, I already don't like you, remember?"

It didn't get me the kind of smile I wanted, but her effort was better than nothing.

"What's with the rubber shoes?" I asked, leading her to the checkout counter.

"Welllll, I'm thinking we're about to experience our first hostel."

I hoped she didn't notice the hitch in my step. "So?"

"So they have communal bathrooms, like the dorms at Whitman. And everyone knows you wear flip-flops in the shower or risk some crazy foot fungus."

Good Lord in heaven, I could not handle this. The mention of the word *fungus* in the same sentence with communal bathrooms made me itch from the soles of my feet all the way to my hairline. Not to mention the nausea burbling in my stomach.

This trip hadn't been as bad as it could have been, at least not so far. Flying coach for almost three days and sitting in a stranger's car had been uncomfortable, but Mari's had been nice enough and even though this Passat was old, it was clean. I'd already blocked out the memory of that bus.

But hostels? I didn't know if I could do it without breaking into hives, but I couldn't tell Blair that. She'd thought from the beginning that I would bail on this whole trip because my life as a spoiled, pampered rich boy hadn't prepared me for any hardships.

While that was true, my germophobia presented the real issue.

Calm down. Deep breaths. Cross that bridge when we got to it, chew sleeping pills if necessary.

"Awesome. Thanks for getting me pink ones, by the way."

"They only had women's. Sorry."

"You don't sound sorry," I observed as we waited in line behind an old man with a twist in his spine that bent him nearly in half.

"Oh, I'm not. I can't wait to see you wear them. Consider yourself lucky if a mysterious photo doesn't end up on some show like TMZ."

I flinched at the reference even though Blair had been kidding. No one who grew up with money and any kind of notoriety at all had patience for that paparazzi crap, but my aversion ran higher than normal after they got hold of that story about my credit card being declined.

The elderly gent finished his transaction and we paid cash for our few purchases, then Blair and I carried them out to the car. She got back behind the wheel and reentered the highway after a quick run through the drive-through at McDonald's.

I tried not to eat that shit after stumbling across the YouTube video that explained the way meat products not fit for human consumption were cleaned with chemicals—the pink slime thing—but there was something comforting about being able to grab delicious fries and a Coke almost anywhere in the world. Blair ordered the same thing, plus a cup of coffee.

The sound of the wheels on the pavement tried to lull me to sleep, but every time I closed my eyes all I could see was moldy walls trapping the stink of homeless kids sweating on sagging mattresses, and laying awake listening to cockroaches and rats wage epic battles through the filth on the floors. My image of the disgusting hovel where she expected me to sleep tonight could be worse than the real thing. Could be. "So, where is this hostel going to be? Do we need reservations?"

"Actually, that's not a bad idea. It's too far to drive all the way to Santorini in one day, unless you want to take turns and sleep in the car, so maybe we should stop halfway. Somewhere in Macedonia? Do you want to check?"

It was on the tip of my tongue to say we'd drive it straight through, but she'd want to know why. Not to mention that, even though we'd had a decent night's sleep in an actual bed last night, there were circles under her eyes that said Blair hadn't rested all that well. It wouldn't be fair to ask her to drive through the night if we didn't have to, and even though some of my exes might accuse me of selfishness, I was worried about her.

Her fatigue had to be more than the will-they-won't-they saga the two of us had going on at the moment. She'd had a strange childhood, and even though her father's influence on her life now remained a bit cloudy to me, it had to be more than she wanted. If she could get him arrested, put behind bars, maybe she could start to build the kind of life she wanted, not the one that he'd forced on her.

Christ, maybe *I* was fucking overtired. It was the only viable excuse for having such sentimental thoughts about a girl I barely knew. One that had, at least in a peripheral sense, turned my life upside down.

Looking up the halfway point between Belgrade and Santorini took my mind off the fact that I was losing my shit. "What about this place called Skopje in Macedonia? Looks fairly good-sized, and there are a few hostel Web sites."

"Do any of them have reviews or anything?"

The way she said it set off warning bells in my mind. "You say that like you don't know any more about finding a hostel in a foreign country than I do."

She cast me an incredulous look. "Do I look like I've led the kind of life where I've stayed in hostels? My father has houses all over the world. He stole millions of dollars from you, and you're nowhere close to his first success story. I went to prep school with the kids of actors and musicians and politicians. Trust me, I *don't* know any more about staying in hostels than you do."

"Oh."

"But I *do* know about this little thing called the Internet. And I know you can find reviews and recommendations for just about anything, so if there's nothing about any hostels in Skopje, then we don't want to stay there."

It made sense. I felt like a moron for not thinking of that myself.

"It looks like there are several that have decent ratings and more than a few reviews." I scrolled through the top recommendations, my hope that this wouldn't be the death of me flickering back to life. "This one doesn't look bad, actually. Even clean."

"Hmm."

"What does that mean?"

"It means you can make pretty much anything look clean in a photograph, Sam."

Chapter 12

*T*he Unity hostel in Skopje should have looked better, considering how hard it was to hold my eyes open even though it wasn't even 6 p.m. We'd had a long day, between the almost-sex in the bathroom, almost getting arrested for breaking and entering, jumping sixty feet into a freezing cold river, and then racing out of town.

My stomach had started rumbling an hour ago, but if I'd seen a bed that looked clean enough, I could have been convinced to forgo dinner and go straight to sleep.

While the community bedrooms didn't look *un*clean, exactly, they left me with a wary feeling that did nothing to encourage sleep. The rooms looked as though they had been decorated by a fifteen-year-old girl who had been fan-girling over her favorite boybands. There were ten or twelve beds in each room, singles mostly, and each bed came complete with a curtain that could be pulled for privacy. The curtains and bedding were an alternating mint green, hot pink, aqua blue, and a bunch of other colors that shouldn't be in the same room. The prints ranged from polka dots to sparkly circles, with a few paisleys and stripes thrown in for good measure.

Alcohol was the only answer.

"Are you hungry?"

Blair tore her eyes away from the perky neon oasis. "What?"

"Are you hungry? More specifically, would you like to find somewhere within walking distance and get plastered enough to be able to sleep here tonight?"

She nodded, slowly at first but picking up speed. "Yes."

The teenage guy at the front desk, who had green spiked hair and so many holes in his face it was hard to know where to look without being rude, directed us a few blocks away to a strip of restaurants and bars.

It surprised me sometimes, how similar things could be in the world while still being so different. Jesenice had been different from Belgrade, and they were both different from Skopje, but there were still couples strolling in the streets, places to eat, and college-aged kids shoving one another in front of a club called Ballet.

The trek from Unity at dusk felt surreal and glowing, so different from the cosmopolitan Belgrade that it was like falling backward in time. My fingers twitched with the desire to reach out and take Blair's hand, and after stopping myself half a dozen times, I gave in.

"What are you doing?" she hissed, looking as disoriented as I felt.

"You said we needed to act more like a couple, right? If you were my girlfriend and we were here, I would hold your hand." I gestured to our surroundings. "It's romantic, don't you think?"

"I suppose." She grimaced as though the idea of romance didn't appeal to her, but a half smile drifted across her lips.

I wanted to kiss them, so I stopped and pulled her toward me, then pressed my mouth against hers.

Kissing Blair surprised me every time—for all of her prickliness in our other interactions, as soon as our lips met she melted into me as though her body wanted nothing more than to be part of mine. This time was less hurried than our previous kisses at first, but when she sighed into me, I stroked her tongue with mine, reveling in the taste of her, the way she was soft but demanding, shy but filled with our shared craving.

Her arms went around my neck and my fingers dug into her back; we might have stood on that street in Macedonia kissing for an hour or a minute. When she pulled away, breathing heavy and staring at me with stars in her eyes, all of the sudden that hostel didn't sound like such a terrible idea after all.

If Blair could make me want to get naked in sheets that had belonged to someone else last night, I might never let her go.

Instead of voicing yet another ridiculous thought, I tugged her down the last couple of blocks to a place called Kapan Han, a pub recommended by my phone as a fun place with authentic Macedonian cuisine, whatever that meant. It sat on the ground floor of an area called the Old Bazaar; between the ancient, uneven stone streets and buildings that looked as though they'd been there since Alexander cut his first tooth, the name fit it perfectly.

I ordered a beer and so did Blair, and we drank them before the waitress returned to take our order. By the time we'd eaten—I couldn't pronounce the names of any of the food, but it was all pretty good, if heavy on beans and olives—we'd killed a six-pack and my fatigue had eased into a desire to explore.

"How do you do it?" I asked, feeling warm all over as I watched Blair sip the last couple drops of her porter.

"Do what?"

"You're at home everywhere. I mean, I don't really have a home, either, but I'm definitely out of my element in the places we've visited. Not speaking the language, or one that can be understood, makes me nervous."

In most of the places we visited on the tennis tour, knowing English, Spanish, Russian, and German, French, and Italian worked well enough. Every place Blair and I had been in central Europe, the people spoke their own languages that were nothing close to what I understood.

"I don't know. I mean . . . I'm not as comfortable as you think. I'm good at faking it, more than anything."

"Fake it till you make it?" The confession made me look at her in a different way, but my brain was too relaxed from the beer to figure out why it bothered me.

"That's how it's done, son."

I leaned across the table, setting my hand over hers and stroking my thumb across the pulse in her wrist. "You don't have to fake it with me."

"We'll see about that," she purred, winking at me over the rim of her mug.

The comment caught me off guard, shooting lust and affection through me in equal measure. The drinks and the flirting had woken me up, which was the opposite of what the plan had been, and I knew I needed to be way tipsier before trying to sleep. We paid the tab and wandered outside, her fingers tickling my palm.

"Do you want to go somewhere else?"

"You're not tired?" she asked, her eyelids drooping.

"Not tired enough to forget that someone else probably had sex on my sheets last night."

A lengthy pause reigned while she stared at me, her eyes sharp and the wheels in her brain turning so fast they were almost audible, sank my stomach. Fooling Blair was no easy task. Not for long, anyway.

"Oh my god. I can't believe I didn't figure it out sooner." Blair stopped outside the restaurant, glowing in the soft lights of the Old Bazaar. The glint in her gaze suggested she was about to say something less than adorable and more maddening "You're a germophobe. That's why the airplane and the public transportation freaked you out so much."

"I don't suppose there's any point in denying it. Since I'm not a faker."

"How crazy are you, like, on a scale of 'carries hand sanitizer everywhere' to 'has a complete zombie virus survival plan'?" The look on my face must have given me away, because she burst out laughing. "You have a zombie plan. Oh my god, that's hilarious."

I crossed my arms, my lips begging to break into a smile. "So what? When the zombies show up you're going to come knocking on my door. You'd better hope that you bring a useful skill set, otherwise you're out on your ass."

She stepped toward me. "What kind of skill set are you looking for, Mr. Bradford?"

"Oh, I think we could probably figure something out," I breathed, mesmerized by the teasing light in her eyes.

It was as if Blair realized in the space of a heartbeat that she was coming on to me, and she shook herself, trademark awkwardness returning. "I'm okay with going for another drink. Let me ask the hostess what she recommends."

She went back inside without looking at me. At least the hostess spoke English—so had our waitress, actually, and the front desk guy at the hostel. I felt more comfortable in Skopje than I had in Belgrade or Slovenia, and stuffed my hands in my pockets, surveying the bazaar while I waited. There were more bars within walking distance—we could have just picked one.

Blair returned a moment later with directions to the place called Ballet that we'd passed earlier, and the tip that it was a popular late-night spot. In Europe, that meant after 4 a.m. Surely the booze would put me to sleep by then.

We started down the street, my hand finding hers again. Blair didn't flinch or pull away, her fingers tightening around mine, and I stopped her for another kiss.

"What are you doing?" She panted into my neck when we'd had enough. For now.

"Hey, if you were my girlfriend I'd be kissing you a lot more. You've got me wearing this stupid hat and glasses. The least you can do is play your part of the disguise."

"Noted."

"More booze?"

"If I were your girlfriend, I would definitely need more booze," she teased. "Follow me."

"As long as it means I get to look at your ass, I'm all for that plan."

"You have a real thing for asses, huh?"

"I have a real thing for yours." I punctuated the statement with a light pat, then fell into step beside her, the excited smile on her face necessitating yet another twelve-o'clock tuck. I hadn't done so many of those since Betsy Reynolds and her cantaloupe breasts quit the junior tour.

*

The whole world was blurred around the edges by the time we stumbled back over the uneven streets toward Unity. My eyelids wouldn't raise higher than halfway, and I seemed to be leaning on Blair's shoulder a little harder than I meant to, which all boded well for my ability to sleep in a bed of communal filth.

The guy at the front desk barely raised an eyebrow, even when I stumbled into a chair and knocked it across the room. Blair giggled, a strange sound, then dragged me toward the bathrooms.

We met back in the hallway a few minutes later, and even though she'd pulled her long hair up and scrubbed her face clean, she was still prettier than most of the girls in the world.

And I would know.

"Stop looking at me like that."

"Like what?" My words sounded far away and probably a little slurred, but the loopy smile on her face said she wasn't far behind me.

"Like you want to finish something we started last night."

"Maybe I do."

"Maybe you should have bought condoms at that drug store earlier today, then."

My lie from last night settled in my gut, making me uncomfortable in spite of the buzzing cloud hovering over my brain. Instead of answering, I held out a hand and led her into the hell pit—or dorm room—and we found an upper bunk that was unoccupied.

The room was half full, with a group of three Arab-looking teenaged guys trying to sleep on one end, a group of two guys and four girls—probably closer to our age—passing a bottle of vodka and talking too loudly in the middle. The talking occasionally turned to shrieks, followed by shushing that was louder than anything else. Somehow, two blond girls snored on the other side of them, their ages a mystery.

I boosted Blair up behind the teal and navy curtains, more as an excuse to squeeze her ass than anything, then managed to get in behind her without breaking my neck. The mental image of how Leo's eyes would bug out if he could see me now—drunk off my ass, eating crap food, not working out, and sleeping in a hostel—made me chuckle under my breath.

Laughter crashed into lust as Blair pulled her sweater off, leaving nothing but a thin tank top to cover what looked like a lacy black bra that barely held her perfect tits hostage.

"What are you doing?" I was horrified and fascinated, my body a giant conflict between desire and honor. I had a policy about sleeping with girls as drunk as she had to be just then, even knowing how close we had come last night.

"It's hot in here, don't you think?"

It was fucking boiling, but no way was I taking my clothes off. "It's fine."

"You're sweating." She wobbled in the process of getting out of her jeans, banging her head into the wall behind the bed. "Ouch."

"Are you okay?"

"I'm fine." Blair made a face, pursing her lips as she swept her eyes over my clothes again. "If you have an aversion to sleeping in the same bed with me all of the sudden, you can move down below. I don't care."

She did care. I sensed it, and couldn't figure out why she was so intent on trying to make me believe that she didn't. Despite the danger of touching her, I ran a hand down her cheek and settled it on her collarbone. Her pulse thudded under my thumb, stirring me to the kind of attention that made me desperate to get out of my own pants.

"I love sharing a bed with you. If we weren't drunk and in a room with fifteen other people, I'd love to share a lot more with you. Which is why watching you take off layers of clothes is making me extremely uncomfortable." I glanced down at my crotch and let her follow my gaze, then watched her cheeks redden.

"If you had protection, I'd be inclined to say fuck it," she mumbled, her eyes glazed and an incredibly sexy smile on her lips.

I groaned, then flopped back on the pillows and shimmied out of my own pants. My boxer briefs didn't do anything to hide my attraction to her, but I left my shirt on because my skin against hers combined with my level of drunkenness would not lead to anything good.

She lay down in my arms, tossing a leg over mine and tucking her head under my chin, fingers toying with the neck of my shirt. The way they tucked underneath the fabric, brushing my skin with the softest touch, made me sigh, and I gathered her closer.

"I have condoms. I lied."

The confession slipped out before I could imagine the consequences. Things had changed so much in the last twenty-four hours—I felt comfortable with her, with the idea that she might be being honest with me now, in a way that I hadn't expected. Lying felt slimy.

Blair stiffened in my arms, her fingers clenching a fistful of my shirt. "Why?"

"I don't understand you, Blair. This whole situation is crazy, and I want to believe that we're in it together, but you don't make it easy. I thought . . . I don't know what I thought. That you would regret it? That I would?" She started to pull away, but I tightened my grip until she stopped moving.

"I'm sorry. I shouldn't have pushed you last night. It . . . we're business partners. I proposed we find my father together, and that's what we're going to do."

"Blair, no. Something changed this morning when you told me about growing up in your life. When you kissed me in the river. I don't know whether it was you, or me, or us, but I know that no matter how our little mission ends, I could never regret being with you. Even if it's only for another couple of days."

The pause went on so long that I wondered if she'd fallen asleep. I was about to let go myself when her soft response fell on my ears.

"I feel the same way. If we have sex, Sam, it will be because we both want to—it has nothing to do with my dad. It can't."

"I should hope not. That's just weird."

She snorted and I smiled into the darkness, the chatter of the hostel's other occupants muted and far away. The seriousness of our discussion had calmed the heat in my blood, and the warmth of her body against mine dragged me further toward sleep. Her breathing evened out and she snuggled closer, sighing and mumbling nonsense into my chest. No matter what she said, no matter what *I* said, I knew that even though the last twenty-four hours had brought me closer to knowing Blair, I still really didn't know her at all.

I fell asleep wondering what it would be like to hold her until she let me past her defenses, no matter how long that might take.

Chapter 13

Blair

1 woke up drenched in sweat with a pounding headache, disgusting morning breath, and an insistent itch on my left leg. While I lay still, trying to get my bearings and the will to move, the events of the night before started trickling through my memory.

Sam and I drinking too much, laughing too much, leaning on each other all the way back to the hostel. Him confessing that he had pretended not to have protection the night before because getting closer to me scared him—but that yesterday he'd felt something change.

The cold fear in my stomach mixed with the oily hangover nausea in a way that made the taste in my mouth even worse. Something *had* changed yesterday— I'd started to wish there was a way to really help Sam. To introduce him to my father and confess that I liked him, that he was a good guy who didn't deserve to be ripped off.

But it unnerved me that Sam had sensed the beginning of that shift. He'd realized even before I did that my heart had gotten tangled up in business for the first time in my life.

He hadn't seen everything—if he knew my entire reason for coming to him in Melbourne had been to assist my dad with the remainder of this con, he wouldn't be curled up against me, hot and solid. He wouldn't kiss me the way he did, or reach for my hand as though he'd been doing it for years, or look at me as though he wanted nothing more than to be able to read my mind.

The longer I lay still, pressed against him, the more the fear eased. It didn't go away—I'd spent years accepting that it never would—but now the idea of Sam learning the truth about the extent of my involvement with my father's schemes scared me more than anything. He would hate me.

It bothered me how much I hated the idea.

I needed time to work this out. To spend time with Sam, to decide whether or not my hormones were somehow impeding my ability to do what was best for my future. Not least of all, to try to guess how my father would react, or the likelihood of his agreeing to return the money.

"Good morning, gorgeous."

I raised my head to find Sam's honey brown eyes smiling at me. He had sleep creases on his face and his breath smelled about as bad as mine tasted, but none of that stopped the tingle that started at my breasts and ended between my legs.

He stirred against my belly as though reading my thoughts, then put a hand over his mouth. "My breath tastes so disgusting. Sorry."

"Bathroom?" I suggested, both because I had the same problem and because I really had to pee.

He nodded and pulled back the gaudy curtain, then swung his legs around and dropped to the floor. I let him help me down without a thought, then remembered that just the other day I refused to let him carry my bag. It had happened, the change in me, and I hadn't noticed.

By the time I'd peed and brushed my teeth, my heart rate had returned to normal. So I let him help me out of a bed. If we were going to sleep together—which I was hoping we were—I was going to have to let him help me with a lot more personal things. I'd never been good at having orgasms during sex. That psychologist I planned to hire in the future would probably suggest it had something to do with my inability to let other people do things for me at all.

The chance that I would tell that person to go fuck themselves seemed high.

Sam had his back to me when I returned to the room, which was quieter in the dawn that it had been in the wee hours of the morning. The other occupants— who all appeared to be around our age, perhaps slightly older—were asleep. I recalled them being louder last night, but the alcohol had done the trick. Nothing could have kept me from sawing logs.

The view of Sam's back, from his muscled shoulders to his ass, held me in place for longer than it should have. I let my mind wander over what it would feel like under my kneading fingertips, what he would feel like inside me, until it no longer seemed like a bad idea.

I swallowed and breathed through my nose until my lust was tucked back under control, then strode over and pulled fresh underwear and my second sweater out of my own pack. I reached down to scratch my leg and pulled the shirt over my head, staring absently at Sam as he did the same until a splotch of red skin caught my eye. "What's that on the back of your neck?"

He spun around to face me, his fingers going to the red rash. "What? That's not funny."

"I'm not joking. Does it itch?"

"I itch everywhere. I thought it was just my paranoia."

I looked down at my leg, suddenly more than a little paranoid myself. A wash of reddened skin, complete with a smattering of bumps, decorated the space between my knee and ankle. "Shit."

Sam's eyes widened when they glimpsed the horror of my leg. "Oh, Christ, what is it? Is it herpes?"

"Dude, calm down." I wanted to laugh at him, but the fact was that I wasn't thrilled about being all itchy after a night in strange sheets, either. "It's probably bed bugs, or maybe a reaction to cheap sheets or detergent. We're not exactly used to those things."

"Bed bugs? Oh my god."

The look on his face, as if someone had told him they'd ground up a turd in his coffee, *did* make me smile. "Sam, it's going to be okay. Even if it's bed bugs, the rash will go away in a few days. We'll stop and grab some cortisone cream."

"I think I'm going to freak out."

I took his hand without thinking, tugging until his eyes focused on mine. In them flashed the kind of panic that can't be faked, and all inclination to poke fun at him fled. "It's okay. It's going to be okay."

I made sure to take deep, even breaths and after a moment, his erratic gasps slowed, starting to mimic my calm breathing. My lips moved on their own to find his, and as my tongue found its way inside his mouth Sam's arms went around me, his bulky frame relaxing against my chest.

The kiss ended too quickly, his forehead pressed against mine. "Thank you. I feel like a tool."

"You don't have to feel stupid, Sam. You're afraid of what you're afraid of. Frankly, germs seem as plausible a possibility to take out the human race as anything else. Maybe more so."

"That's true." He pulled away and took a deep breath. "Let's get the fuck out of here."

*

We were out of Skopje within the hour after a quick stop for breakfast, another for anti-itch cream, and a ten-minute detour to an Internet café so I could tell the Vienna police where to find that first boosted Jetta. The trip to Athens would take about five hours, then we'd have to take a ferry or hire a boat to take us to Santorini. Even so, we would be there by dinnertime.

The Santorini house was the most familiar to me; my mother had loved Greece, so we'd spent a good majority of holidays on the island. It was also the only property situated in close proximity to others, since there wasn't any place on Santorini not covered by some kind of building. I liked it there, too, even though it had too big a tourist population to be one of my favorites. I'd never admitted my affection for it to my father, since saying something like that would be the fastest way to ensure he'd never invite me again.

Nonattachment was a way of life, and even though Dad spent more time in the Caymans than anywhere else, it had more to do with convenience than fondness. Me saying I liked something, or that something made me comfortable or happy, meant losing it the next day.

"I'm not staying in a hostel again, I swear. If you still say no hotels because no credit cards, then we're going to buy some blankets and sleep on the beach."

Sam glanced over at me from the driver's seat, the expression on his face serious. He'd bathed in so much hand sanitizer that it had almost made me barf up last night's vodka, but it had made him feel better.

I kept my mouth shut about all of the studies suggesting people who used too much of the stuff were making themselves more susceptible to germs in the long run, not less.

"Fine. There are some boardinghouses on Santorini that probably take cash up front, but it'll be warm enough to stay outside, too, if you want to do that. I'm game."

I felt game for anything, honestly, as long as it involved Sam. My dad wouldn't be in Santorini. He *could* be anywhere, but as far as I knew, he hadn't lived anywhere but on the *Alessandra*—his sailboat—for the past ten years. Since my mother died.

We passed most of the trip quietly, the person not in the driver's seat sleeping off more of their hangover. A few silly games passed the rest of the time; we played a round of I Spy, then the Alphabet Game. I hadn't played road trip games since I was a small child.

After Mom died I always traveled alone, and always by air.

"Maybe we could find somewhere to play a game or two of tennis," I suggested. "You've got to be itching to practice."

"First of all, please refrain from using the word 'itching.' Second, you would practice with me? I thought you weren't interested." Curiosity made his words curl up at the end.

"I play. I follow tennis. I just didn't want you to see me as some kind of groupie, that's all."

"Blair. You are about as far from a groupie as anyone I've ever met. I'm, like, *your* groupie, with the number of times I've asked you out and been shut down."

That made me blush. It got a little easier, the being honest with him about my feelings, every time I tried. Maybe it took practice. Maybe it took being with someone who didn't seem to have any inclination to judge me. For now, anyway.

"I've never had a groupie." I shot him a smile. "Anything I need to know?"

"Yes. First off, you need to learn how to act busy even if you're not. In public places, take a friend and have fake conversations where you're focused on each other so there's no chance of making eye contact with someone random. Learn to listen to the crazy meter in your gut—there's crazy, and there's special crazy, and the second is the kind that leaves you tied to a bed staring up at a fat lady wielding a giant hammer."

"Which kind are you?"

"What does your gut say?"

"Special crazy. But I don't know what brand yet."

"You might like it."

I was sure that was true. After the scene in the bathroom the other night, there didn't seem to be any reason to doubt that I would like just about anything he wanted to do to me. I wasn't feeling quite comfortable enough to share *that*, though.

The navigation on Sam's phone instructed us to make the last turn before our final destination, which was Piraeus, one of the ferry docks in Athens.

"We could make the one o'clock ferry, or if you want we could change some more cash and buy some tennis rackets?"

"Sure. Tell me where."

"Hold on."

It took me a minute to figure out how to search for sporting goods in Athens, then to find a store we could get to and back in less than an hour.

"You know, I could make one call and have rackets overnighted to Santorini," Sam commented. "No paper trail, since they're free."

I thought about it in the context of the con I'd set up, then nodded. "I don't think that would be a problem, but you can't go through your management. They can't know where we are."

The reasoning was selfish, now. I didn't want anyone else to catch up with us. I loved that Sam had been ignoring his phone calls and messages. The idea that we could let this beautiful, old city keep the real world at bay for another couple of hours.

"Great. So, to the docks?"

"Yep. And if you want to ship the car back to Belgrade, now's the time. We won't be driving to our next destination." My mouth went dry as soon as the words were past my lips.

Was I really going to take Sam to the Caymans?

"How can I do that without using a credit card?"

"We can probably set it up so that they charge your card in a month, and ship it back then. You'll have to pay more to have them store it until then."

We made our way toward Piraeus, the main port in Athens. Cobalt blue water stretched toward the horizon, interrupted by sailboats and cruise ships and industrial boats as far as the eye could see. They were mostly white, and the sun glinted off the paint and the water, blinding me even wearing sunglasses.

"Who's going to do that?" Sam threw the car into park in the queue at the port, then twisted to face me.

I was never going to get used to how handsome he was, or how the way he looked at me made me feel naked in the least scary way possible. "I know a guy."

"You know a guy. In Athens."

"Sure." Xander was my father's caretaker at the Santorini house, but it had been clear to me from a young age that he hadn't been hired for his gardening skills. The guy was six foot seven and had to weigh over three hundred pounds of solid muscle.

We'd gotten along well, mostly due to a mutual love of chess and science fiction and fantasy. He would help me get the car back to Marija, and keep quiet about it, as long as he didn't think it had anything to do with my dad's business. We both knew where his ultimate loyalty lay, but he'd kept secrets for me before, when they were personal. Sam and I would just have to convince him we were what we said we were—lovers.

"We'll take the car to Santorini. I have a friend there who can make the arrangements, though we may have to play up the boyfriend-girlfriend gig to convince him it doesn't involve my father's business at all."

Sam snorted. "Business. Right."

"Well, he does have a legitimate side. And he has a law degree." I didn't know why Sam's comment made me defensive, but even though my dad was a con man, it wasn't *all* he was.

"Do I still have to wear this hat?"

I cocked my head, then reached over and pulled it off, mussing his shaggy hair in the process. It made him look like a little boy. "The hat you can lose, but I'm kind of loving the glasses."

"Oh yeah?" He winked. "I'll keep that in mind."

"Okay, lover boy. Let's go get some tickets and get this bucket on the boat. There will be plenty of time for playacting later."

We strolled over to the ticket office hand in hand. The warm salty breeze ruffled Sam's hair and tickled my cheeks. The green-blue of the ocean, the bright white of the sailboats, the ancient backdrop all filled me with peace and happiness, and I banished the worries of

197

tomorrow from my mind. Tonight, I wanted to pretend. Sam clicked away on his phone, then stuffed it in his pocket.

"Honey, do you think we could go diving tomorrow?" I asked sweetly, looking up into Sam's face as we waited in line behind two other couples and a businessman.

Sam looked down at me, his expression delighted. His carefree attitude was just too adorable, when it wasn't getting us into trouble. "Sure, snookums. Did you bring your certification?"

"Yes. You know I always carry it on me as a second photo ID. You?"

He nodded. "Ditto."

We were speaking off-the-cuff, and it pleased me that we could pick it up without discussing it beforehand. I hoped the exchange meant we actually both had diving certifications and that he wanted to go. It would be a shame to take a five-hour boat ride just to tour another empty mansion and taking a meeting with Xander.

Once we had tickets and made it back to the car, I gave him a look.

"What? Did I say something wrong? Was I not quick enough on the uptake?"

"Snookums? Who the fuck says that anymore?"

"Well, I like it. Do you prefer *snookums* or *devil girl* as a term of endearment?"

"Those are my only choices? Like, I can't choose no term of endearment?"

"Nope. Not at the moment. All sappy couples on vacations call each other something. And apparently I'm honey, so . . ."

"Just drive the car, smart-ass."

He grinned and shifted Marija's Passat into drive, navigating the crowded parking lot and steering us onto the ferry.

We climbed out of the car, leaving the keys in the ignition, then wandered up a slippery, narrow set of metal stairs to the top deck in unspoken agreement. Since hardly anyone else had boarded we had our choice of seats, and Sam settled us near the starboard railing. It felt nice to be aboard a boat again, with the salt air in my nose and the afternoon sun on my face. We'd chosen an express ferry, which would get us to Santorini in a little over five hours instead of eight or nine. It might seem like a long time to some people, but I'd inherited a love of boating and water from my dad, and it had been too long since I'd been able to enjoy it.

"You look happy."

"What?" I'd almost forgotten Sam was here. A hazard of spending so much time alone.

"I've been watching you for over a week now. This whole trip, whenever you think I'm not looking, you have this kind of conflicted expression. You chew the inside of your lips and cheeks, and your eyes get really far away."

"That's not creepy at all."

"Well, you don't talk to me, so I have to resort to creepy stalker tactics to try to understand what's going on in that pretty head." He smiled. "Anyway, just now you looked happy. Your mouth was relaxed, your eyes were on the horizon, and it was like nothing bothered you."

I paused, because that's what I always did. I stopped myself before words came out of my mouth. Analyzed them. What they could tell someone else, what they might reveal that I wanted to keep hidden. Whether or not it was information that would come back to bite me in the ass later.

The old Blair, the one determined to keep everyone out of her fucked-up inner world, would have smiled and shrugged. This one wanted to help Sam learn, because for some reason it didn't feel bad when he inched a little bit closer.

"I love the water. Sailing is one of my father's favorite things—he's really good at it, too—and he started taking me out before I could walk. It was our thing even before my mother died. She never went because she got seasick."

"Yeah, I remember Leo telling me your dad is a world-class sailor. One reason that it's been hard for the authorities to track him down." He paused, looking out across the water. More people wandered up onto the deck, milling around and chatting in low voices. An array of languages, mostly romance, swirled on the light breeze. They were mostly couples and the majority appeared to be non-Greek tourists, but the ferry wasn't anywhere near as crowded as it got during the summer months.

A moment later, the engines rumbled to life. "It's your home. The water. That's why you've never been anywhere you'd want to settle down."

A calm washed over me at the idea of living on the water. Now that he'd said it out loud, it made sense.

"You really want to go diving tomorrow?"

"Yeah, I do. Are you really certified?"

"Sure. When I was quite a bit younger. Even when I have the time now, I'm not really allowed to go because of the potential danger. Same with skiing, which I also love."

I recalled that he hadn't been able to go out on the slopes in St. Moritz, but that he had said more than once how jealous he was of the rest of us. Still, a few years of not doing those things was nothing compared with the kind of tennis career he was building. That would crest and start to fall off, probably by the time he turned thirty. He had the rest of his life to scuba dive and ski, or do whatever life-threatening activity he wanted.

"We don't have to go diving if it makes you uncomfortable."

"No, I want to do something you love. Then later, once my rackets get here, we'll do something I love."

"Did you get ahold of your rep at Head?"

"Yep. Answered my e-mail while we were in line buying tickets. Six new rackets will be delivered to the post office on Santorini tomorrow."

"Bet it's the first time your rackets will be delivered by donkey."

"That would be a yes." He paused. "I am surprised that you want to spend some extra time here if we don't turn up anything at your dad's house. I mean . . . don't you have classes to get back to? Or your life at Whitman in general? Break has got to be over."

Break ended several days ago, but my teachers were under the impression that my father had had a mild stroke. My dad's staff would back up the story if anyone called looking for me. He thought I was out getting Sam to trust me enough to sign over his bank accounts.

Until sometime in the past forty-eight hours, that's what I *had* been doing.

"It's okay. I worked it out with my teachers. The only requirement is that I turn in projects and be there to take a couple of finals before Christmas break. If my dad isn't here or the next place, I'm out of options, anyway. I'll go back to Whitman and regroup, but still work on your specific loss if you'll let me."

The con was harder to step away from than I expected, and I hated that. Hated that maybe all this time I had believed it was something I did, not who I was, and that maybe I had been wrong. Clinging to the familiar was easier than admitting that the real reason I wasn't in a rush to return to Florida sat next to me. Something had started between us, had grown quickly in a few short days, and I didn't want to live the rest of my life and not know what it might turn into.

Sam moved closer, slipping an arm around my waist and tugging me against him. We listened to the waves splash against the ferry's hull in silence. For the first time in maybe my entire life, it felt okay to sit next to someone else and not worry that they would hear a million confessions in the silence.

Chapter 14

*I*t was after eight when the ferry docked at Santorini,

and my stomach felt hollow. We hadn't eaten since lunch on the road, and Sam's belly had been making noises that had him blushing and me laughing for the last two hours.

Unlike Jesenice or Skopje, I felt comfortable in Santorini. I didn't speak a ton of Greek, but I understood enough to communicate. My parents had favorite restaurants, coffee shops they loved, and bars they'd snuck out to after they thought I'd fallen asleep. I had my own favorite—Sea Side. They served the most delicious dish of olives, tomatoes, and shellfish, but I worried they would be closed by this time during the off-season.

I dragged Sam away from the car, which we left in the port's parking lot after a quick disagreement about whether or not it would be safe there overnight. I shoved him into a taxi—not onto a donkey, thank goodness—before he could get a word out.

"Where are we going? And why are you in such a hurry?"

"I'm hungry, and the place I really want to eat might close early."

"Well, since we're staying at least one extra day, we could always eat there tomorrow."

"I know. Sorry. I'm just excited."

"It's equal parts disconcerting and adorable. In case you were wondering."

"I really wasn't."

"That is one of the many things that makes you attractive, devil snookums."

I made a point of ignoring his hybrid term of endearment, choosing to peer out the taxi window at the spectacular view instead. It would be better in the daylight—the sunset had given us a stunning show on the ferry ride—but even at night the island was nothing short of breathtaking. Santorini, like the majority of the Greek isles, had been formed by volcanoes. White-sided, blue-roofed houses and businesses rose on steep cliffs from the crystalline water, zigzag paths climbing the mountain in haphazard patterns. Boats—some commercial fishing, some pleasure—bobbed lazily against the docks down below, and date and olive trees added spikes of green to the picturesque scene. It was a beautiful place, especially in the winter when there weren't nearly so many tourists.

Sam's eyes were fixed out the window. "It's gorgeous here."

"You've never been?"

"No. I've been to mainland Greece but not the islands."

The taxi ride was short, which was normal since Santorini wasn't that big, and I paid the man with coins as we scrambled out. He'd dropped us at Perivolos Beach, which was home to Sea Side and also to a resort where we could buy what we would need to sleep on the beach, if Sam was serious about that.

"Well, are you hungry?"

Sam nodded, tearing his fingers away from the back of his neck, where he'd been scratching his bed-bug rash. I hadn't been brave enough to ask where else the nasty little suckers had gotten him, but I suspected it was a lot like mine—any skin that had been exposed and pressed against the mattress itched like the devil every time the cortisone wore off. I'd done some quick research on his phone while Sam had been driving, just to make sure we weren't going to contract anything horrible, and had verified what I'd said back in Skopje—the rash should go away within a couple of days. In the meantime, I felt spectacularly unattractive, but at least I wasn't alone.

I hadn't felt alone since we'd boarded the flight to Austria.

Sea Side was open, thank goodness, and the sign out front said they would be for another couple of hours. Since setting foot back on Santorini, I hated the idea of being indoors, and the thought of having the beauty of this place interrupted by strangers. It was weird to me that Sam no longer counted as such.

"How about we grab a couple of blankets, and sweatshirts if you want, from the gift shop at Nine Muses and then get the food to go? We're only going to have a couple of days and I'd really rather spend them on the beach."

"We're really going to sleep on the beach?"

I cast a pointed look at the back of his neck. "Unless you want to find another hostel?"

"I'll try the sand."

We gathered two blankets, souvenir candles, a lighter, two resort sweatshirts, and a couple bottles of water from 9 Muses, then ordered enough food from Sea Side to feed half of the pro tour. The sand of Perivolos chilled me even through the blanket we'd spread out, but once Sam's leg pressed against mine and we were shoveling food into our mouths, the temperature felt as perfect as the rest of the night.

"This is fucking delicious," Sam managed around a mouthful of shellfish concoction.

"I know, I told you." It might be rude to talk with my mouth full, but no way was I taking a break for talking.

We scarfed the rest of the food in silence, then Sam poured us each a second glass of wine into the paper cups we'd wrangled from the restaurant. It had taken all of the Greek I knew and then some, but we had managed. The wine was lower quality than Sam was probably used to, but after frat parties at Whitman—even Quinn's fancy ones—I'd gotten used to cheap alcohol. It seemed even rich college kids still slummed it when it came to getting their girls trashed.

"What would you do if this worked out? I mean, if we actually found your dad and you actually had the guts to turn him in to Interpol and they actually caught him."

We both sat with our legs sticking straight out toward the crashing sea, heels dug into the sand, and leaned back on our hands. Sam's right thigh pressed against my left, and in the moments before I answered, there was nothing but the winking stars and the sound of the ocean sucking away the sand.

Like his observation earlier that I seemed happy here, it felt unnatural to respond with honesty—to him or myself. My knee-jerk reaction was to blow him off, give him some pat answer, and it took effort for me to stop and reevaluate in order to find the truth in my own heart.

I didn't know if we could find my father, and if we did, I had little faith in my ability to turn him in—and even less faith in the authorities to prosecute him effectively—but that shouldn't change my answer. Based on the question, Sam didn't have any illusions that we'd be successful in our quest. He was asking what I *would* do. What I wanted.

I didn't know, and that squeezed my heart into a pancake.

I'd imagined a world where my father didn't exist as puppet master. Hoped for one. But even though he'd promised to give me my share when I graduated from college, I didn't really believe he'd cut me loose. He'd never promised any such thing. Despite the fact that I couldn't imagine the authorities ever catching up with him, he was recognizable and on several watch lists. Without me, the majority of his schemes would turn out less profitable, or dry up altogether.

It was a pipe dream—getting out. One I believed because it kept me moving forward, but if I refused to help him today or in two years, he had enough dirt on me to make my life a living hell.

"Blair."

I looked up, startled again at not being alone. Sam had sat up and faced me, concern and confusion darkening his eyes in the moonlight.

"Sorry. I was thinking about the question."

"You're crying. I didn't mean to upset you."

His thumb brushed my cheek. The tears surprised me, but it was the first time I'd accepted, even internally, that that I might never be free of this life. That I would never get to keep a guy such as Sam or a friend such as Audra because if they knew who I truly was, what I did to make the money that kept me in private jets and paid for my Whitman education, they would hate me.

"I'm sorry."

"Why are you apologizing for crying? You can do whatever you feel like doing. If I was in your position I wouldn't be handling this thing nearly as well as you are." He brushed away more tears, the calloused pads of his thumbs scraping my cheeks in a strange and arousing gesture of care. "My parents are greedy assholes, but it took me two years to get up the nerve to file for divorce. Even now, I bring them along to the tournaments. I bought them a house and cars, and they never thank me. Like it's my duty, even though I'm twenty-three years old and I've supported them for almost half my life. And that's nothing, Blair. Nothing compared to your dad."

It felt like a thousand-ton weight lifted off my chest. I felt free, as though I could float after that weight and roll around in the stars as though they were a field of wildflowers.

No one had ever acknowledged the hardship of my life. To be fair, it was because no one knew the truth. People looked from the outside and saw the pretty girl, the rich girl, the girl doted on by her widowed father. They didn't know because they couldn't, but when my dad had forced me into this con with Sam, necessitating my sharing at least a little bit of myself, and there were consequences neither of us had foreseen.

It was as though a dam had broken. I didn't know if the connection Sam and I had back in St. Moritz had sped up the process or if it could have happened with anyone, but it felt amazing to stop pretending I had an easy life.

But I couldn't tell Sam the whole truth without admitting that I was still under my dad's thumb. That the reason I had come to see him was to work a con, not to find my father and turn him in. As much as I wanted to break down, to blubber about how I'd never be free and see if he'd be willing to help me figure out a way, I couldn't risk it. I would lose Sam eventually.

But not tonight.

"Thank you for saying that, Sam. I don't mean to be all weepy and girly—"

"For the record, your being a girl is one of the things I like most about you."

I smiled because that's what he wanted. Still analyzing everything I did and every word that came out of my mouth made me sick. "It's just that no one knows the truth about my dad. I mean, obviously the government does, and so do the people he's conned, but the kids at Whitman don't. Audra doesn't."

"No one? You've never had anyone to talk to?"

"Not since my mom died, no." He looked as though he was going to ask something about my mother, and that was a place I was not ready to go at all. Maybe I never would be. "In answer to your question, I don't know. Be able to live without secrets, I guess. Be myself. Make my own way."

"It would be hard, don't you think. Without the money?"

"Sure. But I'm smart, and in a couple years I'll have a good education." I punched his arm. "Maybe I'll find me a rich husband to make the transition a little easier."

He chuckled. "I have a hard time picturing a guy amazing enough to take you on, devil girl."

My heart sank. He might feel sorry for me, but the thought of taking me on scared him. It proved that I was far more work than I was worth. "Why do you say that?"

"You're special, Blair. You're strong, and there are a ton of guys threatened by that. You're hard to crack, and people are lazy. You're also beautiful enough to intimidate at least seventy percent of the male population right off the bat."

"Oh." I refused to look at Sam, even though his words made my face burn. "I guess you're pretty glad you decided to pretend not to have any condoms a couple of days ago, huh? You dodged a bullet."

"You know, I'm getting a little tired of you assuming that you know everything about me because you watch me chase a ball around a court and give a few interviews afterward." The anger in his tone snapped my eyes to his face. It swirled in his eyes and tightened his jaw, making the muscles in his neck stand out in a way that turned me on.

Maybe I just needed to accept that everything about Sam turned me on.

"I'm not threatened by you, Blair. I'm challenged by you. I love that I didn't know everything about you after one conversation and it speaks volumes about your character that you refused to go home with me in St. Moritz—I was acting like a shallow doofus. Your beauty . . . well, it humbles me that you'd have anything to do with me, but I'm not intimidated." He crossed his arms over his chest. "I'm not the seventy percent. It kind of sucks that, as hard as I've been working to get to know you this past week, you couldn't be bothered to see me."

It was hard to believe that anyone—never mind Sam Bradford, a guy who could have whomever he wanted—cared so much about what I thought. There *had* been something between us in Switzerland; I'd felt it even though he *had* been acting like a shallow doofus, and maybe it spoke more to my lagging self-confidence than anything else that it never occurred to me that it could be something special.

That *I* could be something special.

Since we'd been traveling together, I'd been bitchy and distant, unwilling to keep him in the loop and denying him comforts at every turn. It made no sense that he would like me at all, want me at all, but maybe it didn't have to.

"Sam, that's not it. I don't think you're shallow or insecure. I've never thought that, actually, even on spring break. You like to have a good time and unwind, and with the pressure of the tour and your injuries, it made sense. You've been a saint, putting up with me since we left Melbourne, but honestly . . . I never thought this thing between us was about more than a conquest for you."

"How can you say that? I invited you to sit in my box my first tournament back, that's not a casual-fuck kind of invitation. Do you not feel that something . . . more?"

Sudden shyness overtook me, I'd suspected as much about the tournament invitation, but had been involved with Flynn at the time and, honestly, a little irritated that Sam couldn't take a hint. I wasn't looking for anything more than easy and free, and a guy who didn't ask too many questions. Flynn had fit the bill perfectly. I could admit now that even the prospect of Sam had scared me.

I took a deep breath, thought through the string of consequences, then decided to ignore them. I was so tired of trying to figure out how one misstep could ruin a con down the road. "I *did* feel something more, and that's exactly why I blew you off. I just told you that no one knows about me, about my dad and my life. How could I date someone seriously and expect to be able to keep that kind of distance? And you? You make me want more."

He froze, then broke into the grin that charmed women around the world. "I do?"

"Yes, you idiot. Everything I normally play close to the vest comes spilling out around you, and it makes me crazy. But you're still here anyway." *For now.*

We watched each other, emotions flashing through his honey eyes as fast as they skittered through my heart. Fear. Wonder. Excitement. Distrust, even after everything, that came from not knowing each other as well as we'd like to, a fact that left us vulnerable.

All of the little tidbits that we had shared added up to something, enough to hurt if they were rejected, and that was the root of my fear. That I had finally found a friend, someone to open up to, someone to show myself to, and would be forced to watch him walk away.

"You know, I never think about the future, Blair. My family, the way they are, it doesn't inspire much faith in the validity of long-term commitments."

The piece of information confused me. Not because it didn't make sense, but because I wasn't quite sure why he was telling me. "I'm not thinking about next year, Sam. Hell, I'm not even thinking about next week. I'm just . . . ready to live in the moment. With you."

I'd spoken the truth, but it hurt in unexpected places to agree that we had no future.

Sam stood up, then held a hand out to me. "Grab that bottle of wine. Let's take a walk."

"A walk?" I felt as though my lips weren't attached to my brain.

"Yes." He glanced up toward the resort, which wasn't full this time of year but wasn't empty, either. Its lights reached toward us on the empty beach. "I saw someplace on our way to the restaurant that might be better for spending the night. Less out in the open."

My heart raced at the suggestion. All of me trembled with desire, even ones that were usually slow to wake, and when my palm slid against his, a shock of anticipation moved through me. Sam held one of my hands and my other gripped the bottle of wine. He grabbed our blankets and led me away from the resort, toward the part of the beach that would be crammed with tourists and vacationers in the summer months, but tonight waited, empty, for the two of us.

A thousand yards or so away there was a blue-painted wooden rowboat next to an outcropping of jagged rock. It looked like a painting under the moonlight, with one bench and a pair of oars near the bow, the rest hollowed out—a fishing boat.

I dropped the wine in the sand as Sam stopped next to the hull. He turned, pulling me into his arms and capturing my lips with his in one smooth movement. Our tongues twisted together, hands everywhere, until we were both breathing hard and I was wondering how feasible it would be to have sex standing up.

"Hand me your sweater," he panted.

This had been so long coming that it didn't occur to me to argue or ask why. My sweater landed next to his sweatshirt in the bottom of the boat, and the sweatshirt hoodies we bought at the gift shop went next. I shivered in the breeze that wafted off the water; it wasn't freezing, but the temperature probably hovered somewhere in the mid-sixties.

Sam caught sight of my shudder as he spread one of our fleece blankets over the clothes. "I promise to warm you up in sec."

"You'd better."

He puddled the second blanket at one end of the makeshift mattress, then bowed slightly, gesturing to his creation. "M'lady. After you."

I took his hand as I stepped into the boat, settling on the bottom. He followed a moment later. It was a tight fit with both of us, but it would be more than enough room.

The light touch of his fingers on my belly drew a gasp from deep inside me. I held my breath, then blew it out my nose as Sam lifted my tank top over my head. I returned the favor, ridding him of his T-shirt and taking a moment to stare at the hard landscape of his chest and stomach in the Greek moonlight.

"You are beautiful, you know that?" I breathed, not caring all of the sudden if I sounded like a complete moron. If we weren't going to get repeats of these moments, it seemed to be a mistake to withhold words that begged to be spoken.

He smiled. "I think you should get your eyes checked."

My fingers trailed downward over his pecs, lingering on his abs, then dipped into the waistband of his jeans.

His quick intake of breath shot desire between my legs and brought a smile to my face.

His hands lifted, framing my face. "*You're* beautiful, Blair. I swear, I could watch you for hours and never be anything less than fascinated."

"How about you do a little less talking and get to that warming me up that we discussed?" Compliments made me equal parts happy and uncomfortable.

"As you wish."

I smiled, not knowing if he meant to quote *The Princess Bride* but tickled all the same. Movie references, and thoughts in general, flew out of my head when Sam's lips landed on my neck. They worked downward, hands pushing me back onto the blankets and clothes in the process, until they had trailed down to the swell of my left breast.

He lifted his head, concern visible on his face in the darkness. "Are you comfortable?"

"Yes."

The clasp on my bra flicked open without me even registering that his hand had moved, and the combination of the cool air and Sam's hot breath on my nipples tightened every muscle in my body with pleasure. My hands fisted in his hair as his lips fluttered and sucked; he flicked his tongue at close enough intervals that I couldn't breathe in between, until I writhed with the desire to have him.

I let go of his hair and went for his belt, then the fly of his jeans. He felt heavy in my palm, thick and throbbing and as ready as I was. We had been doing the foreplay thing for over a week—longer if you counted the flirting that had begun last spring—and I couldn't take much more.

The groan I earned in response to my ministrations said we were on the same page. It encouraged me to shove his pants and underwear off his hips, and Sam tugged mine down at the same time. It thrilled me, both of us being naked on the beach, even though it probably should have embarrassed me. I wasn't this carefree, wanton girl—this girl dripping with so much need that she ripped a guy's clothes off in freaking public.

Only tonight, and the other night in the bathroom—with Sam—it seemed that I was.

He kissed me hard, our lips and tongues moving with a kind of desperation that thrilled me, scared me, while his hand dug in the pocket of his jeans. The sound of a packet tearing briefly joined our ragged breathing, then he moved to his knees, shoving mine apart in the process.

Then he was over me, his hands in my hair. "I promise next time we'll go slower but I can't wait. You've hexed me."

"I don't think the devil performs hexes," I croaked. All higher thought dissolved when he pressed against the heat at my center.

He worked inside me, slowly at first, then burying himself deep when he realized I was wet enough from our making out to do what he wanted. The steady rhythm mesmerized me, took me to another place made of sweat and muscled backs and hot breath on my neck. Where there was nothing but the perfect ecstasy of being stretched and full as Sam rocked against me, our bare skin pressed together. His lips trailed over my neck, one hand toying with my swollen breasts until I arched against him. He slid deeper inside me, our hips locking together, and our mouths grew hungry again. We wrapped together from mouth to feet, moving as one person, as though we'd been doing this for months instead of navigating a first time.

"You feel so fucking good," he breathed into my lips.

I opened my eyes to find him watching me with an intense expression in his eyes. It felt unfamiliar, a far cry from the Sam who spent so much time going with the flow, taking each moment as it came, and the sight pushed me over some kind of emotional cliff.

It made me realize that maybe he could see something different, something more real, in my face, too, but I didn't look away.

To my surprise, the expression in his eyes, our slicked skin, and his hardness inside me combined and built the beginnings of an orgasm. In my experience, those things had to be concentrated on, worked at, but the moment he saw the flicker of pleasure on my face he kept up an increasingly rapid pace. Every thrust rubbed me just right, and a wall of pleasure crashed over me without any warning. My legs went around his back, grinding my body against his as it pummeled me senseless, burning as though a wildfire devoured me from the inside out.

When it was over I couldn't breathe. My muscles felt like jelly, except for my arms, which were locked around Sam's neck. There were teeth marks on his shoulder, even though I didn't recall biting him, but my brain was too detached from the rest of me to even think about feeling badly.

"Holy shit," I mumbled, realizing after a moment that Sam had stopped moving.

I pulled back to look at his face, which sported a shit-eating grin and an even hungrier look in his eyes than had been there before my surprise orgasm.

"Good?"

"Good is a giant understatement." I rolled out from under him. "Now it's your turn."

I sat up and traded him places, easing down on top of him and watching his eyes roll back in his head. His fingers were tight on the flesh of my hips, digging in and helping me move against him. I wasn't interested in drawing this out, even though it felt so good I would live with him inside me were it socially acceptable. I wanted to make him feel as good as I felt, to work it so that he couldn't help losing control, too.

It didn't take long, and with Sam, nothing was a secret. Every movement he liked twisted his lips up in a mixture of a smile and a gasp, and when he reached around to give my ass a light smack, I knew I had him. I sat up, using his chest for balance, and pulled him deep inside me, then out, matching his thrusts until my thighs burned, until another orgasm ripped through me.

It sent me burrowing into his chest, holding on for dear life as I came forever, the pleasure tearing at me, lifting me up. Sam thrust into me while I soaked him, hands on my ass, pulling me onto him hard while he joined me underwater. His lips gasped my name into my neck, tickling and spreading gooseflesh over my body.

We both stopped moving slowly, not all at once. Sweat slicked the skin of my chest and between my knees and my thighs. Every time Sam leaned up to kiss me, perspiration from his upper lip slid onto mine—it tasted like salt and sex and Sam, and didn't gross me out a single bit.

I eased off of him a while later, both of us groaning with the loss of weight and heat, then settled on the blankets at his side. Curled into him, reveling in the heat created by our bodies while the breeze cooled my back, nothing had ever felt this perfect.

"That was pretty incredible," Sam mused some time later, twisting his head to kiss my temple. "I mean, I suspected. But. Yeah."

The pause he left was for me to reassure him that it had been good for me, but even though I knew that, it took me a few moments to find the words. To dig up the honesty, to allow my tongue to let it go. "I mean, I had two orgasms in, like, ten minutes. Incredible is a good word."

"Watching you come is quite the turn-on, you know."

I got up the nerve to make eye contact. "Oh?"

"Jesus, yes. I mean, I feel pretty powerful, mentally. And it also feels amazing when I'm inside you and it happens. Like . . . yeah." Sam looked away, an awkward smile on his face.

"Are you blushing?"

"No." He looked back at me, all of the mirth gone from his eyes. "Maybe. You make me feel like I'm back in high school, desperate to make my girl feel good again. I want you to feel good."

"I feel fantastic. But don't you always want the girls you're with to feel good?"

"Sure." His hand trailed lazily up and down my arm. "And, I mean, obviously they do. But usually I care more because of my own ego than really wanting to make them feel good."

"Mmm." My eyelids felt heavy. My whole body felt heavy, as though my blood had turned to lead.

"Are you falling asleep on me? Isn't that the guy's job?"

"Can't help it. You killed me." I shifted closer, smiling into his chest. "Besides, I'm the guy in relationships. Because I don't like mushy."

"You like hard?"

I snorted. "Duh."

He hooked the spare blanket with a toe, dragging it up to his fingers and then over us, then rested his chin on top of my head. We fit together, next to each other or him inside of me, and it scared me more than a little. Despite my strange, lonely life, I had always felt whole. I knew who I was, and had long ago learned to be happy with it.

Now, being so happy with someone else, I worried losing him would make me feel less than whole. As though he had somehow become part of the puzzle that was me, and without him, pieces would be missing.

And there was no doubt I would lose him. The only question was when.

Chapter 15

Sam

*T*he sun woke me up long before I would have liked,

but with a beautiful, frustrating, naked girl pressed against me, at least there was a way to make it better.

Her ass was smooth under my palm. Blair was soft everywhere on the outside, a complete contradiction to the girl hidden away underneath her skin, and the yin and yang made me like her even more. It also made me harder than my typical morning situation, and I worked my hands higher until they found the swell of her breasts.

Her nipples tightened between my fingers. I played with them softly at first, waking her with tiny circles, then graduating to tweaks and pinches, rolling them between my thumb and forefinger as she moaned and arched into me.

"Good morning, you gorgeous little devil, you," I murmured, earning a twitch of a smile.

"Morning," she replied, slipping a hand between our bodies and wrapping it around me.

It didn't seem like I could be any stiffer, but her touch accomplished just that. I moved one hand down her side, over the swell of her hip, then grabbed a handful of her ass again because I truly loved it. I didn't even know why, really—asses typically weren't my thing—but hers was too perfect to miss out on any opportunity to get my hands on it.

Lower, I found heat and a slickness that made my stomach tighten. As oppositional as Blair had been with me, as many times as her words had pushed me away, her body seemed in a constant state of eagerness to welcome me.

Unwilling to wait, I grabbed a second condom and fixed it in place, then rolled up on my elbows and spread her knees. I paused for a second to take in her face. The wrinkle between her eyebrows, plus a soft whimper, communicated her impatience and I pushed inside her, the pleasure of feeling her heat squeeze around me sucking a shudder out through my spine. I held still for a moment, gathering my bearings, enjoying the moment. When she tipped her hips back, pulling me deeper, I took the hint and rocked inside her until our bodies found a rhythm.

Like last night, our eyes locked and some kind of innate, silent conversation flowed between us. The intensity in her gaze frightened me, not because catching a girl as complicated as Blair would have its difficulties, but because I worried that I would fail her. That I wouldn't be good enough.

That despite what she'd said about living in the moment, the inevitability of our failure would leave her more broken than the way I'd found her.

Her feet locked behind my back, knees pressed against my sides as she thrust against me and her eyelashes fluttered against her cheeks. It had been a long time since a girl had come for me with as much ease as Blair did, and watching it fall over her from top to bottom made it almost impossible to hold off on my own orgasm. Made me forget about everything but this moment.

I managed to keep it together, unwilling to end this any sooner than necessary, and after a moment she shook off the cobwebs and bent her legs farther, until I was buried so deep I couldn't think about anything but how it felt. We moved faster, her elbows hooked under her knees, our bodies working together without any help at all from our brains.

Blair threw her head back and writhed when my fingers found her breasts, and as I felt myself crossing a line I wouldn't be able to come back from, I pressed a finger into the slick spot between our bodies. She jerked against me, her fingernails digging into my back, and thrust against me harder. That killed me, and when she clenched around me and came, I tumbled over the edge of reason beside her, riding her and the waves of pleasure with equal abandon, lost to the pounding of my heart, the trembling of my muscles, and the sound of her scratchy voice gasping my name in the dawn.

I don't know how long it took before the world came back into focus—before the sound of the waves against the shore and the shriek of seagulls against the sky broke through the cloud of cotton draping my brain.

Blair's legs shook against my sides, her rib cage expanding and pressing her breasts against my chest, and I dropped a kiss on her sweaty forehead. Her fingers dug into my back, kneading lazily, and her lips smiled into my throat. "That was about the best way to wake up with the sun I've ever experienced. And I am so not a morning person."

"Could have fooled me."

Our fingers twined together and we lay in silence as the sun rose over the ocean. It was new to me, being able to sit with another person quietly without feeling awkward. With Blair, sometimes it seemed as though her silences told me more about her than her words, which were often so calculated that they must be designed to hide things. Her confession about her past, about never being able to be close to anyone because of not being able to share her father's secrets, made sense.

It made me sad for her, but it impressed upon me her strength.

My stomach growled, and I felt her smile. "Hungry? For food, I mean."

"I mean, if you're giving me the option of going again with you or eating food, I would choose the first. Unless you're hungry."

The twinkle in her dark eyes undid every thought in my head.

"I have a feeling you and I will be going again, but at the moment I think we should get a jump on the day. Breakfast. And coffee, for God's sake. And it's best to get out early for diving, so we can make at least two trips. Since we're only here for the day."

I trailed a hand over her belly, watching her muscles twitch. "We can stay longer if school really isn't an issue. I don't have to be back in Australia until the end of the year."

She paused so long I thought she might be considering it, but in the end, she shook her head with a smile sad enough to make me believe she regretted it. "I can't stay away that long. As fun as pretending to be on an international vacation is, that's not why we're really here."

The way her lips spat the word *pretending*, as though that's all we were doing, made the blood in my veins turn to ice. I wanted to protest, but she wasn't wrong. We *were* pretending to be people we weren't, except somewhere along the way we had become more like that vacationing couple than the opposite forces we'd began as in Melbourne.

It was best to play to my strong suit and go with the flow. I had no idea what was happening between us, but I enjoyed Blair's company, we were compatible as hell, and the thought of going back on tour and never seeing her again made my heart sink all the way into my toes. That's what I did know. What I didn't know was how she felt about it, how this trip would turn out, or how either one of those things would affect everything else.

"Let's get you some coffee, gorgeous. Then we'll spend one day with the fishes."

*

The weather had cooperated, with the temperature rising into the low eighties and the sun shining on the deck of the sailboat that hauled us out to a perfect dive site. We'd been down twice, once after breakfast and then again right before lunch, and were waiting two hours before taking one last trip. It had been a long time since I'd dove, but it came back to me pretty well and the supervising divemaster had been meticulous and patient.

I had never seen turtles before, and at the end of the second dive a school of dolphins had shown up to play. The entire experience had been magical. Blair had laughed often, her face brilliant under a smile and droplets of salt water, but every time she looked at me with undiluted happiness, the word *pretending* flashed before my eyes.

Could she be that good of an actress? Had I fallen into Wonderland, a place where Blair had turned into someone else, but only until she unearthed the opportunity to go home?

It killed me to think that, so I decided not to. I was being paranoid, which was unlike me, and the reason for that should stay unanalyzed, too. The enormity of the feelings circling my heart like sharks were too intense for the fact that Blair and I had really only known each other for a couple of weeks total.

I shouldn't have felt so lost at the idea of not having her around. First and foremost, no girl liked a stage-five clinger of a guy, independent girls such as Blair even less so. She wasn't pretending to have a good time today, and neither was I. We were two people enjoying the day and each other's company, end of story.

The internal lecture did little to salve the worry darkening my mind.

"What are you thinking about?"

Blair's question shook me out of my ridiculous melancholy. I rolled my head her direction, squinting in the early afternoon sun and wishing I'd called Oakley rep for a couple pairs of sunglasses after putting the call in to Head.

"What?"

Her body had bronzed in the few hours we'd spent on deck, and looking at her in her plain black bikini gave rise to certain thoughts that gave rise to other things not so easy to hide in my swim trunks. At least the divemaster left us alone.

"You look worried. There's a wrinkle right here." She reached over and rubbed her finger between my eyebrows. "It's weird. Do you not want to go down again?"

"Oh, I haven't gone down at all. But I'm looking forward to it."

"I meant down on another dive, perv." The way she bit her lip said she was thinking about the other kind of going down now, though, and I wished the divemaster would disappear altogether.

"No, it's not that."

"What is it? Your bed-bug rash is already clearing up, if that's it. I think the saltwater helped."

The bed-bug rash hadn't entered my mind for hours, which shocked me. It didn't seem wise to be honest with her about what *was* on my mind, since my concerns could be chalked up to insecurity, which was about the most unattractive thing in the world. But I didn't want to lie to her, either. "I was thinking about how nice today has been."

"And . . . ?"

So much for skirting the issue. I should have known that wouldn't fly with her. "And I'm already feeling a little bit sad that we won't have another."

"Well, one is one more than we expected when we set out, right?" She squinted back at me. "And really, Sam, with the way our lives are, the two of us should take what we can get."

"You two ready?" The divemaster, a short Mexican woman, stepped out onto the deck with her wet suit hanging off her hips.

I smiled at Blair and helped her up, choosing to drop the conversation. Choosing to ignore for as long as possible the fact that I could hardly enjoy the good day for the sorrow over the thought of all of this ending. Choosing, as I had done my whole life, to be happy with what I had.

Chapter 16

"You're better than you let on!"

Blair grinned from the other side of the net, resting her racket on her shoulder and striking a sassy pose. I'd been regretting not asking Head for some clothes, too, because her legs in a tennis skirt would have been a sight.

"Oh, come on. You're taking it easy."

"Well, yeah, but this is my job. You're a great hitting partner." It wasn't a lie. She was quick on her feet, and had an early read on the ball and a killer backhand that had caught the deuce court sideline more than once.

"I'm having fun," she admitted, breathing a little hard. "It feels good to exercise after days of sitting on my ass."

"Diving isn't for slouches, either. I'm going to be sore tomorrow. Can we take the rackets when we leave?"

"I don't care. Don't know if we'll be able to play again, though." Blair squinted up at the setting sun, then wandered over to the benches between the courts and checked the time on her cheap cell. "We'd better go. Xander's expecting us for dinner, and we need to book our flight out of Athens tomorrow."

"So, who is this Xander character?" I asked, trying to sound casual as we packed up our gear in the bag that had been at the post office when we returned from diving.

"Why, are you jealous?"

"As if."

That earned me a snort. "He's the caretaker for our house here. Has been since I was a kid. I trust him."

"You trust him not to tell your dad we were here?"

"If we convince him we're on the island for an impulsive romantic getaway? Sure. He's my dad's man as far as business stuff, but he supports my flights of fancy."

"I have seen no evidence of flights of fancy."

Her eyebrows shot up. "You mean having sex in a boat that smells like fish doesn't count?"

The quick response surprised a chuckle out of my gut, and I leaned down, drawing her lips to mine. Even though we were in public, it wasn't long before she parted her lips for me, inviting my tongue to play with hers, and before we were both sweating again.

"Are we going back to the boat after this dinner? I mean, we did leave our blankets."

"I do like those blankets," she teased, dropping her arms from around my neck and shouldering her bag. "But I do think we should find somewhere to shower before dinner."

"Agreed. How are we going to do that?"

"Do you trust me?"

I decided to not answer rather than lie, which made her laugh, which led to more kissing before we finally left the tennis courts and hailed a cab a few minutes later.

It dropped us off at the base of a narrow path that zigzagged upward. A man kept an eye on a group of five donkeys as people brushed past, some choosing to hike, others continuing on their way. My eyes went up, up, up the side of the volcano, then returned to find Blair watching the donkeys with a wicked grin.

"You ready, Bradford?"

"Really?" I wondered how many illnesses had been passed from donkeys to humans, like the bat-born supervirus that wiped out 80 percent of the world in *Contagion.*

"Okay, don't pass out. I did that to freak you out. We're taking the cable car." Blair squealed when I smacked her ass, then scooted out of range and led me to the queue for the cable car.

I swallowed, trying my best not to look super relieved that I wasn't going to trek up a bajillion stairs on the back of a donkey. "You know, I would have taken the donkey."

"I know. You're surprisingly adaptive, and I kind of love that about you." Her hand reached out and grabbed mine, the motion smooth and natural and heartbreaking. "But they don't treat the donkeys very well. I'd rather hike it than support them."

The sentiment drenched me with affection for this girl, so hard and soft at the same time. The hardness was like a shell, designed to keep others from squishing her breakable parts, and I felt more than a little honored to be trusted with what was inside that shell.

We didn't speak much on the ride to the top. The spectacular view of hillside, water, and sunset distracted me from the thoughts that had plagued me most of the afternoon—all of the worry over what would happen tomorrow—and for the first time in days I settled fully into the moment. With the exception of the time we'd spent naked.

When we headed toward what appeared to be a residential portion of the village as opposed to the more commercial area, my brain snapped to attention. We stopped at a house that looked pretty much like all of the others—open-air patio, small balcony, cracked white plaster. Instead of using a code to open the door as we had in Belgrade, Blair tipped up a flowerpot and grabbed a key.

I put my hand over hers before she turned the key in the lock. "Wait. We don't want a repeat of Belgrade. Are you sure there aren't alarms?"

"No. I didn't think there would be in Serbia, either, but the response time for such a thing would be longer here. Plus, it's much more remote." She shrugged. "Let go in and check. If we see anything suspicious we'll leave, but I could really use a shower."

"With me?"

"Tempting." The hitch in her breath and the spark in her eyes betrayed her desire. "But we have less than half an hour until dinner, and Xander abhors tardiness. I'd need way more time than that to be done with you."

I groaned. "You just had to add the last part, didn't you?"

"You're fun to tease."

"I'm going to make you pay for that later," I murmured, running my fingers down the back of her neck.

"That had better be a promise." She stepped away from me with a saucy grin, then stripped off her shirt on her way down the hall. "Check the living room for cameras, will you?"

She wandered into the other room and my eyes scanned the walls and ceiling, finding nothing that looked out of the ordinary. There weren't vents in this house, given that there was no central heat or air, and the ceiling fans would be the only place to hide anything like a camera or motion detector. The room appeared clean, too, at least to my untrained eye.

I heard the shower come on in the other room, and assumed Blair hadn't uncovered anything suspicious, either. The kitchen was empty, dustier than either of the other places we'd stopped, and smelled like stale air. No refrigerator or microwave. Nothing to suggest Neil or anyone else had been here in some time, though this world was simpler than most to begin with.

It made me wonder exactly what kind of caretaker this Xander was, since this property didn't appear to need much support, and my instinctual nerves over meeting him ratcheted up a couple of notches. Anyone who had worked for Neil for twenty years had to know enough about his business to at least suspect criminal activity. Which pretty much ensured Xander was some kind of criminal himself. I was going to shove what was left of my cash into my underwear before we sat down to dinner.

The shower went off in less than ten minutes, followed by the sound of Blair's voice hollering that it was my turn and to hurry up. She was gone from the bathroom when I walked in, which disappointed me, but the spray of lukewarm water took my mind off her naked body for the seven or eight minutes I stood underneath it.

A record since we'd left Melbourne, probably.

"I have to say, I'm not a fan of the towel."

I startled, my heart leaping into my throat, when Blair spoke from the shadows outside the bathroom. "Christ."

"You're jumpy."

"I'm sorry, after having to jump off a balcony at our last checkpoint, should I not be?"

She didn't answer, just held out a pair of jeans and a yellow button-down. "Here. My dad and you are about the same size. They should fit, and they're clean."

Once my heart rate returned to normal, I noticed she wore a gauzy red sundress that tied at the shoulders with little bows. It dipped low enough in the front to show off the cleavage that had so intrigued me last night, and the sun from the day had kissed her skin with a golden hue. She'd twisted her wet hair into a braid that hung down her back.

I stepped forward, snagging her into a hug. "You look like the most beautiful devil in hell."

"What kind of devil would I be if I couldn't seduce you," she joked, swatting me away. "You're getting me wet."

"That's the point."

"Get dressed, would you? I promise not to ask you to put clothes on for the rest of the trip."

"Fine." I shut the bathroom door after stealing a kiss, because getting naked around her would lead to us being late for dinner, no matter what she said. Her eyes betrayed her.

The clothes fit fine, and the comb, toothbrush, and toothpaste under the sink combined to make me feel almost human again. The deodorant in my pack took me the rest of the way, and for two people who had been halfway around the world and through most of Europe in a little more than week, we looked damn good.

"Four minutes to spare. Are we going to make it?"

"Yep. The restaurant isn't far. Nothing is really far on Santorini, as a matter of fact."

We left the house without incident, Blair locking the door and replacing the key under the pot. The walk to the restaurant, with Blair's hand in mine, made me forget again that we were merely pretending to be a couple on vacation. Which worked in our favor, given that we were about to try to convince a man who knew her as well as anyone of that very same lie.

The place was called Fanari, part of another resort hotel type place. A young, bored-looking host led us out onto a stone patio. White-clothed tables with flickering candle centerpieces overlooked the ocean, which had turned a deepening blue in the twilight.

The sun set early here this time of year, before six, which had come and gone. It had dipped below the horizon a good fifteen minutes ago, spraying a golden halo above the waves and giving the evening a surreal glow that artists of every kind had been attempting to capture for thousands of years.

I stopped for a moment and took it all in. There were so many things that I loved about technology, but one of the things I hated was that no one ever stood and stared. Off into the distance. At the beauty in front of them. If we were lucky enough to see something amazing, we were reaching for a phone or a camera to photograph it, not just seeing it.

It occurred to me that neither Blair nor I had reached for our phones for anything other than navigation in days. I should be more vigilant, since Leo wasn't above sending out an international search party, but life felt good this way. Right. As though it really could be simple.

"It's beautiful, isn't it?" Blair stood at my side, as still and silent as I had been, her bottomless dark eyes chasing the spot where the ocean met the sky.

"Yes."

She caught me looking at her and whacked my arm. "I meant the view."

"So did I."

As hard as she tried to keep the smile from twitching up the corners of her mouth, they wouldn't obey. I slipped an arm around her waist at the same moment a huge, burly man of indeterminate race swaggered up to us with the kind of confidence that only came from being sure you could kick a man's ass—any man's.

"Well, if it isn't little Blair Paddington." He gave me a hard look. "How about you take your hands off her."

Blair grabbed my hand, trapping it against her waist before I could snatch it away like a little boy caught with his hand in the cookie jar. "Sam, don't move. Uncle Xander, it's good to see you."

After she'd held on to me long enough to make her point, Blair stepped forward and into the giant oaf's arms, giving him a squeeze. He lifted her off the ground, making her squeal like a child as I tried to figure out what kind of caretaking he specialized in.

He set her down and turned his black, beady gaze on me. "And who in the hell are you, other than handsy?"

"I'm Sam Bradford."

"The boyfriend?" He cocked his ear toward Blair, refusing to peel his hard look away from me.

"Yes. Now stop acting like you're a father. Not mine, because obviously he doesn't concern himself with who I date, but someone's. Is the table ready?"

The man harrumphed, then stuck out his hand my direction. "Xander."

"It's nice to meet you. For what it's worth, I promise I'm treating her with as much respect as she'll allow."

He bellowed, laughing until he bent over and put his hands on his knees to catch his breath. Half of the people on the patio were staring without trying to hide it by the time he recovered. The wide set of his shoulders and the thickness of his gut suggested it didn't take much to wind him.

Good to know. In case I needed to run.

The three of us sat at one of the tables closest to the short stone-and-mortar wall that separated the restaurant from the steep drop down to the sea. Single-sheet menus waited on our plates, glasses full of water and ice. Xander ordered what turned out to be a bottle of white wine. He poured for all of us and then drank his glass down in one gulp, refilling it while I tried not to stare.

Blair paid him no attention, studying her menu even though it was in Greek. I followed her lead, peeking at him while he drank the second glass in two gulps, then refilled and stared at his own menu. Some of the words were familiar enough, and when I looked closer I saw that there were English and Italian translations in lighter print along the sides.

A waiter appeared, and Xander ordered another bottle of wine along with his dinner. Blair ordered next and I requested what I hoped was fish with a mushroom risotto, or something similar. The waiter wrote everything down on his pad with quick strokes, then left the three of us alone.

Xander sipped his third glass of wine, which meant it went down in five swallows instead of one or two, then leaned forward on his elbows. "So, what are the two of you doing here?"

"We're having a little holiday."

"Shouldn't you be at school?"

Blair shrugged. "This was the best time for us to get away. Sam's a tennis player, Uncle Xander."

"Tennis?"

"Yes. Quite a good one, too."

"What does that have to do with anything?"

"Nothing, I suppose. Except it means he only gets six weeks off a year and they're right now."

"That's horrible. You work too hard, boyfriend." The waiter scurried back up to the table, setting down a basket containing an assortment of breads and crackers. "You said in your message that you needed a favor. Oh! And I have your spare phone."

He pulled an iPhone identical to the one that Blair had dunked in the Danube from his pocket and tossed it across the table. She caught it, dropping it in her purse without looking at me. It didn't bother me that she hadn't mentioned asking for a new phone, but it *did* bother me that she clearly didn't want to talk about it.

Maybe she'd been enjoying life without one, too.

"Sam and I borrowed a car from a friend in Belgrade. We're going to leave it at the port in Athens, but we need to get it back to her. Also, I need some cash. Five thousand should do it."

A chunk of bread stuck in my throat. She'd asked for five thousand dollars as though it wasn't any different from asking for a mint after dinner, and Xander hadn't flinched. My curiosity about him, about her father, about the life they led ramped up every time she let a new bit of information slip, but this encounter had increased it by leaps and bounds.

The phone rang in her purse. Blair leaned over and peeked at the incoming call. If I hadn't been looking at her I would have missed the flash of resignation that crossed her face, so sad and poignant that it made it hard to breathe. Our eyes met for the briefest of moments, and in the space of a breath her expression settled back into the contentment we'd enjoyed over the past thirty-six hours—but it didn't look quite right around the edges. An ill-fitting mask.

"Okay, so return a car to Belgrade and hand over some cash. Do I get to know details? What's the money for?"

"Nothing in particular. We just aren't quite ready to go home yet."

"You've been in Serbia and Santorini." His eyes narrowed. "Where next?"

"I'm going to take him sailing."

"Hoo-boy, tennis boyfriend, you're in for a treat. I've only ever met one sailor in this whole world better than this girl's daddy, and that's this girl. Could sail rings around anyone in the world by the time she was ten."

It was on the tip of my tongue to ask where and how we were going sailing, but that was probably the kind of thing actual couples talked about before bringing it up in public.

Xander took another swig of wine, then winked at me. "Course, our girl learned many things from her daddy, and she keeps them honed, too. Practice makes perfect, and all that."

Blair winced as food appeared in front of us, the waiter so quick and quiet that I didn't hear him come or go. I had a hard time tearing my eyes from her face, trying to see past the mask, to guess what exactly Xander meant by her keeping in practice. Blair's breathing quickened enough for me to hear it sitting next to her, and I heard her swallow.

Xander dug into his plate with as much gusto as he'd attacked his wine a few minutes ago, oblivious to the fact that he'd caused a quiet panic attack in his honorary niece. He sounded exactly how I imagined a pig would sound, snorting supper up from its trough.

I ate on autopilot, my mind a million miles away trying to make sense of the jumble of feelings inside me, the girl beside me, the days ahead. Whether or not I would ever see that money again, whether I even cared anymore. I felt stronger than I had in months. The tennis Blair and I had played had been energetic; I hadn't pulled many punches, and my abs felt great. This was going to be a good season, and with any luck, it wouldn't be the last.

And I would be fine.

I would be fine without Blair, without the money. So why did it make me so sad to think about walking away, about going back to the world where I belonged—the world I loved?

We finished the dinner with me adding little to the conversation. Blair snapped out of whatever had set her off, chattering with Xander about tides and the woman from the village, musings about what resorts would be the biggest sellers the coming summer.

Once the plates had been cleared, Blair cleared her throat. "There is one more thing, Uncle Xander."

"There's always one more thing with you, girl. Out with it."

"If you talk to my father, please don't tell him I was here. He might be upset with me for missing the last couple weeks of school."

"Aw, you know I never rat you out to your pops. What he don't know won't hurt him, and your daddy knows everything he needs to know about you."

We all got up and Blair gave him a hug. "Thank you."

"You're welcome. I'll meet you at the docks in the morning with your cash, and get the keys for the car, too."

"Can you meet us there in an hour? We were hoping to catch the last boat to Athens tonight so we can grab a flight to Jamaica tomorrow."

My eyebrows went up before I could stop them. We had been planning to go back to the beach, to spend one more night in our pretend world before moving forward, but apparently she'd changed her mind at some point. I didn't know when, but I could guess: somewhere between that mysterious phone call and Xander talking too much about her relationship with her father.

"I can send one of my boys. No way I'm running anywhere after that feast. Delicious, as usual." He tossed a few extra coins down on the table, even though he'd already left a generous tip, then kissed Blair on the side of the head. "You guys be safe."

He walked off, guffawing at his own double entendre all the way out the front of the restaurant. Blair and I stood until the sound of his laughter faded, then I glanced down to find her looking up at me.

"We're leaving tonight?"

"I think we should get going. It's too easy here to forget why we're together."

245

She started to walk off, but I grabbed her hand to make her stop. "Why *are* we together, Blair? I thought it was because we were enjoying it."

Her eyes closed, then opened. Just like that, she was the detached girl who had come to get me in Melbourne. But, as with her expression at the table, there was something else trying to push out from underneath. It said she had changed, but wasn't ready to admit it yet. Or perhaps that was what I wanted to see.

"I'm enjoying it, Sam. I am. I just . . . we set out to accomplish something, and longer we sit around soaking up the sun and having sex on the beach, the farther we are from reaching our goal." Her eyes pleaded with me to understand. "We need to find my dad. So we can get your money back, and so I can get my life back."

"You said that you wanted to find your dad so you could turn him in, so you could put all of that out of your head and get on with your life." My gut tightened at the question bubbling up from the depths. "Are you still part of your father's schemes? Is that what Xander meant by you keeping in practice? Is that why you really want the authorities to put a stop to him?" I hated that she wouldn't look at me. "It's wrong of him to ask you to do that, if it's true. You don't have to do anything you don't want to do."

She snorted, then walked away, tracing Xander's path out the front door of the restaurant. I followed her onto the street and down the steps to the water, until we were both sweaty and out of breath. Only then did she turn and look me in the eye. "You don't have to worry about me, Sam. We're having fun together. This is easy. Don't make it hard."

"Don't make it hard by trying to actually be your friend, you mean? It's okay if you let me between your legs, but the rest of your insides are off-limits?" The crude comment made me cringe the moment it left my lips, but it was too late to take it back. I didn't think I wanted to, anyway.

"That's about the size of things. Take it or leave it." She stuck her chin out, challenging me.

We both knew I would take it. Somewhere along this road she had wriggled her way under my skin, and even though it had always seemed certain that we would part ways at the end of our adventure, I wasn't ready for that day to be today.

But no matter what Blair thought, no matter how much distance she thought she'd kept between us, there were holes in her armor that, for some reason, I could see through.

I sensed her fear—I just didn't know what scared her.

"Okay, Blair. Let's go to Athens tonight. And then we're flying to . . . ?"

"Jamaica," she said, looking me in the eye hard enough for me to catch a flicker of relief.

Our next, and maybe last, destination had to be at least two days away. Two more days for me to try to make the holes bigger, until I could see enough to figure out whether or not Blair's mysterious fear was unfounded, or whether it would make me feel better about the inevitable end.

Chapter 17

Blair

It had been another long day. Another twenty-plus hour flight, though at least the one from Athens to Kingston was direct. Unlike our first hellacious and never-ending trip, from Melbourne to Austria, Sam decided not to take advantage of his prescription sleeping pills. I was torn between wanting his company for every second of these last couple of days and wishing he would sleep so that I could feel guilty in peace.

There had been a slew of text messages on my backup phone after Xander had it activated. A bunch from Audra, just checking in. Two from different professors letting me know what final projects had been assigned. Two cryptic messages, one from Kennedy Gilbert and one from Cole Stuart, with strangely similar wording, piqued my interest, but one from my father drove any thought of getting involved in Whitman drama from my head.

There are better ways to get the rest of Bradford's money. You have two days to get it done, or I'm going a different direction. I'll call for the update 12/2.

He'd only sent one, because he wouldn't deign to tell me anything twice. One was enough to remind me why Sam and I had come together, and that pretending otherwise would hurt us both. Being with him, feeling the physical manifestation of our connection, had been the tipping point. I couldn't treat him like everyone else when he wasn't like *anyone* else. Regardless of my change of heart, my determination to help Sam instead of steal from him, it wouldn't alter the outcome. Sam would find out the truth, and this—pretend or real—would be over.

December 2nd was tomorrow. We'd land in Jamaica in the next twenty minutes, according to the pilot. We needed to find a boat and haul ass to the Caymans, come up with a plan, and confront my dad before my deadline expired. I thought seeing the two of us in the flesh, maybe looking at my face and glimpsing even just a fraction of how much I liked Sam, would convince him to drop the act. If not, I was prepared to threaten to go to the authorities with all of the information I had accumulated over the years.

I thought. It would implicate me, too, but there were things such as immunity, right?

Maybe I watched too much television, but all my years of conning wouldn't go to waste. I could play the poor, abused little girl forced to participate in her daddy's games or get tossed into the street. It might have even been true, once. Before I started to like the challenge.

I glanced at Sam, taking advantage of his fascination with the island landing to watch him without being caught. He had a gorgeous, strong profile, and his brown hair curled a bit at the ends now that it was too long. If he looked at me, his eyes would poke holes in all of the misdirection and sarcasm that served me well as protection with other people. Even so, I loved his eyes.

Every guy I'd ever dated had been good-looking. Especially Flynn. But, that's *all* they had been—shiny toys I'd picked up, then tossed aside when they grew boring. While Sam was handsome by anyone's standards, it surprised me to realize his looks were the last thing I would use to describe him, and far from my favorite thing about him. Mostly it was his patience. His surprising determination and depth. His easygoing personality and wry sense of humor.

Not that I didn't enjoy his body. I thought that I could spend years learning every groove, and never tire of how it tensed and rippled under my fingers. The weight of him on top of me, watching his eyes close in pleasure, feeling his hands squeezing my hips—the experience had been almost surreal. Otherworldly. As though fitting together with another person so well, so easily, couldn't quite be real.

Spending another night having sex in that boat would have pushed me over the line—one where there was no way he wouldn't take my heart with him when he went. I had no illusions that these twenty-four hours would end without Sam learning the real reason I'd come to get him, the real reason I'd dragged him halfway around the world. My father would rat me out, or I would have to do it myself in order to get Sam's money back.

But that was the most important goal. Get Sam's money back. If I could accomplish that, I would go back to doing my dad's bidding for the next two years. Sam had poured his heart and soul into his career for way longer than that. He deserved the money more than I did my freedom.

For the first time in my entire life, the right thing to do was more important than what my father wanted, than what would keep me safe. It was more important than the knowledge that Sam would hate me. Keeping him with a lie would be so much worse than fixing this and letting him go.

Sam's hand found mine, startling me out of my head. I realized he'd caught me looking, and when he gave me a sly smile a lump formed in my throat. My eyes burned, but I didn't look away.

His gaze turned concerned. "What's wrong?"

"Nothing. I think I'm just sorry this is almost over."

"Really? You're going to miss the two-day flights, the dirty trains, smelly buses, hostels and bedbugs?"

I forced a smile. "Don't forget the balcony jumping."

"How could I?"

My heart had leapt into my throat when my confession had spilled free that not only did I know this was about to be over, but that it made me sad. Maybe nothing could come of this relationship, even in perfect circumstances, but the ferocity with which I wanted to try to hold on to it terrified me.

It had come out of nowhere. Chemistry had turned into friendship had turned into attraction had turned into . . . was turning into more. The thought of not being able to turn and talk to Sam made the lump throb. Tears pricked my eyes. "I'm going to miss you, that's all."

"Holy shit." He unbuckled his seat belt even though the wheels hadn't touched down, pulling me into his arms in one swift movement. "I can't believe it."

"Believe what? After all of this, after the other night, you didn't think I would miss you?" I mumbled the words against his shoulder, trying so hard not to cry.

He pulled back, thumbs smoothing the heat of my cheeks. "Honestly, Blair? I didn't think I'd hear about it one way or the other. You're so . . . bottled up. After the other night in that boat, there was no denying the way we're connected, but I didn't expect you to admit it."

"I didn't expect me to admit it, either."

"This doesn't have to be the end, Blair. I know my schedule is crazy and you have two years of school left, we still have to figure out your dad and everything. But as stupid as it sounds, I've never felt this way about anyone—like nothing would be real if I couldn't tell you about it. Don't give up before we give it a try."

It sounded wonderful, coming out of his mouth. The way he described it, like life would feel wrong if we couldn't share it, mirrored the desperate desire to keep him that was ripping apart my own heart. The memory of my dad's text message trampled the joy threatening to burst me open. There were too many things Sam didn't know. I was falling for him, but I knew the real him. The girl Sam thought he was falling for wasn't the girl who had spent the last ten days at his side—not totally.

He couldn't possibly want to rearrange his life to include Blair the con-artist liar.

Sam watched me, a cautious hope in his posture, fingers gripping my waist. I wanted to make him happy, but more than that, I didn't want to lie to him ever again. "Let's figure out my dad first, then see where we go from there."

A smidge of the light went out of his face, but he covered it quickly, pecking me on the lips. "It's a starting point. That's more than we had three days ago."

The wheels touched down, humming along the short runway. Sam sat back in his seat, watching out the window with a faint smile, while I gathered my things from under the seat. If only the conversation could have meant the same thing to me as it did to him. For Sam, saying we would figure things out after we dealt with my dad was a reason to have hope.

For me, it meant I knew when we'd say good-bye.

*

The nice thing about convincing Sam that my father's vast, imaginary network of spies would find us if we traveled in our typical style was not having to wait for baggage. We climbed off the plane and went through customs before most of our fellow passengers had left the bathroom. I watched the agent stamp my passport, my mind going again to the vaguely threatening message from my dad. For the first time since spinning the yarn to try to talk Sam out of joining me on a fake quest around the world, I wondered how much truth there might be to it—if Dad had been notified about the "break-in" in Belgrade, and he probably had, he could have pulled the footage and seen us there.

He didn't have any reason not to trust me, I reminded myself. He might think my methods were excessive, especially if he checked out how much money I'd taken out of my spending account in the past two weeks, but he wouldn't think I'd gone soft.

I tried hard to recall if we did anything or said anything in Belgrade that would make him realize I had feelings for Sam that were getting in the way, but it didn't matter. My dad had a perceptiveness that didn't seem human. If he was in the Caymans, if he saw Sam and me together, there was no way he would miss the pull between us. It could make him nervous, but it more likely would make him angry. People did what my father asked. *I* did what my father asked.

"I can't wait to go sailing."

"You know how to sail?" My eyebrows went up. "You never mentioned it."

"You never asked. I have many, many talents I plan to let you discover."

His arms went around my waist from behind as we waited in line for a taxi. A thrill went down my spine before I could think about stopping it. "Is that right?"

"Mmm-hmm." He murmured into the back of my neck, leaving a kiss in its wake.

"Next!"

The valet gave us a stern look that would have made me smile if my heart wasn't in my stomach. Sam and I climbed into the backseat, and the cabbie, who was too much of a Jamaican cliché to make fun of —because he could probably put a voodoo curse on us—turned to ask where we were going.

"The Yacht Club, please."

"Is the house here? Does your dad have a boat at the marina?"

I didn't answer, unwilling to say anything incriminating in front of the cabbie, who stared into the rearview mirror without reservation. Sam got the hint, reaching over to hold my hand and then watching out the window. As was the way with all taxis, for some reason the guy had the windows down. In Jamaica, as in Greece, there wasn't anything sweeter than the fresh, salty smell of the warm air. Going back to Florida would be downright dreary after the last two stops of our trip.

The Yacht Club had security, but the taxi driver just waved on his way through. I hadn't spent a ton of time in Jamaica, but I knew the island had a growing problem with corruption and crime that worked in my favor. The plane tickets had soaked up over four thousand bucks for the two of us, which mean only about a thousand remained in my pocket. Sam had five or six hundred left at last check, and even though it would be plenty of money to get us *to* the Caymans, it was little enough to make me nervous about *leaving* the Caymans.

"You can just let us off at the docks," I instructed, pulling out cash and a tip that might be generous enough to keep his mouth shut if news of a stolen boat reached his ears later tonight.

He took the money and sped off, then Sam turned to me and raised his eyebrows in a silent question. I didn't answer, wandering down the dock looking for a sailboat with specific specifications—not too big, since the two of us would be sailing it alone, but too small wouldn't do, either. It would only take us six hours or so, depending on the wind and the chop, to make it to Grand Cayman. Too fast for anyone to notice their boat was gone, report it, and chase us down.

Especially if we found the right boat.

Third from the end, a little Catalina 335 series, gleamed like the answer. The sails and cushions were a tad faded and weathered, and the gorgeous teak interior needed a shine. It hadn't been attended to regularly, which meant a higher likelihood that no one would miss it right away.

"I thought your dad's boat would be bigger. And what's with the name?"

I walked around to the rear, snorting when the boat's painted name came into view. Who the hell named their boat *Wiggler*?

"I don't know," I replied, tossing my backpack in and climbing on board. I grabbed Sam's backpack and tennis bag, stowing everything in a locker by the anchor.

"You don't know why your dad named his boat the *Wiggler*?"

He hadn't moved from the dock, squinting down at me in the bright midday sun. The set of his posture, the clench of his jaw, said he knew the answer to his question but still wanted me to say it.

A sigh spilled out before I could stop it, even though it would have sounded more at home coming from a petulant five-year-old or an exhausted mother of seven. Ever since I'd heard from my dad, I'd wanted nothing more than to get this over with and go home.

To stop pretending and accept the inevitable.

"It's not our boat, Sam. We're borrowing it."

"Stealing it, you mean."

"No. Same as the car in Austria. We'll give it back. We're just taking it on a short trip to the Caymans. No big deal." He didn't move. "This is it, Sam. What we set out to do. If my dad is on dry land, he's in the Caymans, and this won't be the first crime you've committed since insisting you come along instead of giving me your information and letting me use it. If you want out, give me what I need and go. If not, get your ass in the boat."

He got in after the briefest hesitation, reaching for the mainsail and rigging without being asked. I checked the rudder then slid the jib into place, leaving both sails unfurled until we puttered free of the marina and sluiced into the open water.

We worked together to unfurl the sails and secure the mainsheet and boom, until the wind caught us and drove us forward at a comfortable pace. The day was beautiful, lending to the serenity of the sounds of the slapping waves and the light spray cutting off the bow. We tacked into the wind, then settled back to let the boat and the water do the majority of the work.

"So, your phone was going nuts at dinner last night. Your friends at Whitman miss you?"

Talking about the messages on my phone tightened the muscles between my shoulder blades. Even though the question could be innocuous, it wasn't. "Audra was checking in, which is pretty normal. She's not worried or anything."

"And . . . ?"

"How do you know there's an and?"

"Isn't there?"

Sam reclined in the bow, arms behind his head, legs stretched out and crossed at the ankle. Sunlight bounced off the waves, bringing out the sparkling chestnut highlights in his hair. He looked like an impossibly perfect guy, and the fact that the way he acted backed that up made it hard to believe he was real, and that he could want me.

"I'm worried about her, I guess. She's dating this guy that rubs me the wrong way."

"Why?"

"I don't know. Just a bad feeling. Don't you ever get those?"

He nodded slowly, his eyes never leaving mine. "Sure. Have you said anything to her?"

"No. She's so happy. It doesn't seem right to rain on her parade without anything to back it up." I tugged the rudder, adjusting our course slightly. "But I had a couple of weird texts from her brother and my old roommate. I'm a little worried something happened."

"You should call her."

"I'll see her in a few days. We need to keep the focus on my dad."

"Is that why you didn't want to spend the night in Santorini last night? You wanted to put the focus back where it belonged?"

There was nothing I wanted to talk about less than why I'd shoved us out of our fantasy and back into reality with such abrupt gusto. One of the only bad things about being trapped on a sailboat with another person was having nowhere to run.

"Yes. I liked pretending that it was just you and me on vacation a little too much. And I'm not saying I didn't love everything you said on the plane—I did. But we can't figure out where we go from here until we get past this, you know?"

"You're a very practical girl, Blair, and I like that about you."

"But . . . ?"

"How do you know there's a but?" he parroted with a smile.

"Isn't there?"

"Not really. It's just . . . there's a difference between being practical and being a pessimist. You've spent your life alone. I worry you don't know how to let me just be there."

Quiet returned to the boat for several moments. If Sam loved my practical side, I adored his ability to sit in silence, to not push me, to wait for the right conclusion.

"I *don't* know how to let anyone be there, Sam. But I know that these past couple of weeks, I've gotten used to looking over and seeing your face. I've loved leaning into your arms, and kissing you, and I'm going to be seriously disappointed if we don't get to have sex again before we part ways. I like having you around. It makes me sad to think that soon you won't be." I paused, swallowing my panic at sharing so much, terrified of the pain to come. "I'm trying."

"I would have taken advantage of another night on the beach. Just saying."

I rolled my eyes, hiding the fact that it killed me that we might never feel that impossible connection again. Another first for me. Not that I didn't enjoy a good romp, but it was another thing that bored me quickly. With Sam, I couldn't imagine ever being within five feet of him and not thinking about what I would do with him naked.

"We're not having sex in another boat, lover boy. I demand a bed."

"As long as there's no bugs in it." Sam shuddered at his own attempt at humor, his hand going to the back of his neck.

My eyes dropped to the back of my leg to find that the rash had almost disappeared. "Right. As long as there aren't any bugs in it."

Chapter 18

$\mathcal{W}$e switched places with about an hour to go because

I couldn't keep my eyes open anymore and Sam insisted I lay down. The warm sun, trusting someone else enough to let them take over, to doze off and know we would be okay—that Sam would be there, not asking anything from me that I wasn't ready to give—it all felt too perfect.

For the first time in my life, I sank into feeling good instead of pushing it away.

In my dream, dolphins swam up beside the boat, happy and chirping. They leapt and sprayed water my direction, and my heart felt light, as though I didn't have a single worry in the world. Then the sun disappeared. The waves grew choppy and gray, disturbing the dolphins until the fear in their eyes made me feel slimy and cold, dragged the lightness away and replaced it with a drowning dark. Panic stole my breath as strings of seaweed crawled over the edge of the boat, clawing and grasping like human hands, tugging me by my feet toward the abyss. A scream built in my throat and I kicked in a fruitless attempt to struggle loose.

It sounded as though the waves were calling my name when I woke up with a start, panting, my heart beating a million miles a minute. My mouth went dry when I saw the look on Sam's face and my phone clutched in his hand. He'd seen the text message my dad had sent yesterday. Or maybe my dad had called early. Either way, the jig was up.

Instead of the kindness, the concern, that had been so often in his face, his maple eyes boiled with anger. I could have dealt with that, but the betrayal and pain swimming alongside it . . . that broke me in half.

"You were playing me this whole time?"

"Sam, no. I mean, yes, at the beginning, but—"

"Jesus. You fucked me for information? How could you? How did I miss that?" Anger reddened the tips of his ears and his hand shook around my phone. "All of that shit you told me about growing up alone, it's all sob story? You've been happily helping your dad this whole time, right? And you were going to get more information out of me so he could steal the rest of the money I worked for? Lost my family over? Destroyed my body for? How could you do that?"

"I wasn't going to, Sam. I didn't lie to you, not after we got started. I swear."

"Yeah, well, the word of a con-artist and a whore doesn't really mean much to me."

It felt as though he'd landed an actual slap across my face. For all of the bad things I'd done or helped do, none of my marks had ever caught on in front of me, had ever been the wiser until I'd long fled the scene, had ever had the chance to yell at me and damn, it hurt.

I knew it hurt because it was Sam. Because no matter what I said, he wouldn't hear anything but lies. He wouldn't see anything but a girl willing to do anything to steal from him.

So I didn't say anything. Maybe that made it worse. In his eyes, a silent admission of guilt. But there didn't seem to be any point to worrying about it now. Emotions swirled in the boat, in the air between us, building the longer we stayed silent. The pain, the anger, the aching, empty sense of loss brought tears to my eyes that I turned away in order to hide. They refused to be contained as the blue of the water grew lighter and shaded toward jade, then sea green, signaling our arrival in the Caymans. Sam made no move to comfort me, never stirred to speak. More insults would have been easier than the silence, which signaled to me that he had nothing left to say.

After what felt like an eternity, Sam spoke again. "Let me guess—your dad isn't going to be here, either. You want to go ahead and give me your big speech designed to earn my trust now, or were you saving it until we were naked again?"

I closed my eyes, trying to will away the rest of my tears. It took forever before my throat stopped burning long enough to let loose the words it was squeezing to death. "Can we get the boat moored and then talk about it? And there's no point in asking me questions if you aren't going to believe a word I say."

Sam moved without agreeing or disagreeing, and the two of us brought *Wiggler* smoothly into the North Sound, dropped anchor, and made our way ashore. A flurry of shops and places to eat awaited the arrival of tourists and sailors, but we had to go through customs first. Sam crossed his thick arms over his chest while we waited in line. His refusal to look at me left my heart feeling stomped on and my body cold, as though I'd been tossed out in the Manhattan winter.

"Nice touch with the tears, by the way. Brilliant."

The disgust in his voice hit my skin like pellets, diving beneath and dumping agony into my blood. "I know that you don't have any reason to trust me, Sam. But I think my dad is here. I want to talk to him with you, just like I said in Melbourne." I took a deep breath, hardly believing I was about to give him more ammunition. More truth to throw in my face. "But the reason I blew you off in St. Moritz . . . that was the truth. It seemed inevitable that we would be different. Not easy. I didn't want to come on this con at all, but he forced me. And things changed along the way. You have to know that."

"I don't believe anything you say," he spat, handing over his passport.

"Sir, you need to come with me." The customs agent had his hand on his hip, over his gun. He spoke softly into the radio on his shoulder, his eyes flicking between Sam and me. "Are you Blair Paddington?"

I nodded dumbly.

"You'll need to come with us, too."

Neither Sam nor I spoke while the rest of the people in the customs building stared at us as though we'd just bombed a village inhabited by kittens wearing party hats. I had almost convinced myself that this had to be some kind of misunderstanding when the police showed up to escort us away.

My legs went numb and my heart pounded in my ears as they put us in the backseat of a police car outside the terminal instead of taking us to a room for questioning. No use pretending this was a simple immigration issue, then. Not if the police had flagged our passports.

"This is fucking fantastic. If you can't ruin my life by stealing all of my money, you'll get me arrested so I get fined or suspended from the tour. Or banned."

"Sam, I swear I have no idea what's going on."

He snorted. "Right. It has nothing to do with your penchant for *borrowing* things?"

"Would you shut up?" We were in a fucking police car and he was basically admitting to stealing multiple items. I normally abhorred telling people to shut up, but cripes. This was my territory. No matter how pissed off Sam was, he needed to use his fucking head.

He seemed to realize the same thing, sitting back and pinching his lips together for the remainder of the ride to the police station. It was a dingy, one-story building too close to the ocean to be so depressing— clearly not the main station, which I assumed was in George Town. The inside held a couple of metal desks, a small, square conference or interrogation room, a kitchen with coffee stains on the counters, and a single cell, where they dumped both Sam and I. The walls were cinderblock and the linoleum floors peeled up at the corners. Two wooden benches sat along the back wall of our cell, one end far too close to a stinky latrine.

"Hey, don't we get a phone call or something?" Sam shouted at their retreating backs.

Neither of them replied, leaving us alone without an explanation for plucking us off the streets like vermin.

It could be the sailboat, but I doubted it. The longer I had to think, the more I suspected my dad was behind our arrest. He'd seen the footage from the house in Belgrade, I was willing to bet, and had deduced that, for the first time in my life, I was not going to get the job done. Having us arrested smacked of him taking matters into his own hands, though how he thought it would get him the rest of Sam's money I hadn't the slightest idea.

Sam slumped on the other end of the bench, sticking to his plan of not speaking to me. I guessed I wasn't speaking to him, either, but there wasn't much more to say. He knew I was a con, that I'd been willing to help my dad steal from him. He refused to hear me when I told him the truth—that the days we'd spent together had changed my mind.

Changed my life, maybe.

I didn't have a clue how to convince him otherwise, and maybe I didn't deserve the chance, anyway. This had always been how it was going to end. At least we had one good day.

One of the officers returned, a young guy with a sexy British accent, shining blond hair, and muscles that tested the limits of his cheap uniform that would make half the girls at Whitman drop their panties, but he wasn't looking at me.

He crooked a finger at Sam. "You have a phone call."

Sam left without asking any questions, even though a bunch of them tumbled through my mind. First and foremost, who knew we were here? The answer could only be my dad, unless the press had somehow gotten ahold of the information—which, in the age of cell-phone cameras, wasn't impossible—and why would my dad ask for Sam and not me?

The answer to that question also provided clarity as far as my dad's endgame in getting us arrested. Sam returned to our cell, a storm cloud of anger obscuring what was left of his "go with the flow" demeanor. He didn't sit, instead pacing along the front of the cell.

"Who was it?"

"Who do you think it was, Blair?"

I recoiled from the anger in his voice, but tried not to let the hurt show. "I think it was either my dad or that sleazy dude from TMZ."

The joke didn't get me a smile, but that was probably too much to ask.

"It was your dad." He glanced down the hallway, maybe to make sure it was empty, then back at me. In his eyes, it was clear that his pain over my betrayal outstripped his anger, and the knowledge that I'd hurt him punched me in the gut.

I'd been prepared for his anger, but not this. Not pain.

"He says all I have to do is give you the information he needs and I'm free—no charges, no one will know. I don't know how he can promise that, but that's what he said."

"Sam, no. I'm not taking anything from you."

His lips twisted, a hateful edge glinting in his smile. "That's the whole reason we're together, Blair, right? Don't wimp out now. I'm sure I'm not the first mark you've gotten *close* to in order to carry out your daddy's twisted games."

My heart broke, but out of it boiled unexpected, indignant anger. "Hey, asshole, I understand you're mad. But you don't get to fling insults at me, or call me names."

My chin trembled despite my best efforts, and horror replaced the disgust in Sam's eyes. He rubbed a hand through his hair, looking away from me and then back, opening and closing his mouth a few times before getting words out around clenched teeth. "I'm sorry. You were honest with me before we slept together. I just heard it wrong."

The tiniest scrap of my hope had somehow survived, and it floated to the surface with his apology.

"I'm sorry, Sam. So, so sorry. I knew you were going to find out how this all started, and that you would be angry and feel stupid, and I should have been strong enough to resist the spark between us so this wouldn't happen. If I would have known this would hurt you, too, I would have tried harder." My feet begged me to take steps his direction. A twitch infected my fingers with the desire to touch him, the desire that had somehow become second nature in such a short time, and I hated that I couldn't give in. Not anymore. "I like you, Sam. I wanted things to be different. But this is what I am. This is my life. I tried to tell you."

"That things can't be different for you. Yeah, I get that now."

"Don't you think I want them to be? Different?"

"I want to, Blair. I do. I guess neither of us can get what we want today."

His words bled the remaining strength out of my legs and I flopped down on the bench, letting the tears wash out of my heart and drip out my eyes. It had been forever—years—since I'd cried at all, but it was all that I'd wanted to do since Sam looked at me with hurt and betrayal in his face earlier today. It felt good and terrible at the same time, to let go of the façade that had passed for the real me all of these years, to let someone else see me, even when I felt gross and hateful.

Sam sat at my side. He didn't touch me, even though it felt as though maybe he wanted to, but the warmth of his presence, of the idea that maybe he was my friend even if we were fighting right now, dug my fingers into that scrap of hope. That even if things weren't different today, it didn't mean they couldn't be. With my roiling emotions drained, my intellect snapped into use again, and an idea took root in the back of my mind.

Not a way to make Sam consider a future with me again, because I didn't think that would be possible. Relationships were all about trust—that was the reason I'd never had a real one of any kind. No one could trust me, and I couldn't trust them.

But I could still find a way to make things right. I could do what I'd decided to do between Belgrade and Santorini—get Sam his money back. Get him out of this sticky situation without compromising his career. Figure out how to get out from under my dad's thumb.

Get my life on track, so that the next time I felt the way I felt when Sam stared into my eyes, I'd be able to believe in the possibilities of love, of a future.

Just thinking of caring about anyone else the way I did about Sam made my heart rebel. Right now, it felt as though that would never happen. But Sam and I would never happen, either, and the time had come to do the only thing I could. One last gesture to what might have been before moving on with my life.

Clinging to any part of my past wouldn't be healthy. After today, that included Sam.

I took a deep breath and got up, then walked over to the bars and shouted for the guard. Sam's eyes burned a hole between my shoulder blades. I smiled when I felt them slide down to my ass, resisting the urge to wiggle as the handsome British accent stopped, eyebrows raised.

"I'd like to talk to whoever is in charge. It's important."

Chapter 19

Sam

I wanted to be surprised at the way things turned out but I believed in being honest with myself. As hard as I'd tried to ignore my gut feelings when it came to Blair, as close as I'd come to convincing myself everything was simple, there had been more than one red flag— none of them bigger than the fear inside her I couldn't place, couldn't assuage.

Turned out my gut was right. That fear in her was born of the idea that I might find out what she was up to before she managed to wrangle whatever account information she needed, not any worry that stemmed from her childhood or her inability to form attachments.

It hurt my pride and my heart, which had been dangerously close to being in her palm when everything went to shit. There was no denying the chemistry between us. I knew in my soul she hadn't faked that— *couldn't* have faked that. The way we connected in bed, in conversation, in silence, was real. There *was* something between us, something I'd never felt before and worried I would never feel again, but it didn't mean shit now.

Blair had been gone long enough for me to start to worry about the Cayman cops mistreating her, which made me angry and contemplative at the same time. It seemed that finding out she'd been trying to make me look like a fool wasn't enough to dislodge the emotional attachment we'd formed. It had almost killed me not to hold her while she'd cried as though her soul had ripped in two. The desire to make her feel better about treating me like every other moron she'd ever met confused me.

It was the friendship. The one that had grown around us in the days before we'd gone to bed together, solid and formed before we'd noticed what had happened. One that meant I worried about her and wanted the best for her, no matter what that meant for me.

The good-looking cop returned, turning the key in the lock and holding open the metal cell door. "Let's go, lover boy."

"Where are we going?" I wanted to be more suspicious, or possibly more of a dick, but the events of the last several hours had exhausted me, body and soul.

"Cap wants to talk to you before you go."

Go? "Where am I going?"

"Wherever you want, as long as you have the cash to get there. Come on."

"Wait, are you saying you guys aren't pressing charges? And I don't have to do anything?"

He didn't respond, motioning again for me to come along. When I paused next to him, free from handcuffs or even a strong grip, he smiled. "Cap's got the details, but yes. You're free to go, after a brief chat."

I didn't know what to say to that—not to mention the worry that saying anything at all might jinx my good luck—so I followed him down the hall to the conference room in silence. There was an older, portly man inside with Blair, whose wrists *were* locked in handcuffs as he helped her up and out the door.

Our eyes met as she squeezed past me into the hall. The look on her face, her eyes filled with sorrow and guilt, made it hard to swallow. To breathe. But the solid strength running underneath her pain had been one of the things that intrigued me from the beginning. Blair would survive.

The British guard took her and left me alone in the doorway to the conference room. The older man, whose badge identified him as the police captain, escorted me to the table after shutting the door behind us.

"Have a seat, Mr. Bradford."

I did as I was told, trying not to fidget. "Sir, I—"

"No. I don't want you to say anything just yet. I'm going to tell you what's going on and why you're being detained, then you can agree or disagree with the statement that has been provided by Miss Paddington. Is that clear?"

I nodded even though it didn't make a whole lot of sense. In the movies when the police brought in two suspects, they interviewed them separately to see if their stories matched up.

"There was an alert placed on your passport, and Miss Paddington's, due to a break-in that happened at the Belgrade home of one of our residents. It has also been discovered since you have been in custody that a sailboat was stolen from the yacht club in Jamaica, a boat that is now anchored in our North Sound."

"Okay . . ."

"We've spoken to Miss Paddington about both of these incidents, given her connection to the Cayman resident who initiated the complaint."

"She's his daughter."

"Please keep your mouth shut, young man. I'd hate to see that Spaniard win another Aussie Open." He winked, taking me by surprise. "Miss Paddington has admitted to being in the Belgrade house and to stealing the sailboat, but insists that she told you that both belonged to her father and she had legal access to the property. She will remain here until her father decides whether or not to press charges—or the owners of the *Wiggler* can be located—but you are free to go. There is a ticket to Melbourne waiting for you at the airport in George Town."

Blair was taking the fall. She was taking the blame for everything and putting me back where all of this started, but her father had insisted nothing but access to my accounts would spring me from prison. She had thwarted him, gone against his wishes to manipulate the police, and I knew I should take advantage of her kindness and run back to my life before things got worse.

It would be horrible luck to ask how exactly they could get worse, because even when it didn't seem like it, the worse was always waiting to sweep in from the wings.

But I was worried about her. Who knew what her father was capable of, how long she would be stuck here, or how he would handle her rebellion?

"What's going to happen to Blair?"

"I wouldn't worry too much about Miss Paddington, Mister Bradford. I daresay the girl can take care of herself, and besides, disputes between family members are resolved sooner or later."

"So I can just go?"

"Yes. We can take you to the airport."

"Can I talk to Blair first?"

He watched me for several moments, his expression impregnable. Finally, he shrugged. "I suppose it can't hurt anything. You have five minutes, then I'm reconsidering this entire situation."

I nodded, standing up and stretching my legs. It was weird walking around without an escort while Blair was handcuffed in a cell, but the captain was right. Blair could take care of herself. I was already too involved with this thing between her and her father, and it was time for me to exit this world that I didn't understand. I'd lost thirty million, but at least I'd gotten out with the rest intact.

My heart was a little worse for the wear. So was my confidence.

Her face lit up when she saw me outside the cell, but she rearranged her expression quickly into one of indifference. I couldn't blame her. I'd said some terrible things in my embarrassment and anger, and we had both fallen back into the mode of protecting ourselves first.

Still, she did get up and walk over, until we were less than a foot apart even with the metal bars separating us. I wrapped my hands around hers, which clung to the bars, even though the feeling of her skin against mine shredded my heart into tinier pieces.

"Thank you. You didn't have to tell them I was ignorant."

"Yes, I did. None of this is your fault, Sam. You don't deserve to pay for my lifetime of sins." Tears filled her eyes for the third time today.

Every bone in my body wanted to lean forward, to capture her lips in mine and kiss her until we both forgot what had brought us here. In the end, I couldn't resist a portion of that and our lips connected for too short a time. She tasted salty and pure, exactly like the Blair I'd made love to in that boat, like the one who had jumped into the Danube at my side.

The one who had been lying to me. How could she be the same?

"Thank you," I whispered again. "You'll never know how sorry I am that this turned out to be what was real. I could have fallen in love with that girl in Santorini."

I waited for Blair to say something in response but she only gave me a sad smile and pulled her hands away from mine, leaving me cold and lonely in a way I couldn't remember ever being.

"Good-bye, Sam."

"Good-bye."

Chapter 20

Blair

Saving Sam the embarrassment of being charged with breaking and entering and theft had been a no-brainer. An easy decision, even though the idea of my dad finding out—and he *would* find out—caused an itchy sweat to break out on my palms. The captain had understood what was going on, and knew I was lying about Sam's level of complicity, but lucky for me had turned out to be a huge tennis fan who also happened to have six daughters of his own at home.

Instead of making Sam's life harder, he had simply put him on a plane. I had to believe my dad wouldn't let me rot in prison. If not because I was his daughter, because he needed me, but Sam had left the Cayman Islands three days ago. My confidence in fatherly instincts had started to wane when the cute British accent, whose named turned out to be Darcy, came to get me.

"Your attorney is here to see you."

My eyebrows shot up. "Attorney?"

I had expected my dad to come himself, but then again, he was a fugitive wanted for fraud on six continents. Even with the inherent secrecy of the Caymans, taking unnecessary chances wasn't part of his modus operandi.

Darcy led me to the conference room. I spent the short walk wishing they had given me a shower, or a brush, or fresh clothes. At least they had provided a toothbrush, toothpaste, and food three times a day, but prison outside the United States left something to be desired. Not that I'd ever been in prison *in* the United States, but it had to be better than this place.

My rank smell took a backseat to my curiosity when the man at the conference table came into view. He wasn't my dad, and he wasn't anyone I recognized as being in my dad's employ. It shifted my curiosity into overdrive, along with my nerves.

Darcy unlocked my handcuffs, which was kind of him. He'd also played a couple hours' worth of gin rummy with me, for which I would send him a basket of his favorite liquor if I ever got out of here.

I sat down at the table and gulped water from the glass in front of me while I studied my "lawyer" over the rim. His silver hair looked dull under the poor lighting, and had the look of an athlete—strong shoulders and a slim frame. He wore an expensive suit, navy-blue pin-striped and designer, and watched me with an obvious interest.

"So, you're my lawyer."

"I am Mr. Bradford's attorney, but I am retained on your behalf. So, yes."

My throat hurt, my heart hurt. If I believed I had a soul, it would hurt, too. Sam had walked out of my life without a backward glance, but he hadn't forgotten me. The wafting scrap of hope that the friendship at the foundation of our time together had survived wrapped around me like the warmth of Sam's body.

I'd never had a friend before, but it turned out losing one was the pits.

"Sam sent you?" I managed.

"Yes. We've arranged your bail, but I'm afraid you won't be able to leave the country until the charges are resolved."

"But I'll be able to leave the building?"

"Yes. It's the best we can do, but I will continue to work on the charges as long as Mr. Bradford wishes it."

"What's your name?" My voice shook. I wasn't even sure what I was feeling; it was too many things to articulate or pick out at one time.

His face, which had been stern and devoid of emotion, softened. "Renaldo."

"Renaldo, please tell Sam that this is more than enough. I need to resolve things with my father before I leave the country, anyway."

"As you wish." He opened his briefcase and extracted an envelope with my name on the front, sliding it across the table. "You're free to go."

"Thank you." I picked up the letter with weak fingers. It would be a while before I would get up the nerve to read it.

An hour later I'd been given a shower and the clothes that had been stowed in my backpack. I felt better, I smelled better, but part of me was missing. I knew it was Sam's presence, but there was nothing that could be done to get it back.

It was time to go see my dad. Alone.

*

"Dad, I know you're watching me on the camera right now. Open the gate or I'm climbing it."

I stood outside the gates barring strangers from my father's massive island home. He spent the majority of his time in the Caribbean but only had one house—the *Alessandra* was his home.

The gates swung open a few seconds later and I hiked up the sandy, stone-covered drive. The circle of green grass in the middle sparkled with spittle from the stone fountain, the burbling sound peaceful in the morning. I was so tired I could sleep for a week, but more than anything I wanted to go back to Whitman. I wanted my stupid, uncomfortable sorority house bed and the sound of Audra grinding her teeth. The idea that Sam might have ratted me out to Quinn, that I might not be welcomed back, made me sick to my stomach.

The front door was unlocked, so I let myself inside. Unlike the houses in Jesenice, Belgrade, and Santorini, this one had been decorated with warm colors, potted plants, and antique furniture. It felt rich and homey even with the ceramic tiled floors that led me onto a patio complete with a table and chairs. Beyond lay a swimming pool in the middle of another expanse of rich, green grass.

"Hello, dear daughter. I must say I'm surprised to see you. And a little impressed." My father sat at the table dressed in what passed for island wear for him—a loose, pale gray linen suit and a lightweight white shirt. He still had shoes on, but it weirded me out to see him so relaxed.

I shut down all of the emotions that had spilled out of me so readily with Sam, knowing they would work against me in any negotiation with me father. "I got tired of waiting. How long were you planning on leaving me to rot in prison?"

"School's out for the holidays in less than a week. I figured I could keep you there until January, if that's what it took to teach you a lesson."

"Kind of an unnecessary burden on the Cayman economy, don't you think?"

"I pay them enough for their assistance and discretion."

I wasn't surprised the police were at least somewhat under my father's influence, but I worried how dearly the cap would pay for letting Sam go.

"Well, I guess I've picked up a few tricks of my own over the years."

"Yes, seducing a world-class athlete. Once again, I'm impressed."

My face felt hot. "I didn't seduce him, Dad. We're friends. Were friends, anyway."

He didn't answer, leaving me with the impression he didn't believe me.

"And this friendship is the reason that you did not finish the job? Have I taught you nothing? We don't make friends, Blair. Because we don't get to keep them."

This was it.

I called on the tatters of courage left inside me, the ones planted by Sam's staunch belief that I could be that girl—the one ready to shake off the life she'd been born into and step into the one she wanted. One full of honesty and, maybe someday, trust.

"*You* don't get to keep friends, Dad. *You* live for the con, not me. I liked it when I was younger. It was a fun game, and an easy way to live, not having to form attachments. Especially after Mom died, because it hurt to think that I would lose the next person I cared about, too." He flinched at the mention of my mother but I soldiered on. "But I don't want to live like that anymore. I want friends. I want to fall in love. I want to work for my money."

"I thought we were partners, you and I. That we had each other."

"I'm your daughter. I'll always be your daughter, and I'm thankful for the things you've given me. But you're never around, Dad. You're wanted by international authorities and you'll never be able to come home. Never stay in one place. I don't want what you want. I need more."

He gave me a sad smile, then shifted to stare out over the pool, into the distance. "You're not like your mother. You're not like me." His gray eyes, so unlike mine, returned to me. "Where did you come from, Blair Louise?"

"Maybe wanting a normal life is a recessive gene."

"Perhaps." He paused, his gaze wandering away again. "And what if I refuse to grant it to you? There are many things to consider, not the least of which is that this is going to put a serious damper on my business pursuits."

Keep going. Don't let him con you.

I took a deep breath. "Then I go to the FBI and tell them everything I know—how you work, how you choose your marks. Your safe houses, your favorite banks. I don't want to, but I will."

His lips down in a grimace. "I taught you well. I can honestly say I didn't think the day would come when you'd use your formidable skills against me."

"You and me both."

"Can I ask what changed? Is it Sam? Did you fall for the boy?"

I started to shake my head, then stopped. "I don't know. I think I could fall for him, in a different world. But he's not the reason I decided this life isn't for me. The idea of being happy with him pushed me to demand it sooner, that's all."

The breeze ruffling the leaves of the fruit trees cooled the sweat on my skin. My insides trembled, and I was sure my dad didn't miss the evidence of my nerves in my shaking voice, yet he made no comment. I hated confessing Sam's importance to me, because Dad would see it as weakness, as a point of leverage, and he'd taught me never to give those up.

But this wasn't a con. This was my life.

"I think it's in both of our best interests to part ways, as business partners."

Relief so potent that it brought tears to my eyes flooded my blood and lifted my heart until it floated, weightless and pounding, in my ears. It gave me the courage to keep pushing.

"There are two more things."

My dad tensed. "Don't make me regret my generosity, Pear."

"Don't forget I'm your daughter."

"Go on."

"I want a million dollars. I've earned at least that much, and it will get me through the last two years at Whitman and give me some breathing room afterward." I could have asked for more. Probably *should* have asked for more, but it was dirty money. I wasn't stupid enough to think I was prepared to live the way Sam and I had on our trip, but I didn't want to be greedy.

"And the second thing?"

"Give Sam's money back. All of it."

"I'm inclined to negotiate the second request."

Despite the hard edge in his voice, I steeled my nerve. "I'm not negotiating. Those are my requirements."

"I find it insulting that you're not concerned about whether or not I'll let you leave this island at all, never mind give in to your demands."

"Dad, you're tough, and you're a criminal, but you're not violent. We both know it."

Another seemingly endless pause preceded his acquiescence in the form of a tight nod. "Fine. One million dollars to your account, and thirty-two million returned to Mr. Bradford. I'll make the arrangements right now."

To my surprise, he did. It took four phone calls to four different banks, but less than ten minutes altogether to move the money. I checked my spending account and verified the pending funds, then used my phone to log into Sam's accounts with the passwords my dad had given me at the outset of this ill-fated venture.

Well, ill-fated in my dad's view. Never mine, even with the pain.

The money was pending there, too.

"Okay, well, I guess I'll go."

"Please stay for lunch, Pear. You can have a quick nap, a shower, fresh clothes. I would like to hear more about school, and about Sam, before you go. There's no telling when we'll see each other again." He paused, smiling a real smile this time. "I suppose I'm a little proud, that you've grown into such a strong woman, even if it is inconvenient for me."

I had a strange, sad feeling that, now that he no longer needed me, I might never see my father again. That it made me sorry was a surprise, though I didn't know why. He was my dad. As much as I wanted to get back to my life, having one last meal together wouldn't hurt.

"That sounds nice."

*

The sight of Whitman's campus squeezed my heart with pleasure—it's faux brick and manicured lawns, the kids laughing between finals, the tickle of anticipation in the air. I'd made it back in time to take the two finals that my professors demanded be completed in person, which meant that if Sam didn't rat me out, I could come back next semester in good standing even after missing the last three weeks of class.

There had been another text from Kennedy waiting on my phone asking me to please call her as soon as I could, but nothing that suggested everyone knew of my moonlighting career as a con artist.

The state of my room unsettled me, since it appeared Audra hadn't been there for some time; there were no sheets on her bed and her toiletries were gone from the sink. The cold, abandoned feeling on Audra's side of the room worried me more than the idea of being ostracized, and I called Kennedy. No answer. I tried Cole, too, just in case, but got the same nonresponse.

The fact that no one answered made my nerves twitch, but they would return my message.

My two finals weren't until Friday—two days away—but I did need to go to the library to finish one last project. When I dumped out my backpack, intent on repacking it with marketing textbooks, the envelope Sam's lawyer had given me fluttered down onto my bed.

My stomach clenched and my fingers shook as I picked it up. This was my new life. Starting over had to be done, and leaving this letter unopened would chain me to the past. The seal broke under my fingernail and I held my breath through the two quick sentences.

Devil Girl,

Even though sex with you was the best thing ever, I considered us friends first. You may not know this, since friendship is more of a concept for you than an experience, but friendships don't end after a fight—or even a slight (hey, I'm a poet and didn't know it!).

Keep in touch.

Sam

Hope, too fragile to look directly at, rose inside me until tears bubbled down my cheeks. I wanted more than friendship from Sam—I wanted everything from Sam—but having him in my life in any small way was better than nothing. It was almost too much to think possible, and a hesitant smile found my lips on my way to the library.

I had a new life, and I was determined to make it amazing, all on my own.

Epilogue

Sam

My first Aussie Open match started in less than half an hour, but my mind couldn't have been further from analyzing my opponent, warming up, focusing, or anything else I should have been doing. All I wanted to know was whether Blair's face would be in my box when I stepped out onto the court for the first time in months.

Even after I'd written the note letting Blair know that, despite my anger, we were still friends, even after I'd woken up with all thirty-plus million dollars back where it belonged, it had taken my pride a week or so to cool enough to realize I was being an idiot. Not because I felt angry or betrayed, but because I assumed we couldn't get past it. Start over. Blair had shown me, from the moment she realized I knew the truth, that she meant what she said about a new life. I wanted one, too.

It would kill me if I were too late, if she'd decided she didn't want a dumbass guy who held on to grudges and ego instead of her beautiful, brilliant, maddening face. Because no matter how epically bad this whole thing began, I knew in my gut that the kind of innate connection the two of us had might never come around again.

Marija had even said as much when I'd told her the entire sob story a few weeks ago. I'd been surprised to hear her support Blair, given that they hadn't exactly been cozy in Belgrade, but she seemed certain that she'd never met anyone else who got under my skin enough to make me so mad . . . or so happy.

One of the tournament employees came to get me, listening to his walkie-talkie as he led me down a tunnel. I stopped briefly to say a few words to the media about the upcoming match, a ritual I hated, then stood just out of sight behind my French opponent. The announcer called his name first, then waited for the crowd to clap politely before announcing me. I received a bigger round of applause but hardly heard it. My heart was in my throat as the crowd came into view, my eyes whipping to the players' boxes.

She was there. Blair stood in the front row, in between Leo and one of my trainers, a hesitant smile— a real one—on her beautiful face.

I forgot about the match. Forgot about protocol, expectations, warm-ups, and the fact that cameras feeding live to half the world were trained on me. I dropped my bags and broke into a jog, making it across the side of the court in a flash, then threw my arms around Blair and hauled her over the barrier. I heard the rustle of security, someone vaguely asking me to leave the spectators in their seats, but nothing could distract me from how she felt against my chest.

The smell of her—fresh and clean, familiar but exciting, filled my nose and I let her go long enough to look down into her face, beaming and flushed.

"You're making a scene," she whispered, peering over my shoulder at what had to be a crowd of people and cameras.

"I don't fucking care," I growled, lifting her up so I could press my lips against hers.

Tasting her after all that time was heaven. Her lips parted for me, inviting my tongue to tangle with hers, and her fingers found the hair at the back of my neck. My body responded, pressing into hers, desperate for something I couldn't have right then. When we broke apart, struggling for breath, the look on Leo's face said he knew I was considering forfeiting the match to get laid, and that he would kill me if I did.

It made me chuckle. "Don't worry, Leo. I'm not going to do it."

I lifted Blair back over the railing, setting her in her seat and leaning in to sweep my tongue over hers for one last taste. "Thank you for coming."

"Oh, I'm not coming. I'm just breathing hard."

I laughed at the unexpected joke. "Wait until later."

"I believe you," she replied, her dark eyes searching mine.

"I believe you, too."

*

I woke up the next morning a little more sore than I should have been, and not from the first-round win I had under my belt. Blair's soft, warm body was curled up against me, our skin damp where it touched. I ran a hand from her shoulder down to her hip, cupping her bare ass to pull her closer. She shifted in her sleep, burying her nose in my neck and whispering something incoherent. The movement of her lips against my pulse jumped my body to attention, even though I'd lost count of how many times we'd done it since yesterday afternoon.

Four, I thought. Maybe five.

Even so, my fingers walked toward her breast until they landed on the spot that I'd learned gave me the quickest route to waking her up ready to go. Her nipples tightened between my fingers and her hips moved against mine, a moan escaping her as she shook off sleep and ran her tongue along my neck, up to my ear.

I pulled her on top of me, then joined her groan as she guided me inside and sat down, rolling her hips across mine. She moved slowly, her breasts brushing my chest in a maddeningly soft movement, teeth nibbling my lips, tongue pressing against mine until her breathing quickened.

"Sam," she gasped, moving faster, the sheet on either side of my shoulders balled up in her fists.

"Yes, devil girl. Come on," I encouraged, enthralled by the desperate pleasure twisted on her features as she sat up, riding me until she came with a cry. It seemed as though it lasted forever while I lost myself in the feeling of her tight around me, until we were both soaked with her pleasure.

She collapsed on top of me, breathing hard, her lips forming a smile against my chest. "Okay. I'm dead now. Are you happy?" she mumbled.

"You don't feel dead."

I thrust into her hard enough to earn another gasp, to get her moving, then flipped us both over and buried myself between her thighs.

"Christ, Sam. You feel so good." A sly smile replaced her passion. "You're the best friend I ever had."

"Since I'm the one teaching you about friendship, let me tell you something—you do not let all of your friends fuck you. Got it?"

"Audra's going to be very disappointed."

"Now, that might actually—"

"Do *not* finish that sentence." She hooked her elbows under her knees until I fell deeper. "You're welcome to finish something else, though."

She laughed at my inability to reply to her challenge through clenched teeth, but our mirth dissolved as we slipped against each other with more intensity until I couldn't see anything but the way her brown hair tumbled over her breasts, until I couldn't feel anything but her heat wrapped around me, her hands holding on to my ass to pull me in harder and faster. Until she came again and I couldn't hold out, our tongues dancing while we gasped pleasure into each other's mouths and everything was slick with sweat and happiness.

"That's what I call a finish..." She panted underneath me, fingers toying with my hair.

I propped myself up on an elbow, touching her because I could. It would be a long time, probably, before it got old. If it ever did. "I'm never going to be finished with you. You realize that."

Tears made her eyes shine. "I'm so glad you sent me the ticket."

"I'm so glad you came."

"Twice." She smiled, but it fell away quickly, replaced by that serious, probing gaze. "Do you think we can really make this work after the way it started?"

I hesitated, wanting her to know that the answer was real. Not off-the-cuff, not the result of amazing sex. "I think we've probably got a better chance than a lot of people, Blair. Relationships never stay the same. People change. The ability to know that, even though things don't go the way you planned, you want to be with the other person enough to fight your way though it isn't something you find every day. That's why I wrote you that note. That's why I wanted you to be here. Because after everything, I couldn't make the idea of life without you make sense."

"I have a lot to learn. It's not going to be easy."

"Why in the hell would I expect easy? I want you to be Blair, and easy isn't something that comes naturally to the devil."

She chuckled and rolled into me, hugging my neck and kissing me in a way that made me think number six probably wasn't far off. Leo was going to kill her if I couldn't walk well enough to play my second round match tomorrow.

I didn't know how long we would be together—no one could know such a thing—but I meant what I told her. We made an interesting couple, were yin and yang in so many ways that the disagreements and fights would be inevitable, and probably epic.

But for the first time, when I peered into what might come to pass, I saw the potential for a family of my own. One I could create with a girl determined to be honest from here on out, to build something solid and normal like neither of us had been fortunate enough to have until now.

Whatever lay out there, in the days far beyond this one, I was looking forward to it.

"I'm glad I met you in St. Moritz, Sam Bradford. You changed my life."

"You changed your life. But I'm proud to be part of it."

"Part of the future."

"Part of *our* future."

She kissed me again, her tongue sweeping lazily over my bottom lip, and I forgot about everything except today. There was plenty of time to think about tomorrow, and with Blair beside me, I had no doubt that every last moment would be worth the one that came after it.

Thank you for reading *Staying On Top*! If you enjoyed this novel, I would appreciate so much your taking the time to leave a review for the book on Amazon, iTunes, Barnes and Noble, or Goodreads!

If you haven't, please check out the other Whitman University books - *Broken at Love, By Referral Only, and Be My Downfall*, and visit us at www.whitmanuniversitybooks.com.

ACKNOWLEDGMENTS

No book is a solitary effort, and this manuscript is no different. I owe a debt of gratitude to my critique partners and constant cheerleaders - Alessandra Thomas and Denise Grover Swank. My copy editor Lauren Hougen, who gave me back a manuscript a million times cleaner than the one I sent her. My cover designer and graphic artist, who is always on call and never complains - thank you, Eisley Jacobs, for everything that you do.

I have a fantastic street team, the Whitman U Hooters, whose support and enthusiasm and general wonderful-ness warms my heart on a regular basis. They, along with the rest of my readers, make this all worthwhile.

Last (but certainly not least) to my family and friends for putting up with my moodiness, my unwashed hair, and every other hardship that goes along with love me. I appreciate it.

ABOUT THE AUTHOR

I've long had a love of stories. A few years ago decided to put them down on the page, and even though I have a degree in film and television, novels were the creative outlet where I found a home. I've published Young Adult under a different name, but when I got the idea for Broken at Love (my first New Adult title), I couldn't wait to try something new - and I'm hooked. In my spare time I watch a ton of tennis (no surprise, there), play a ton of tennis, and dedicate a good portion of brain power to dreaming up the next fictitious bad boy we'd all love to meet in real life.